MW01125468

Heaven Sent Copyright © 2019 Cherié Summers. All Rights Reserved.

All rights reserved. No part of this book may be reproduced in any form or by any electronic or mechanical means including information storage and retrieval systems, without permission in writing from the author. The only exception is by a reviewer, who may quote short excerpts in a review.

Cover designed by Cherié Summers
Editing by Laura McNellis EIC AlternativEdits

This book is a work of fiction. Names, characters, places, and incidents either are products of the author's imagination or are used fictitiously. Any resemblance to actual persons, living or dead, events, or locales is entirely coincidental.

Cherié Summers
Visit my website at www.cheriesummers.com

Printed in the United States of America

First Printing: August 2019

ISBN 978-1-0861-4333-1

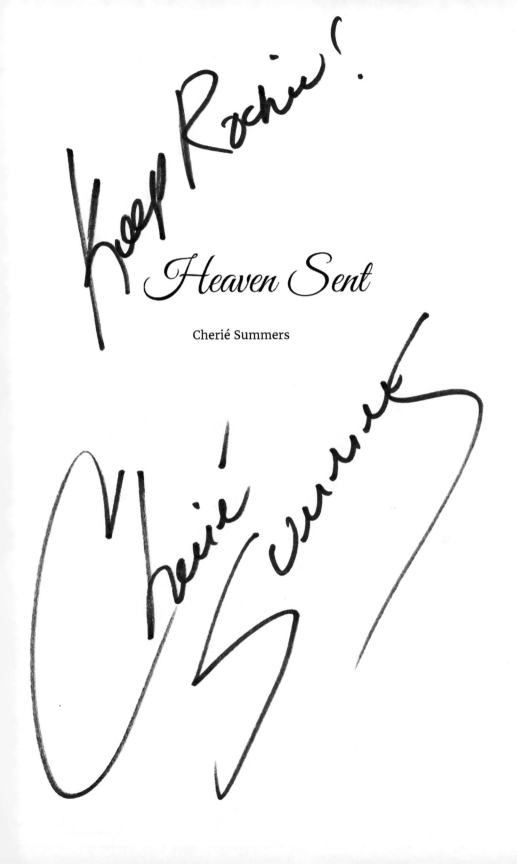

Heaven Sent

Cherié Summers

For Michael Hutchence
and Jon Farriss
Without your inspiration
there would be no story.
A story of music, love and loss, and most of all, friendship.

For friends, family, and fans who continue
to support my creative endeavors.
It means so much to have you believe in me.

Prologue

"Caesar! Johnnie! Where the hell are you?"

Johnnie Vega stirred from a deep slumber. Heat surrounded him. *Where am I?* Rolling away from the mountain ledge, he lay on his back and squinted through swollen eyes at the bright, Arizona sky. His mouth was dry, his throat sore.

"Johnnie! Caesar!"

Is that Rhett?

Memories from the previous night came drifting in slowly...painfully, pushing aside the cloudy haze in his mind. His eyes widened in horror.

No. It didn't happen.

"Johnnie...where the fuck are you?"

Kurt's voice. His friends were looking for him...and Caesar.

Shit. It had been his idea to hike up this mountain. His idea to try peyote with Caesar. His friend hadn't wanted to do it. After all, Caesar had been sober for a year...and then.

It didn't happen.

Then where was Caesar? He brushed back the sweaty curls from his forehead. *Look over the ledge, you idiot.* Prickly shivers crept through his body. *I don't want to look.* But still. He needed to see. See his best friend. He rolled back over, hanging his head over the ledge as he'd done the night before. Caesar's bright white shirt stood out amongst the brush in the ravine.

"Johnnie!" Rhett's exasperated voice. "We've been looking everywhere for you. What the fuck? Didn't you hear us calling?"

When Johnnie heard his other two bandmates approaching, he scrambled to his feet, stumbling around, trying to regain his proper balance. "Don't come over here! Stay right there!"

"What's going on?" Ignoring his drummer, Kurt continued his forward path.

"Where's Caesar?"

At Rhett's question, Johnnie charged toward them. Tears streamed down his face. "Stop! Please! Go back! Stay away!"

His gaze darted wildly between his two friends. Frantic, he grabbed hold of Rhett. The guitarist seemed to sense his desperation and wrapped his arms around him. Johnnie sobbed uncontrollably against Rhett's shoulder. The red dust from his face smeared across Rhett's pale blue t-shirt.

"Shit man, what is it?"

"It's that peyote he ate." Kurt straightened his eyeglasses, then folded his arms across his chest. "I told him that shit's too powerful to mess with."

"Oh, my God." Johnnie fell to his knees and continued sobbing. "I'm so sorry. It's my fault. I brought him here. Caesar...no, no, no."

Kurt and Rhett stared at one another, clearly confused.

"What's going on?" Kurt knelt beside Johnnie and placed a gentle hand on his back. "Where's Caesar?"

Johnnie looked up, his lips trembling, his nose flowing down the bottom half of his face. He pointed to the horizon beyond the mountain's ledge. "He flew away."

"Sir...sir...excuse me, are you alright?"

Johnnie snapped awake. A flight attendant was shaking him. "What the hell? Have we landed?"

"No, sir," the curvy brunette replied. She appeared concerned as she moved in closer and lowered her voice to a near whisper. "You seemed to be having a bad dream. Talking in your sleep a little loudly. Some of the other passengers were alarmed."

Johnnie sneered as he glanced around the first-class section of the plane. Bunch of corporate types. "Fuck em."

"I brought you a towel to wipe your face. You're all sweaty."

"What I need is another drink." He really didn't. He'd already had two since leaving London. But drinking chased the bad dreams away. The same dreams that had been haunting him for sixteen years. The ones where he relived his best friend's death.

The attendant placed a gentle hand on his shoulder. "What can I get for you? Another whiskey sour?"

"Sure." He grinned. *Women love my smile.* "And keep them coming. It's a long flight to LA."

She smiled back. "Do you have someone picking you up at the airport?"

"Don't worry about me. I'll make it home safely."

She nodded and left to get his drink. Johnnie's gaze followed the sidewinding motion of her rear end. *Nice ass. Definitely attractive.* She'd been a bit flirty during the flight. Perhaps she recognized him, although she seemed a bit young to have been a Lush fan. Plus, he didn't exactly look the same as he had when he flew the friendly skies as a rock star. Not with grey sprinkled throughout his dark, wavy hair, or the slight pudge he now carried around his midsection. Still, he liked to think he was somewhat good looking. When the attendant stopped to talk to a couple, he watched as she smiled and touched the gentleman's arm. *Just doing her job. Too bad.*

"You sure this is the right address?" the cab driver asked as he pulled up to the gate of Johnnie's Malibu beach house.

I must really look like hell.

"Two-five-three-two Beach Road. Yep, this is my place. Well, it was my friend's house, but he died, so I inherited it."

The driver let out a low whistle. "Wow. Nice friend."

"The very best," Johnnie mumbled. "I'll get out here. I can carry my shit in."

Johnnie opened the car's door and tried to stand. He teetered a bit but managed to stay on his feet.

"Dude, let me help you." The cab driver switched off the car and hopped out. He unlocked the trunk and retrieved Johnnie's luggage.

"Thanks, man." Johnnie squinted in the dark. Everything was a bit fuzzy. "Had a few drinks on the plane. I hate flying."

"I understand. Don't much care for it myself."

Johnnie punched in the numbers of the security code to open the gate. The driver handed him his duffle bag, and he draped it over his shoulder. Then, he pulled up the handle on his suitcase so he could roll it in.

"Are you sure you don't need help getting inside?"

"I'm good." Johnnie saluted, before reaching into his pocket and pulling out his wallet. He took out several bills. "This should cover it."

"Alright, thanks, man." The driver smiled, nodded, and went back around to his side of the car. "Have a good night."

Johnnie yawned as the car drove away. He grabbed his suitcase, dragging it inside the gate. After locking it back in place, he lumbered to the front door.

As he fumbled with his keys, he heard waves crashing. He took a deep breath and happily sighed. The scent of ocean air was exhilarating. It was good to be back at the beach house. His best friend, Caesar Blue, had willed him two houses, this one and one in London. He spent late summers, fall and winter here, and then would return to London in the spring.

"Home sweet home," Johnnie muttered, pushing the front door open. Immediately, he sensed there was something different about the place. He dropped his luggage in the living room, kicked off his shoes, and looked around. *Definitely different.*

The house smelled wonderful. Clean and fresh. A hint of vanilla. Caesar's favorite scent. Usually, it was musty and dusty when he returned each summer. Instead, everything was neat and tidy.

In the kitchen, he discovered more surprises. A loaf of bread on the counter. A couple of apples in a bowl. A bottle of wine and a wine glass on the counter next to the sink. *Where did this shit come from?*

"Who the hell cares?" He poured some wine into the glass and sipped it. "Mmm...not bad."

In no time, the bottle was empty, and his head was spinning. He headed to the downstairs bathroom to relieve himself.

He snapped on the light. "What the fuck is going on?"

Again, the room was spotless. A brand-new bottle of hand soap sat by the sink faucet. Neatly folded towels hung on the rack. Maybe Caesar's lawyer had sent someone over to clean the place. The man had always been cordial. Calvin Matthews handled Caesar's estate and was the one who'd handed Johnnie the title and keys to both houses after Caesar's death. The attorney also made sure the housing expenses were paid for and signed the checks Johnnie received every month. Not a large amount, but enough money to get by on. Allowance, Johnnie liked to joke.

The very best. Caesar. Because of their wild rock and roll lifestyle, they'd willed one another their houses and money. They'd done it just in case the worst happened. And then it did.

Johnnie checked himself in the mirror. He indeed looked like shit, unshaven with red-rimmed eyes and a tangled mess of dark brown hair. *It should've been me.* Caesar had been clean nearly a year when he died in the Sedona Mountains while Johnnie was still down to party. Even now. *What else is there to do when you're a has-been with no direction in life?*

Slowly, he lifted his t-shirt over his head, then let it drop to the floor. When his head spun again, he realized he was too tired and too drunk for a shower. After a good night's sleep, he'd worry about cleaning himself up and finding out who'd been in the house.

His legs were heavy as he plodded upstairs to Caesar's old room. Just past the top of the stairs, there was a night light on in the hall. *Where did that come from?*

When he stepped into the bedroom, the mystery was solved. The faint light from the hallway spilled into the room. It was just enough to illuminate a sleeping form on the bed. When he crept closer, he saw that it wasn't just anyone. *A woman!* She was lying on her back, blonde hair spilling around her head like a golden halo.

Do I know her? He wiped his eyes and rubbed his temples. *Hell, maybe I'm dreaming. Or hallucinating.* Caesar had never given a woman keys to the house, preferring to keep his romantic entanglements separate from the peaceful bliss of the beach house. And since his friend's death, Johnnie hadn't had anything resembling a romantic relationship.

That would make this beauty a criminal. Breaking and entering. *And cleaning house? Supplying food, wine, and soap?*

When she turned to her side, the blanket shifted, revealing to him that she was nude beneath the bed covers. His groin stirred. *Just what I need. A hot criminal.*

He grinned as he went to the opposite side of the bed. Quietly, he slipped out of his jeans, underwear, and socks before pulling back the covers. Ever so carefully, he slid in beside her. *She'll be in for a surprise when she wakes up.*

When he awoke later that morning, he was still rock hard. He snuggled closer to the woman, pressing his erection into her curvy backside and wrapping an arm around her waist. She smelled delicious. Like sugar cookies. Caesar's vanilla oil. The scent made his heart ache. His friend had bought it years ago in Thailand while they were on tour and wore it every day afterward. *Where did she find it?*

"I've missed you so much." She sighed dreamily.

Maybe I do know her. Being an addict made those one-night stands even more difficult to remember. He nestled his bristly chin against her silky-smooth neck. He felt her inhale sharply.

"Oh, my God!" She scrambled out of the bed. Her beautiful blue eyes were wide with shock.

"Where are you going, baby?" His mind filled with the wicked thoughts of what he'd like to do with those luscious curves that were on full display to him. Smiling widely, he patted the bed. "Come back. We were just getting started."

"You're not Caesar." She yanked the comforter from the bed and wrapped it around herself, leaving him bare in the process. Her eyes went even wider.

Hands supporting his head, he lay back against the pillow. *Let her look.* His waist might be a bit thicker these days, but his cock had always been thick. It was something else women had always loved about him.

"Sweetie, if you're expecting Caesar, you're in for a big disappointment. But I promise...with me...you won't be."

She cast her eyes downward before turning away from him. Part of the blanket fell away, leaving her exposed again.

"Nice ass, babe."

"Stop looking at me!" She wrapped the blanket around her twice this time, creating a cocoon. "Can you please pull up the sheet or put some clothes on?"

He laughed. "You break into *my* house and have the nerve to tell me what to do?"

She stood with her back to him. "Please."

"If you insist," he told her and draped the sheet over his crotch. "Okay. Done."

She turned around, and her mouth dropped when she saw the tent he'd pitched. Quickly, she turned away again. "Johnnie, please."

"Do I know you?"

"If you cover yourself completely, we can talk."

"Damn, woman. You're fucking bossy."

He threw back the sheet and got up. She peered over her shoulder.

"I see you peeking," he said as he slipped on his jeans. "Alright, done."

She turned back around.

He covered his eyes, mocking her. "Oh, please cover yourself. My eyes are burning! I'm melting!"

Her face flushed red with anger as he doubled over and began laughing hysterically at her.

She picked up her pillow and threw it at him.

"Oh, you want to play games?" He grabbed the pillow from the floor, ran to her side of the bed, and pelted her with it.

She struggled to block the blows and stay covered at the same time. "Johnnie, stop!"

Grabbing the comforter, he yanked her close and wrapped his arms around her waist. "Who the hell are you?"

"My name is Melanie." She wriggled, prying herself loose. "If you wait for me downstairs, I'll be right down to explain everything. I promise."

"Yes, boss man." He saluted, then *pretended* to march down the stairs. He peeked around the doorway. "Mmm...nice tits, too."

"Johnnie!" Again, she pulled the comforter around her. "Go. I'll cook breakfast as soon as you let me get dressed."

He grinned widely. "Now you're talking."

Quickly he flew down the stairs. Feeling dehydrated, he drank a bottle of water he found in the fridge. *What's taking her so long?* He knew he'd unnerved her, but her frustration and feistiness were keeping his dick hard. He ran back up the stairs. *Where is she?* There was movement in the master bathroom.

Johnnie banged on the door loudly. "Hey! I'm waiting on breakfast, and I'm starving. Hurry up!"

She slung open the door. "Who's being bossy now?"

He laughed loudly. "I'm starting to like you."

Chapter One

Past

"You almost died!" Caesar paced the floor of Johnnie's hospital room, waving his arms around. "You have to quit doing this shit!"

"You do the same shit!" Johnnie yelled just as loud, startling a passing nurse.

"I've never been as bad as you. You're out of control."

"In all the years you've known me, I've only OD'd this one time."

Caesar slammed his hand on the bed next to Johnnie. "One fucking time too many! Jesus Christ! If I hadn't come back to the hotel early, you might be dead."

"But you did, and I'm fine." Johnnie lay back on his pillow and chuckled. "Caesar. My guardian angel."

"Stop making light of this." Caesar rubbed his forehead, then stared at him. "I'm quitting everything. No more drugs. No more drinking. Let's do this, Johnnie. Together. It's time!"

"You're out of your fucking mind."

"I can't lose you, man. You're my best friend. My brother." Caesar wiped a tear away as he plopped down in the chair nearby. Johnnie watched his friend drift deep into thought.

"I've been thinking," Caesar finally said.

Johnnie rolled his eyes. "I am not going to rehab again. I suck at it."

"Which is exactly why I've been thinking. I talked to my lawyer, and I'm writing a will. I'm leaving my two houses to you. And money, too."

"What the hell for?" Johnnie mocked. "I thought you were quitting."

Caesar stood and came to his bedside again. "In case it doesn't happen. In case something bad happens to me. You won't be able to sell the houses though, which means you'll always have a place to go, something to live on, no matter how bad things get. I want to make sure you're taken care of."

Johnnie closed his eyes tight, trying to prevent himself from crying like a baby. Caesar was the greatest. No one else cared about him the way his best friend did.

"What do you think?"

He opened his eyes. "Do you think your lawyer can draw me up a will as well?"

Present

Johnnie Vega sat on a large rock, watching the glowing sun melt into the horizon. The orange globe colored the ocean with glorious hues of pink and gold. He sighed blissfully. This was his favorite spot to think...to reflect. In years past, his thoughts and recollections had brought nothing but heartache and anger at his shortcomings. But these days, things were different. Life was good. *All thanks to Caesar Blue.*

The seventeenth anniversary of his best friend's death had passed a few months ago, but instead of pain and anguish, he'd sat on this very rock, watching dolphins play nearby, his heart filled with love and contentment. Those were feelings that were completely foreign to him until the past year.

Today's anniversary was even more special. Last year, in August, Caesar had sent him a precious gift. A gift sent from the very heavens above. And that gift had finally prompted him to get clean. To be done with alcohol and drugs finally, and all the strife they'd brought to his life.

"Thought I'd find you here."

While smiling, Johnnie's gaze drifted from the ocean to Melanie—a sight more beautiful to him than any sunset. His heart fluttered as she walked toward him, the wind lifting her blonde hair from her shoulders, the waning sunlight softly kissing her face. She reached his rock and climbed up beside him. He wrapped an arm around her shoulder and pressed his lips against her neck.

"Did you get some work done?" he asked. She'd been working on her third romance novel when he'd left the house for a swim.

She smiled and raised her arms in victory. "First draft complete!"

"Another book." He snuggled closer. "You're amazing."

"There's something so special about this place. It inspires me."

He kissed her forehead. Melanie was right. The house and their private beach *were* special. Since meeting her here last summer, she'd published two romance books. With his help, she'd also written and produced a documentary of his band, Lush. And with Caesar, Kurt, and Rhett's help, they'd also written the band's autobiography. It had been released alongside a new album of previously unreleased music. The last year had been a rebirth of creativity for both him and Melanie. *All thanks to Caesar.*

Johnnie smiled, remembering the day Caesar had shown him the beachfront property for the first time. Caesar had fallen in love with the house immediately and wanted Johnnie's opinion. Even though Malibu was worlds apart from Philadelphia where they'd grown up, Johnnie had encouraged Caesar to buy the house. Johnnie had also suggested Caesar turn part of the large garage into a rehearsal area for the band. His friend had loved the idea, and with Johnnie's blessing immediately offered a bid to the realtor.

"That's why Caesar chose it. Said it got the creative juices flowing. He wrote a lot of great songs here."

She placed her head on his shoulder. "Thinking about him today?"

"Can't help it. He's the reason..."

"No." She lifted two fingers to his lips. "This is *your* accomplishment. *You* did it. And you keep doing it every day."

He took her hand in his and kissed her palm. "Without Caesar...without you...I don't think I would've ever gotten clean.

Allow me to at least give you two credit for providing the motivation."

She nodded, brushed a soft kiss against his lips, then stared out at the ocean.

He ran a hand through her shoulder-length hair. *Melanie.* He sighed, thinking back to the day he'd found her asleep in the house and had slipped beneath the covers beside her. When she awoke, she'd been shocked and appalled. And he'd been completely turned on by her spirit. Later, he discovered she'd been sent to the beach house by Caesar himself. At first, Johnnie hadn't accepted the idea that his best friend had returned from the dead, but once Caesar appeared to him as well, he'd been convinced.

Those weeks with Caesar and Melanie had been wonderful. His friend had returned to help Melanie overcome a personal tragedy and had fallen in love with her after their meeting in Atlanta. Caesar had also encouraged Melanie to pursue her writing dreams and offered the beach house to her, telling her where to find the spare key—even the money he'd hidden away. In motivating her, Caesar had set her on a collision course with Johnnie. As soon as they'd met, Johnnie had fallen just as hard. When he and Melanie were both reunited with Caesar, at first things were uncomfortable, but eventually, they'd come together and shared the love Melanie wanted to give them both. It was during this time that Johnnie resolved to once and for all beat his addictions. Caesar's return to the world had helped him, too. Although Johnnie had been in and out of rehab several times, knowing that he had a life with Melanie waiting for him had prompted him to complete the program he'd entered last year successfully.

One year. One year of complete sobriety. Johnnie had gone two years previously, but it hadn't lasted. While he'd cleaned up then, he hadn't dealt with the issues that had caused him so much personal pain. This time, he had. He'd come to peace with his father's abusive treatment. And even though his two older brothers were still pricks, he accepted that nothing would change their attitudes toward him. It no longer caused him pain. Their loss. Their problem.

"Are you hungry?" Melanie broke the silence as she hopped down from the rock. "The roast should be done."

He slid from the rock. She'd had a pot roast with vegetables in the slow cooker all day. "We should've gone out to eat. It's a special occasion, after all."

"It is, isn't it?" She moved closer and wrapped her arms around his neck. "Tomorrow we can go out to dinner."

"How about a movie, too?" He grinned.

"As long as it's not some super violent, action movie," she protested.

"Well, surely you're sick of romance. You've been writing about it for months."

She ran one hand up his torso, then to his face, caressing him. Her fingers then worked their way through his thick, wavy hair. The look in her eyes was pure seduction.

She pushed her bottom lip out. "Are you sick of romance? Of love and everything that comes with it?"

"Hell to the no."

Their lips met, and his whole body came alive wanting her. This woman drove him crazy with lust. Around her, he was a teenager again, not a forty-five-year-old man. He liked to joke that her pussy was magic. It certainly had cast a spell on his dick.

She pulled away. Her blue eyes sparkled like sapphires in the dwindling light. Grabbing Johnnie's hand, she turned toward the house.

He refused to budge. "No, baby. I want to make love to you."

She smiled back at him. "Let's go then."

"Too far away. I need you right now." He led her hand to his crotch.

"But dinner," she said coyly. His cock hardened even more as she softly touched him.

"It can wait." He moaned as she unfastened his swim trunks and slid them down over his hips. "Not like you're going to eat pot roast, Miss Vegetarian."

She knelt and ran her tongue along the underside of his cock. He shuddered as she gently kissed the tip before wrapping her lips around it. He thought he might explode. She looked so beautiful and so incredibly sexy on her knees pleasuring him.

"This won't do." He tapped her shoulder, then tugged her arm.

She stayed put. "Don't tell me you don't like it, Johnnie Vega."

He threw his head back and laughed, loving when she said his full name—his rock star name. She'd been a fan of Lush as a teen, and he'd been her favorite band member. Her enthusiasm for the band...for its music...had made him long for those days again. After Caesar had died so tragically, the band had been broken. Eventually, he and the remaining two members, Kurt Rain and Rhett Star, had drifted apart, and he'd not seen them for many years. Now they were brothers again. Melanie's doing. And of course, Caesar's. His return had healed Johnnie in so many ways. The documentary and autobiography were a success, and the new album still sat near the top of the charts. These projects had placed Lush back into the media spotlight, and the money was rolling in again. Not that he was desperate for money.

After Caesar's death, the band's manager had prompted Johnnie's parents to take control of his money. At the time, he was really messed up and spending uncontrollably on liquor, pills, and anything else that would alter his state of mind. Johnnie had lived off Caesar's generosity for sixteen years until his father passed away last year. Then his mother had returned what remained of the millions he'd earned as the drummer of Lush. It should've been more, but he'd squandered so much of it on his addictions. Caesar had rescued him from a sleeping pill overdose. Heroin had nearly done him in on another occasion. Johnnie had always wondered how he'd managed to stay alive when he'd worked so hard to kill himself.

"Do you really want me to stop?" Melanie asked then ran her tongue up and down over him.

This is why. Why I'm alive.

He was feeling...loving...*really* living for the first time in his life. Caesar had brought Melanie back to life, and Melanie had brought him to life. He smiled at her.

"Come here." He tugged her arm again, scooted back on top of the rock, and kicked his trunks off.

She crawled onto his lap and straddled him. His cock throbbed as it brushed against her pussy. He moved his hand under her dress and in between her legs.

"No panties. How convenient."

She laughed lightly, playing coy again. "I knew I forgot something."

"You seem to do that a lot."

"It's easier than trying to locate my panties later on."

He laughed as he slipped two fingers inside her. He *was* always stripping her of her underclothes and throwing them wherever.

"You're so wet, babe." He spread her moistness up to her clit and began to rub tenderly. His other hand went to her hair, brushing it aside, exposing her neck so he could kiss her there. He knew it drove her wild.

She took his cock in her hands, then sank onto it, filling herself.

"I love you so much." He nibbled her neck. "You love me, don't you?"

"Yes, Johnnie," she said, breathlessly, moving sensually on his lap. "I love you."

"Say my whole name."

She laughed and tapped the side of his head. "That really goes to your head, doesn't it?"

He pressed his forehead against hers. "Yes, both heads absolutely love when you play fangirl."

She covered her mouth, feigning surprise. "Johnnie Vega, I didn't realize how enormous your stick would be."

He grinned slyly. "Are you feeling the rhythm?"

"Mmm...yes." She leaned back, ran her hands through her hair and moaned. "Like heaven. I can't believe I'm fucking Johnnie Vega. It's a dream come true."

"Ahh...you've dreamed of me?"

"All the time." She ran her fingers over his eyebrows. "These gorgeous blue-grey eyes."

He slid down the straps of her sundress, then pulled off her bra, freeing her gorgeous breasts. "What else?"

She lightly stroked his lips with her index finger. "These thick, luscious lips."

"Did you dream of this?" He bent to capture one of her nipples in his mouth.

"Yes." She gasped.

"Anything else?"

She slid her hands up and down his arms. "These muscular arms."

"All those years of drumming paid off. You like them, huh?"

"Love them. It feels so wonderful being wrapped up in them."

"Stand up."

She stood, and so did he. He turned her away from him and pulled her dress off her. At five-foot-ten, he was only a few inches taller than her. He bent his knees slightly, then slid into her from behind. As the stars began to appear above them, he made love to her, moving slowly, one arm holding her close, the other squeezing a breast. She pushed her hair aside, and he kissed her neck. He felt her shudder and grow even wetter. She was close.

"Oh, Johnnie, this is better than any dream I ever had."

His hand drifted to the juncture of her thighs where he quickly homed in on the magical spot that would make her even wetter, make her pussy tighten around him.

"Is it now?"

"I'm going to cum, Johnnie."

He withdrew and turned her around. "Johnnie who?"

"Johnnie Vega." She came closer and wrapped a leg around his hip. Her hand went into his hair. "My favorite rock star."

He pulled her leg higher up. Fingers slipped inside her to again spread her wetness.

"Johnnie...please."

"What is it?" he teased, and her body tensed. "You need my big stick inside you again?"

"Yes."

He waited until he felt the first quivers of her orgasm, then plunged inside her. Immediately, her pussy tightened on his cock, making him work even harder to fuck her. But it felt amazing. This thing between them was indeed magical.

He pulled out and turned her around again. She gasped as he shoved hard into her, but then she quickly fell into his rhythm, meeting his thrusts with her own backward thrusts. His hand went back to her clit.

"I'm going to cum again."

"Shit." He groaned, filling her just as her pussy hugged him tightly once more.

When he finally withdrew, he jumped from the rock. He grabbed her around the thighs, hoisting her up over his shoulders. "Let's get washed up for dinner."

"Oh no, Johnnie!" She squealed. "I need to check on the food. Let me go!"

"No way in hell." He laughed loudly as he trotted into the water.

"No, really. We *have* to get back to the house."

"Okay." He was waist-deep and tossed her into the ocean. "But a swim first."

She came up sputtering. "You are rotten, Johnnie Vega."

He drew her close, wiping the wet hair from her eyes. "And yet you still love me."

"Guess I have a thing for bad boys." Pressing her palms against his chest, she kissed him.

He widened his eyes with fake surprise. "Boysssssssss?"

"Okay, I have a thing for one *very* bad boy." Slipping away, she trudged back to shore.

"Good. So, that leaves out a hippy, dippy, *I-love-everyone-and-everything*, lead singer named Caesar Blue."

She turned and placed her hands on her hips. "Stop being jealous of Caesar. He's gone."

"Who's jealous?" He shrugged.

"You are." She fastened her bra back on, then slipped her dress over her head. "Always have been."

Johnnie leaned back and floated on the water. "And wherever Caesar is right now, I guarantee you...he's jealous as hell that I'm the one who just fucked you."

Suddenly a dolphin broke the surface, leaping up beside Johnnie, then crashing down hard, splashing him.

"Holy shit!" Johnnie stood and raced toward shore.

Melanie burst out laughing.

"I swear that dolphin will not leave me alone." Johnnie grabbed his trunks and put them on. The dolphin made loud, squeaking noises and nodded its head as if it were mocking him. "Damn horny dolphin! Go find your pod."

Melanie hugged him from behind, giggling. "Guess he's a Johnnie Vega fan, too."

He took her hand in his, and they walked back to the house. The lanterns on the deck were lit, and plush towels were waiting on a lounge chair by the back door. *Melanie thought of everything.*

"Let's shower off." Johnnie tugged her toward the outdoor shower.

"I have to check on dinner," she reminded him. "And if I get in that shower with you, things will happen."

He winked at her as he turned on the water, stripped off his shorts, and dipped beneath it. "I got news for you. Things are going to happen even if you don't get in here with me."

"Later." She threw him one of the towels. "Besides, I have a surprise waiting for you inside."

"You do?" He grinned as he caught it and draped it over the shower stall. "Is it in the bedroom?"

"Maybe," she replied, blew him a kiss, and disappeared inside.

Chapter Two

Past

Johnnie was eating lunch with Caesar in the courtyard when he saw two young men approaching. Johnnie knew one of them. The Irish guy who was in his Biology class. Rhett was his name. The other one he'd seen around school but had no clue who he was.

"Hey." The Irishman waved. His hair was reddish-blond, his eyes green. Despite it being warm, he wore a leather jacket. "I'm Rhett. From Biology."

Johnnie nodded, then chuckled. "If you need help studying, you've come to the wrong place."

"Nothing like that," the other one said. He was sort of dorky looking with thick-rimmed glasses. He reminded Johnnie of Elvis Costello. "I'm Kurt. Rhett told me you guys want to start a band."

Johnnie narrowed his eyes. He hadn't mentioned that to anyone.

"I overheard you two talking about it at your locker," Rhett explained.

Caesar smiled, stood, and held out his hand to Kurt. "I'm Caesar. I'll be lead singer. I play a little piano, and write lyrics, too."

Kurt shook Caesar's hand. "I play bass. Rhett plays guitar."

"Good enough to lead?" Johnnie asked.

Rhett smiled. "Been playing since I was six."

"We practice at my place," Caesar informed them. "Can you come by after school?"

"Sure thing," Kurt promised. "You have a name for this band yet?"

"Nothing official," Johnnie told him. "Caesar has some ideas."

They all stared at Caesar.

"Lush," Caesar announced, then closed his eyes and sighed deeply. "Like a woman's lips."

"I like it." Kurt nodded. He turned to Rhett, who nodded as well.

"Give me your address, and we'll be there."

Present

"Dinner smells amazing, babe." Johnnie wrapped a towel around his waist as he headed into the kitchen. He didn't find Melanie. Instead at the kitchen island, Rhett was chopping vegetables, preparing a salad, while Kurt iced a cake.

Johnnie rushed in and hugged each one of his bandmates. "What the hell, guys. I didn't know you were coming."

"We're a surprise from Melanie." Rhett mixed the salad, adding a dash of salad dressing here and there as he tossed it. "To celebrate. Hope you don't mind, but we're staying the weekend."

Kurt looked Johnnie over, then shook his head. "I know what kept you and Melanie down at the beach for so long."

"What?" Johnnie feigned innocence. "I was just washing the sand off me."

"She said she was going to get you and would be right back. How long ago was that, Rhett?"

"Long enough for us to know better than to go looking for you two." Rhett laughed.

Johnnie's face warmed. *Really? Me? Johnnie Vega? The bad boy of Lush? Blushing?* "Let me get some clothes on."

"Please do." Rhett smiled. "Melanie's upstairs showering."

"No more hanky panky until after dinner." Kurt went back to icing.

"No promises, Kurt." Johnnie slid a finger across the cake, then sampled the icing on his finger. "But I'll try."

"We're proud of you." Kurt raised a glass of raspberry lemonade as the three bandmates relaxed together in the jacuzzi after dinner. "A full year of sobriety."

"With many more to come." Rhett raised his glass as well.

Johnnie lifted his own and clinked it against his friend's. "I'm glad you guys came out to celebrate with me. It means a lot."

All three of them took a synchronized drink. Johnnie smiled. It was great having his friends with him tonight. Rhett was usually on the road, playing guitar, backing some famous singer who was out on tour.

Kurt had mostly settled into a home life although he still got steady work as a session musician. He was married with two young kids and lived on a ranch where he and his wife raised horses.

Caesar's death had ripped apart their friendship. Because Johnnie hadn't been able to remember much about the events that led to Caesar falling from the mountain ledge, some in the press had jumped on the theory that he was somehow to blame. A few even suggested he'd pushed his own best friend to his death. The one thing Johnnie had been sure of was that he'd taken peyote and had been drinking earlier that evening. The guilt he already felt was worsened by the speculation from media and then the fans. His drinking and drug use worsened. He had lashed out at Kurt and Rhett time and time again, until they had slowly slipped from his life. *Until Melanie brought them back to me. And Caesar.*

The back door slid open, and Melanie appeared. She shed her cover-up, revealing a simple one-piece swimsuit, then joined them in the jacuzzi.

Johnnie kissed her cheek. "We could've helped clean. You didn't have to do it all by yourself."

"It's alright. You guys deserve some time together. It's been a while since all of us were together at the release party."

"We'll be spending a lot of time together on this book signing tour. You'll all be sick of me."

"Those days are over, man." Kurt splashed him with a little water. "No more trashing hotel rooms or having to pull your ass down from hotel roofs."

Johnnie grimaced as he thought about all the dumb shit he'd done in the past. His friends had put up with a lot when they'd traveled the world together. He was lucky to have them still, even if one of them was gone.

Is Caesar really gone? Since meeting Melanie, Caesar's presence always seemed to be near. She had a way about her, a calmness, the same as Caesar. And she smelled exactly like him. After she and Caesar had fallen for one another in Atlanta, Melanie had picked up the scent of the vanilla. The exact fragrance his friend had always worn. It never went away. And since Johnnie had bought Melanie her own bottle of the oil, it probably never would. She seemed to love it. And Johnnie loved her. *Whatever makes her happy.*

"It's a gorgeous night. We should swim in the ocean before it gets too cold," Kurt suggested. "How's the water temperature?"

Johnnie finished his lemonade. "Feels great. Just be on the lookout for that horny dolphin."

"Horny dolphin?" Rhett's eyebrows shot up, and he looked at Melanie.

Melanie bit her lip and averted her eyes.

"That damn thing is huge." Johnnie held his arms out to his sides. "Almost every single time I go for a swim, he messes with me. Always jumping around and splashing me."

Rhett smiled, and Kurt chuckled.

"Sure, laugh all you want, but it's weird. I've lived in this house for a long time and never seen any dolphins. Only since Melanie moved in. And now I get one that's a complete mental case."

Rhett burst out laughing. Melanie joined in.

"Sometimes there's two little ones." Johnnie sighed. "They don't bother me. And when they're around, he leaves me alone."

Kurt's eyes narrowed as he rubbed his chin. "How do you know it's a he?"

Johnnie shrugged. "Just guessing because of how big it is."

"So, you haven't seen...you know..."

Johnnie's eyes widened, and he splashed Kurt. "Hell no, and I don't want to."

Rhett was laughing so hard tears were rolling down his face. Melanie stopped laughing and held a finger to her mouth in an obvious attempt to shush his guitarist friend.

Cocking his eyebrow, Kurt glanced at Melanie. She shook her head.

Johnnie's gaze shifted from Kurt, to Melanie, and then to Rhett. "If you don't believe me, you go out there and swim with him."

"You should tell him, Melanie," Kurt suggested, then took a sip of lemonade. "You told us."

"Tell me what? What the hell's going on?"

Rhett hoisted himself out of the jacuzzi. "On that note, I'm going to get ready for bed. And for more of that cake."

Kurt stepped out next. "Yeah, me, too. Think I'll pass on swimming with horny dolphins."

Rhett threw his arm around Kurt's shoulder, and the two of them burst into laughter again.

Johnnie's brow furrowed as he watched them go, knowing the guys were giving him time alone with Melanie so she could tell him *something*. Some secret the three of them obviously shared— something that had to do with that dolphin.

He stared at Melanie. "Spill it."

She scooted closer to him, put her arm around his shoulder, and then her legs over his lap. "Think about it, Johnnie. Really think about it. When does that dolphin bother you? What are you usually going on about when he suddenly appears? Like tonight? Who were you talking about?"

His mouth dropped opened. "No fucking way. Caesar sent a dolphin to harass me?"

She took a deep breath and slowly let it out. "Caesar *is* the dolphin."

"Okay." He flicked water on her. "Now you're messing with me. And the guys are in on this joke?"

She grabbed his hand. "It's no joke."

Something told him she was telling the truth. After all, he hadn't believed her when she first said she'd met Caesar's ghost in Atlanta and that had turned out to be true. He stared out at the calm ocean waters. *Can Caesar really be a dolphin?*

His gaze shot back to hers. "No games? You're for real?"

She sighed, closed her eyes, then opened them again. "Yes."

"Why haven't you told me? You told Rhett and Kurt, but not me?" Johnnie turned away, hurt that she'd kept a secret from him. Especially one involving Caesar. *My best friend. My best friend who she loves. And who loves her.*

She touched his chin and pulled his gaze back to hers. "Remember I told you I first saw the dolphins when I was sad about our breakup. I said it almost seemed as if Caesar had sent them to cheer me up?"

"Yeah." He frowned, remembering how he'd cheated on her and the aftermath of that horrible decision. "When I disappeared after fucking things up between us."

"I saw them again while you were away in rehab. First, the two smaller ones visited when you'd left without saying goodbye. Then all three of them right after Caesar left."

She paused, glanced away for a moment, then turned back to him. "And then again...when he came back to see me."

His eyes narrowed. "You told me he never came back to visit while I was away."

She caressed his cheek. "I'm sorry, Johnnie. I lied."

Johnnie raged as the jealousy over her special relationship with Caesar returned. He scooted away and sat opposite from her, squeezing the bridge of his nose, trying not to cry. He hadn't felt this vulnerable in a long time. Images of Caesar making love to Melanie played in his mind. He'd accepted it and enjoyed it when the three of them were together, but once he'd gone to rehab, he'd expected Caesar to disappear. After all, Caesar's mission to help the two of them had been completed. The whole time he'd been away, he worried about leaving Melanie alone. He worried that she might find someone new to love. But she hadn't. At least that was what she'd told him. But she'd also told him Caesar left two days after he'd left for the rehabilitation center and had never come back.

"Tell me everything." He crossed his arms over his chest and huffed. "Did you and he..."

"No." She shook her head. "Nothing like that."

"But you two love one another. And I was gone for so long."

"It was after your mom called the rehab center and learned you weren't there anymore...that you'd completed the program and left. I didn't know where you were. I didn't know if you were coming back to me. I was crazy with worry, not knowing what was happening."

Guilt stabbed his gut. He'd gone through the program, then left and lived on his own for a while. He'd needed to know he could make it, to be sober and to stay sober without the complications a relationship might bring to his life. Then he'd surprised her at the book release party by showing up and confessing to the world how much he loved her. It had seemed like a great idea, and it had put an even more positive spin on that night. But in the interim, he knew she'd been hurting. He'd kept in touch with Kurt and Rhett who'd told him how miserable she was.

"I'm sorry." He shook his head, frustrated. "Maybe I shouldn't have handled it the way I did."

"It doesn't matter now. What's done is done. Things are perfect between us."

His body trembled. "Except for the lie about Caesar."

"I couldn't stop crying when I found out you left rehab and had not contacted me. Caesar returned again to cheer me up."

"By fucking you no doubt," he grouched. He knew he shouldn't be upset. Or jealous. Caesar was his best friend. And Melanie had loved Caesar first. Without Caesar, there would be no Melanie in his life. No sobriety. No joy. No love.

Frowning, Melanie stood. "No. By bringing my daughters to me."

Johnnie's heart sank, and he felt like shit. *Leila and Lily.* Melanie's twin daughters who'd been killed in a car accident eleven years ago. An accident caused by her late husband. They'd been only four when she lost them.

"You saw them?" He stood as well.

When tears slipped from her eyes, he wrapped her in his arms and held her tight.

"I saw them, but they couldn't see me. They were the ones who found CJ and gave him to me to help."

Johnnie looked over at CJ, the stray cat she'd taken in while he was away. The ginger cat was sleeping soundly on a nearby lounge chair.

"The dolphin connection didn't sink in until Caesar left me a note with three dolphins drawn on it. He told me he and the girls were always nearby, and that he'd been taking care of them since he'd left me in Atlanta."

Johnnie wiped her tears away. It must have been a wonderful thing for her to see her children again. "Was that the only time you saw them?"

She shook her head. "The last time was the morning after the release party. I was on the deck. Caesar and the girls were taking a walk together along the shoreline."

His head pounded, and he rubbed his forehead. "But I was there with you. I didn't see them."

"I know. It's why I didn't say anything. You couldn't see Caesar anymore. I don't know why. In my mind, I heard his voice saying you didn't need to see him."

Johnnie fought back the tears again. He would've loved to have seen Caesar that day.

"Because I was sober. Because I didn't need him anymore." He left the jacuzzi and wrapped a towel around his waist.

Melanie followed. "I suppose that's why. I also knew...felt it in my heart...that it was the last time I'd see them. In human form at least."

He handed her a towel. "That was when I first saw the dolphins."

Melanie nodded as she took the towel and began drying off.

Johnnie sat down on a lounge chair, and Melanie sat beside him. "I wish you'd told me."

"I'm sorry, Johnnie. That day felt like a whole new beginning. Just you and me and our new life together. Part of that was letting go of the past. Which meant letting Caesar and the girls go and moving on with you."

"Don't you miss them?"

"Of course."

"I still miss Caesar. I think about him every day."

Softly she stroked his arm. "I know you do."

Tears slipped from his eyes. "He was the best friend I ever had. And he sent you to me. And I love you so much. I'm forever in his debt."

"I love you." Melanie kissed his tears away.

He ran his fingers through her hair, then lay back in the chair. She stretched out beside him. He took her in his arms and kissed her softly, pushing her mouth apart. His tongue danced with hers. Soon they were shedding their swimsuits.

"You feel so good," he murmured against her ear as he filled her with his cock.

"You make me feel so good."

He made love to her slowly, deliberately, his thick cock stretching her, making her wetter with every thrust. She wrapped her legs around him and ran her hands down his back to his butt. She squeezed his butt cheeks as she thrust her hips up to meet his.

"Yes, baby, cum for me," he whispered hotly in her ear.

"Magic tongue, please."

He chuckled as he pulled out and slid down her body. "Of course. Whatever makes you happy."

He lapped at her juices first, fucking her with his tongue before heading for her clit. She squirmed, and her hands plunged into his hair. He adored fucking her like this because she loved it so much. It turned him on to taste her, to make her cum with his mouth. He sucked her clit and slid two fingers inside her.

"Yes, Johnnie...yes"

"Are you going to cum?"

She lifted her hips from the chair. "Yes, I'm cumming."

As her body tightened on his fingers, he withdrew them and stretched out over her again. He shoved his cock inside her, pushing her over the edge. He ground into her over and over, loving the feel of every quake her body made as it tightened around him.

He gazed into her eyes. "You are my life."

She stroked his face. "And you're mine, Johnnie Vega. My sexy rock star."

He moaned and filled her.

In silence, they lay wrapped in one another's arms. But thoughts of Caesar plagued him. "If you see Caesar again, will you please tell me?"

"I will." She kissed his cheek.

"Do you feel him? Because I do. It's like he's always here and not just as that damn dolphin, but his spirit...his essence. I never felt it before when I lived here alone. Only when you came."

"You weren't sober then. Your mind was clouded. Now it's clear. And your heart is open."

She was right. Once he'd met Melanie, he'd only gotten messed up a couple of times. At first, the cravings were still there, but he'd fought them, preferring to be clear-headed when he engaged with her. They'd started as friends and business partners, but he'd been intrigued by her from the start and had quickly fallen in love.

Johnnie had been hesitant to begin a relationship with her. He feared hurting her as her alcoholic husband had done—as he'd done with previous girlfriends and his family. But eventually, living with her, being around her every day had broken him...broken the both of them and they'd given in to their feelings. At that point, he knew he'd do anything to get sober and stay that way.

"That might explain why I enjoy fucking you so much."

"I suppose you haven't had much sober sex."

"Are you kidding. You're the first sober sex I've ever had."

She sat up and looked down at him. "Should I feel good about that? Or should I worry that you might want to try it with others?"

"You've got to be kidding." He sat up and rubbed a thumb over her bottom lip. "There is no other. Only you."

She gazed deeply into his eyes. "You're the only man I want."

"Really?" He leaned back in the chair and grinned. "Oh, wait...you said man. That doesn't include dolphins."

"I don't want to be with a dolphin." She giggled.

Johnnie cupped his hands around his mouth and yelled, "Do you hear that, Caesar? She doesn't want you!"

The dolphin suddenly appeared, leaping out of the water, splashing down, and vocalizing.

"Uh oh, someone's jealous!" Johnnie laughed.

"Yes. You!" Melanie playfully smacked his chest. Then she turned her gaze to the ocean. "And him! I swear the two of you are too much."

He grabbed her and pulled her down on top of him. "He's probably been watching us make love."

Melanie rolled her eyes. "Yes, and if he wanted to, he would be the Caesar we know and love and join us. He knows we're happy together. That we belong together. That you are mine, and I am yours."

"Prove it!" He tickled her.

She squealed as she sat back up and looked to the ocean. "I am not hurting that dolphin."

Johnnie's eyes widened. He tapped the side of her head. "What a dark, twisted mind you have. That's not what I meant."

She gasped. "That was a horrible thought. I know you'd never hurt Caesar."

"If we're swimming and he tries to hump you, I might."

Her face was panic-stricken. "He's never done that."

"I'm kidding." He pulled her into a hug, then kissed her lips. "You're right. I'd never hurt Caesar."

"Then how do I prove you're the only man for me? Road head? Anal sex? Public sex? Perhaps make a video?"

"Well, I was going to ask you to marry me...but your list is pretty damn enticing. Hmmm. What will I choose? A video could be interesting. Maybe a little role-playing."

She sat up again, stared at him, her mouth open, her eyes wide.

"What?" He grinned devilishly.

"Did you just ask me to marry you?"

"Do you want to marry me?" He shrugged and traced her jawline with a finger. "I mean I'm no longer the young, hot, sexy, rock and roll drummer you crushed on as a teen."

"That wasn't you banging on the drums for hours yesterday?"

"Okay, so I'm still a drummer."

A tear slid down her cheek. "You're all those things to me, Johnnie."

"Except young." He felt his own tears welling up.

"You're right." She laughed through her tears. "Which means we better get married soon before you fall over dead."

He sat up. "Do you really want to marry me?"

"I should be asking you that. You're the bad boy rock star who said he'd never...ever...get married."

"I did?"

"In an interview I once saw. I believe I was around twenty then. In college."

He rolled his eyes. "Which means I was twenty-four and knew absolutely nothing."

"So now you know everything?"

He lightly stroked her cheek. "I know I love you more than anything, Melanie. That morning I woke up snuggled next to you in my house...I knew you were special. I knew I wanted you."

She sighed. "Yes, I seem to remember feeling, then seeing your cock all thick and hard. I wanted you, too."

"I knew by the end of that day I was going to fall head over heels in love with you. It excited me and scared the shit out me." He took her hand and kissed it. Then he put her hand over his pounding heart. "It's been over a year, and you still have the power to make me feel that way."

She placed his hand over her heart. It beat wildly against his palm. "What do we do about this?"

He moved his hand down and cupped her breast, teasing her nipple into a hard bud. "See a heart specialist?"

"No, silly." She playfully slapped his knee. "Let's get married."

Johnnie stood, took a deep breath, and howled like a wolf into the night air. CJ jumped from his chair and raced off the deck.

Laughing, Melanie left the chair and hugged him tightly.

The back door slid open, and Kurt asked, "What the hell was that?"

Melanie shrieked and quickly wrapped a towel around her. Johnnie didn't bother. Instead, he jumped around wildly.

"What's going on?" Rhett asked as he and Kurt stepped out onto the deck.

Johnnie ran to Rhett and hugged him tightly. "She said yes!"

He started to hug Kurt.

Kurt grabbed a towel and held it up in front of him. "Wrap yourself first."

"Ah, come on." He slapped Kurt on the back and ignored the towel. "You've seen me naked plenty of times."

Kurt grimaced. "A long time ago. And you were usually passed out after a long night of partying. That wild man's gone, remember?"

Johnnie grabbed him anyway. "Says who? Sober doesn't mean boring."

"I guess not." Kurt shook his head as Johnnie continued to jump around the deck.

"Did he ask you to marry him?" Rhett asked Melanie.

Melanie nodded, and fresh tears sprang from her eyes.

"And she said yes!" Johnnie yelled.

"I think we got that." Kurt smiled, holding the towel out to Johnnie once again.

"Congratulations." Rhett hugged Melanie, and then Kurt did as well.

Finally, Johnnie grabbed the towel and wrapped it around his waist. He ran to the railing and shaking his fist, yelled out at the ocean. "I'm marrying her, Caesar!"

A strong gust of wind swept across the deck.

It's about time. Caesar's voice.

Johnnie jumped back as if he'd been electrocuted and fell to the deck.

"Are you alright?" Melanie rushed over and knelt beside him. "Perhaps you *should* calm down. Before you hurt yourself."

She loves you so much. Congratulations.

He gasped and stared wide-eyed at Melanie. Rhett and Kurt bent over him.

"What happened?" Kurt snapped his fingers. "Johnnie, you okay, man?"

Melanie smiled. "Is it Caesar?"

Kurt helped him to his feet. Johnnie stared at Melanie, then tapped his temple. "I heard his voice. In here."

She kissed him. "What did he say?"

He gave her a sly grin. "He said, *you win.*"

Melanie rolled her eyes. "He did not."

"He said he was super jealous."

Rhett and Kurt shook their heads and groaned together.

From the ocean, the dolphin loudly vocalized.

"Okay. Okay." Johnnie yelled at the animal. He turned back to Melanie. "He said congratulations."

Melanie fell into his arms, and he held her tightly.

"Look!" Rhett pointed to the water.

There were three dolphins now. They jumped high, spinning in circles as they did. They swam together in perfect synchronization just inside of where the waves began to break.

"Looks like you're not the only one excited about this proposal." Kurt patted his back.

"Let's get married now."

Johnnie whirled around. "Are you kidding? Don't you need months to plan some huge shindig?"

"Not if we go to Vegas."

He laughed. "Now I know you're kidding. You've got to find the perfect dress, have someone do your makeup and hair, invite the families."

"I just need you." She ran her hands through his damp hair, then turned to Rhett and Kurt. "And a couple of witnesses."

"It's a long drive," Johnnie protested.

"We could fly."

"We could, couldn't we?" He grinned. "Are you sure that's what you want? I haven't even bought you a ring."

Another strong gust of wind flew past, whipping Melanie's hair around her face.

Use my mom's diamond ring.

"Damn it. Stay outta there." Johnnie smacked himself on the side of the head. He looked at Melanie and shrugged. "We can use Mrs. Blue's diamond ring."

"That will be perfect. And when we get back, we'll get matching bands."

Kurt stretched. "A Las Vegas wedding? Does it get any more rock and roll than that?"

"Sure." Rhett laughed. "Have an Elvis impersonator perform the service."

"Now that sounds like a great idea!" Johnnie shook Rhett's hand. "Good thinking."

Melanie grabbed her swimsuit. "I have a million things to do. I have to pick out a dress and do something with my hair. We'll need to call the airport and see when the flights are. Johnnie, go find CJ and bring him back inside."

Johnnie leaned into Kurt. "So like I said, this wedding will take months to plan."

He, Kurt, and Rhett roared with laughter.

Chapter Three

Past

"You bought another house?" Johnnie groaned.

"A small one." Caesar pinched two fingers together, then faked a British accent. "In jolly old London."

"But you love the beach house."

"The beach house is a place to chill, relax, and create. London's full of life and music. Great club scene nearby. We can run around at night and catch some new sounds."

"You could've just rented an apartment."

"Investment."

"You and your investments." Johnnie shook his head, smiling.

"Better than wasting money up my nose or pouring it down my throat."

"Don't start with me."

Caesar wrapped an arm around him. "At least buy a house. Aren't you sick of that dumpy condo in LA yet?"

"It's all I need."

"What's the use of having money if you're not going to invest in nice things?"

"Those pills I took last night were very nice."

"Well, I'm sure you'll find lots of drugs in the clubs near my new place."

Johnnie lit up. "Really? When do we move in?"

Caesar pushed him. "Stupid fool. One day that shit's gonna kill you."

"I'll die smiling."

Present

"I should've brought you here before we got married." Johnnie fidgeted in the backseat of the taxi. His foot repeatedly tapped against the floor of the car.

"Why would you say that?" Melanie took his trembling, sweaty hand in hers.

"You'll see when we get there."

Johnnie rubbed his neck with his other hand. Melanie was about to come face to face with his former life. After their Vegas wedding, he'd whisked her away to Paris for a few days. And since they were so close, he'd decided to take her to his London home. The other one left to him by Caesar. The one he stayed in about five months each year. The one that he'd left in a horrendous mess over a year ago.

There was something comforting about the beach house in Malibu. Even before Melanie arrived, it had always been his refuge. A place where he felt close to Caesar, and far enough away from Los Angeles that he could avoid the nightlife and any trouble it might bring. But the London house was in the heart of the city. And he'd always indulged in his weaknesses when he was there.

"Here we are." The cab driver steered the car to the curb.

Johnnie exited the vehicle, then took Melanie's hand and helped her out. After paying the driver, he wrapped an arm around her shoulder.

"Brace yourself."

"It doesn't look that bad. And you've only been gone a year."

Johnnie stood at the door and took a deep breath. He unlocked it, then motioned for Melanie to go in. "See for yourself."

He hung back a bit, then followed her inside. The stench of stale liquor and trash was in the air.

Her nose wrinkled. "You didn't clean before you left?"

"I usually called someone in to clean up after me." He opened a few windows in the living area. The air was cool, but at least it was fresh. He flashed her a devious grin. "But when I arrived at the beach house last year...there you were. I got distracted."

Melanie turned slowly in a circle, taking in the bare walls and floors. "No furniture?"

Johnnie stared at the floor. "Sold most of it."

"Oh." She frowned. "I thought you weren't supposed to sell anything."

"It's not like Caesar was ever going to find out." He gazed back up at her. "Although I suppose he does know."

Sadness...pity...crept into her blue eyes. That was the last thing he wanted from her. *She needs to see this, no matter how hard it is.*

Although they'd been together over a year, they'd been in each other's physical presence less than that. And even though she'd been a fan of Lush, she really had no clue who Johnnie Vega had been for so many years. Her late husband might have been an alcoholic, but Logan had nothing on him.

"I told you before. Addiction is an expensive disease."

"Yes, you did," she replied glumly, walking over to the wall that separated the living room from the kitchen. She ran her hands over the wall. There were a few holes in it—fist-sized holes.

"It's also a disease that brought out my anger."

She snatched her hand away and shoved it into her coat pocket. Then she walked into the kitchen.

"This is where the smell is coming from."

Johnnie strolled in behind her. The trash from fast-food places littered the table. Bottles of every shape and size lined the countertops. Most were empty. But there was one bottle of whiskey with a swig or two left in it. His mouth twitched. Sweat began to bead on his forehead. He closed his eyes and pushed the idea of drinking, the remembrance of the taste back into the recesses of his mind. Without further hesitation, he took the bottle and emptied it into the sink.

"Did you have a party before you left?"

His face warmed. Melanie turned to him, her eyes questioning. He placed the empty bottle back on the counter and shrugged. "A one-man party."

"You drank all of this yourself?"

"Not in one night."

"Why keep the bottles here? And this trash? Why not throw it out?"

He lumbered over and picked up an empty vodka bottle. "I was fucked up, Melanie. Who knows?"

She threw her arms around his waist, and he rubbed her back.

"Don't feel sorry for me."

"It's hard not to. You were in so much pain."

"I don't need your pity. Just love me."

She pulled away. "You know I do."

"This could come back, Melanie. This ugly side of me. You've only had a small glimpse of what I used to be."

"Don't talk like that. You're doing so well."

"I have to take things one day at a time, and I'm determined to do it, but I don't want you to think I've magically been cured. I'll always be an addict."

She was frowning as she left his side. "Did you at least have a bed?"

Johnnie sensed her apprehension. *Damn!* This was something that needed to be done, but it was terrifying. He could lose her. Melanie had never shown any fear in the face of his problems, but she'd only seen the tip of the iceberg. And since rehab, he hadn't wanted to discuss his disease. Every day with her had been blissful. *Why ruin that? Fuck! Why am I ruining it now?* Because things were serious. It was legal. She was Mrs. Johnnie Vega. Wife of a recovering addict. If she couldn't handle it, then she could get out. Leave him. *Better now than in a few years when she can no longer stand the sight of me.*

He grasped her hand, guiding her upstairs where there were two bedrooms. One had a mattress on the floor. No bedding on it. Bare like the walls. A lamp sat on a small nightstand next to the bed. Unused condoms lay by the lamp.

Johnnie turned away from her. "I used this one when I brought women over."

"I don't need to see this." She wrested her hand free from his, then hurried away to the other bedroom, stopping in her tracks at the door. "Oh my."

He came into the room behind her. The four-poster bed was enormous. The wood all hand-carved. Caesar's dad had been a painter, a sculptor, and a photographer. Art was in his blood, and Caesar loved commissioning artists to make him beautiful things.

Melanie moved her hands up the post, closely inspecting the woodwork. "It's beautiful. Is it an antique?"

"Caesar had it made." He couldn't contain a wicked grin. "For when he brought women home."

She continued to admire the wood, lightly tracing her fingers along the carved flowers and filigrees.

Johnnie sat on the bed. The unmade bedclothes smelled musty, and he pushed them aside. "So, you're not jealous that Caesar had women in this bed?"

"That was a long time ago. You were here just last year."

He sighed heavily. "Sometimes it seems like a million years ago, and other times seems like yesterday."

She shifted her attention to the headboard, pushing the pillows out of the way. He heard her sharp intake of breath when she ran her hands over what was carved there. Nothing an artist had created but what he'd crudely engraved himself...with a pocketknife.

Sorry, Caesar.

It should've been me.

It pained him to see the beauty of Caesar's bed marred by his drunken stupidity. Especially now. For years, he'd blamed himself for Caesar's death, mostly because he could never clearly remember what had happened on that mountain. Now he knew. Caesar had shown both him and Melanie. It had been an accident. He and Caesar had been goofing around. Caesar slipped, then fell from the edge. Johnnie had tried to pull Caesar back up, to save him, but it had been futile. When they both concluded that it wasn't going to happen, he'd told Caesar he wanted to die with him, but Caesar insisted that Johnnie had unfinished business and that he needed to live. Caesar had slipped away from him and fallen to his death.

Johnnie fought back the tears, leaned over, and rubbed the etchings alongside Melanie. "Man, I fucked it up. Damn shame."

"We could get someone to repair it. Another woodcarver could sand it out perhaps."

"We're not going to live here, so does it matter?"

"This bed is gorgeous. We could have it sent to the beach house."

"We could." He glanced at her. Melanie's eyes were wide with wonder as she touched a carved hummingbird. She was smiling, obviously enamored with the bed. "We will."

He watched as she finally slipped away from the bed and opened the closet. She rifled through the clothing. "You left a lot of your clothes."

"How do you know those aren't Caesar's?"

She removed a black t-shirt emblazoned with a red skull on the front. "I know your style. You wore this during the last world tour."

He shook his head, chuckling. "You're good."

"Superfan, remember?" She returned the shirt and began sniffing. She pulled out a denim jacket and held it to her chest. "This is Caesar's"

Johnnie walked over and sniffed the jacket's arm. The slightest hint of vanilla lingered on the fabric.

"We should take all these clothes with us, too," she suggested.

He nodded and left the room. "There should be a suitcase or two in one of the hall closets."

When he returned with the suitcase, he saw Melanie opening a wooden box. One that he'd put away on the top shelf of the closet and forgotten about.

"Melanie, don't."

But it was too late.

As if it contained a poisonous snake, she flung it to the ground. The contents spilled out onto the floor.

He gathered up the syringes, the spoon, the lighter—his drug tools from his heroin days.

She started to wheeze. Her eyes pleaded with him as she patted her chest. "Fresh air."

"Is it a panic attack?" He'd seen her pass out before. It had been one of the scariest things he'd ever experienced. She'd hit her head on the way to the ground, and he'd had to call an ambulance to rush her to the hospital for stitches.

Tears fell from her eyes. She nodded and squeaked out, "Maybe."

He scooped her up in his arms, took her downstairs, and went out the back door to what used to be Caesar's garden. It was overgrown from years of neglect. But somehow, there were flowers that had managed to hang on.

Gently, he put her down but held her close just in case.

"I'm okay," she whispered.

He kissed her forehead. "Are you sure?"

"Just surprised. You told me you quit doing hard drugs years ago."

"I did. I don't know why I kept that shit. Maybe the same reason I kept the empty bottles around. Sick trophies for a sick man."

"None of that is coming back with us."

"Of course not." He squeezed her tight. "I'm sorry you had to see that."

"You overdosed on heroin once, didn't you?"

He drew away and stared at the ground. He pushed a large stone with his foot, loosening it from the dirt. "About a year after Caesar died. The media was coming down hard on me. My parents had taken control of my money. Luckily, the people I was partying with got me to the hospital in time, although my heart stopped beating on the table. When I got out of the hospital, I went to rehab and got off heroin."

"But not the alcohol and pills."

He sensed it. He didn't even have to look at her to know. Her mood was different now. *Probably wondering what she's gotten herself into.*

Melanie walked around the perimeter of the backyard, looking around. She picked a flower, then turned back to him. "What are you going to do with this house?"

"Well, I can't sell it." That was a stipulation in the will. It would always give him a place to live even if times were bad.

"We could stay here sometimes." She came back to him. "You're used to living here during the year. The spring, right? Do you want to still do that?"

"You'd be okay with that?"

She kissed him. "If it's what you want."

"It needs work." He ran a hand through his hair. "Those weren't the only walls I punched."

"We could do some work." She forced a smile. "Make it our own."

Gently, he caressed her cheek and kissed her forehead again. "Honestly, I prefer the beach house, Melanie. All my good memories are there, not here. My life with you is there."

Melanie smiled, then wandered back into the house. He followed her in and watched as she started looking through the kitchen cabinets.

Is she looking for more drug paraphernalia? Pills? Liquor?

"Can I help you find something?"

She found a box of garbage bags and pulled it down from the cabinet.

"Why don't we fix up the house and give it away?" She took a bag from the box and began stuffing trash into it.

He grabbed a bag to do the same. "Give Caesar's house away?"

"He barely used it. You only used it a few months out of the year. We can take anything important back home. But maybe there's a family out there struggling. Maybe a single mother with kids and not enough money for a home. You could help them. It would still be yours in name, but then it would be put to good use. It would have a new life."

He traced a finger along the edges of another hole he'd punched into the wall. *Nothing but bad memories here.* But, if someone new lived here, they could make good memories for themselves. Johnnie smiled. Caesar would like that. His friend had loved helping people.

"What do you think?"

He turned to her. "Caesar gave money to charities all the time. I bet we could contact one to find a mother in need of assistance."

She threw down the bag, wrapped her arms around him, and kissed him.

They parted, and he grinned. "But what happens when you get sick of me, or we fight and you throw me out of the beach house? I'll have nowhere to go."

"You can live in the rehearsal studio." She laughed.

He brushed the tip of her nose lightly with a fingertip. "Aren't you supposed to say, *Oh, Johnnie, that will never happen?*"

"No. Because given how stubborn both of us can be, it might."

"And given my past, I might fall off the wagon."

She shrank back into herself again. Her body shuddered against his.

"Melanie, it's a reality we have to face."

"You've been sober a whole year." She stared at him. "You'll be fine. We'll be fine."

He smiled at her faith in him. Her light always gave him hope...gave him the strength to be a better person. To be the man she deserved. *God forbid, I fail her.* He'd never forgive himself.

"You definitely *are* my biggest fan."

"Always."

"Hope I can live up to the hype."

"You already have." She kissed him, parting her lips, inviting his tongue to invade her mouth.

"Damn," he muttered between kisses. "You know what this is doing to me?"

"Call for a cab so we can get back to the hotel. We'll come back tomorrow and pack things up to ship."

Overcome with desire for her, Johnnie glanced around the room. *No. This isn't the place for us to make love.* He knew it, and so did she. He nodded, pulled out his phone, and secured a cab.

"Take your clothes off extra slowly, babe." He sat on the bed, eager to watch her undress. They'd flirted madly in the cab all the way back to the hotel, each whispering to the other what they planned to do once they were alone. He was hot and hard for her, but still, he wanted to simmer some more.

She slid off her coat and tossed it onto the chair behind her. Sitting on the chair beside it, she slowly unzipped her boots and slid them off each leg. Then she stood again and wiggled out of her jeans. Her black satin panties barely showed beneath the plush sweater she wore.

"You're so beautiful," he whispered, sliding his shirt over his head before tossing it across the room.

She strutted over to him and swept the palm of her hand sensually across his chest. "And you're so incredibly gorgeous."

"Come here." He grabbed her arm. "I can't wait any longer."

He unbuckled his belt, then unbuttoned and unzipped his jeans. She kissed him deeply as he slid them and his boxer briefs from his hips, then kicked his way out of them. She immediately climbed onto his lap and rubbed herself against him. The fabric of her panties felt silky soft next to his hard cock.

"How much do you love these panties?" he whispered, hotly in her ear.

She nipped his ear lobe before whispering back. "Not as much as I love your cock."

A cry of surprise escaped her lips as he grabbed the crotch of the panties and yanked hard, ripping them away from her body.

"Johnnie Vega. You are a naughty boy," she purred, then pressed soft kisses along his neck.

He shivered, his body aching for her. "Now, the sweater."

"I like this sweater." She slid her now naked pussy up and down his cock.

"I'll be gentle then." He tugged the garment over her head and slung it across the room. With his tongue, he teased her nipples until both were protruding through the thin fabric of her bra.

"What are you waiting for?" he asked as he unclasped the bra, slipped it off her, and sent it flying. "Are you going to fuck me, or keep teasing me?"

"I like teasing you." She ran her tongue across his bottom lip.

He flipped her over onto to the bed, dragged her to the edge, then knelt in front of her. "As I do you."

"Johnnie, no. I want you inside of me." She pouted and clamped her legs together.

"Too late." He wrenched them apart, then slid his tongue right up her crevice from her pussy to her clit where he went to work. She sighed dreamily and lay back against the bed.

"You taste so good. I could do this all day long."

She tossed her head to one side and moaned. "You're going to make me cum."

He halted and laughed huskily. "No, because I'm going to stop every time you're about to cum."

"How will you know?"

Instead of answering, he put his mouth on her again. He slid two fingers into her while his tongue flicked across her clit. She moaned again, and when her body began to tense, he stopped.

"I know you, and I know your body, Mrs. Vega."

"Because it belongs to you, Mr. Vega."

He stood and leaned over her. His fingers moved inside her again, working their magic. "Does it now?"

She placed her palms on the sides of his face. "Forever."

"Promise?"

She started laughing.

"What?" He smiled, loving that he could make her so happy.

"I believe I already made that promise a few days ago, right in front of Elvis."

He laughed, too. "Yes, you did, didn't you?"

Suddenly, she went quiet. She stared at him with awe as she caressed his face. "Make love to me, Johnnie."

She didn't take her eyes off him as he crawled onto the bed with her. She backed away until she was lying against the pillows.

He slid between her legs, resting his cock near her wet entrance. "I love you, Mrs. Vega."

"Show me how much."

Johnnie's lips never left hers as he entered her slowly, taking his time to fill her with his thick cock. She spread her legs wider and lightly raked her nails down his back to his butt, then back up again. Soon she was pushing up, matching his movements with her own, forcing him deeper. Holding her tight, he rolled over, letting her take control. She threw her head back and rode him, sensually grinding her hips into him. Lifting his upper body from the bed, he sucked on a nipple as she worked.

"Yes, Johnnie." She moaned, and when his hand drifted back to her clit, she moaned even louder. Her pace quickened. "Don't stop."

His tongue flicked over the second nipple before he tugged on it with his teeth. "I want to cum with you baby."

A cry of passion tore from her throat as her body began to shudder on him. He rolled her to her back and shoved himself deep into her. Her pussy clamped down tight around him, squeezing him until he was cumming himself. Melanie held him tight as he released inside her. Then he cuddled and kissed her tenderly as they came down from their lovemaking high.

"I'm gonna need a nap after that one." He finally moved to his side of the bed and wiped the sweat from his brow.

She snuggled under his arm. "Already tired?"

Johnnie kissed the top of her head. "I'm getting old. Forty-five. Damn, how did that happen?"

His phone vibrated on the nightstand. Melanie scooped it up and glanced at it before handing it over. "Uh, oh. We've been caught."

"Hi, Mom," he answered and switched it to speakerphone. He chuckled. "What am I up to? Are you sure you want to know?"

Melanie smiled. "Hello, Mrs. Smith."

"Hello, Melanie. It's Judy, remember? Can you put me on that *FaceTime* thing so I can see the two of you?"

"We're sort of naked, Mom."

"Don't tell her that." Melanie scrambled under the covers.

Judy Smith laughed. "That's my boy!"

Johnnie turned on the app and kept it focused on their faces.

"There you are," his mom said when her face appeared on his screen.

Melanie waved.

"How have you been, Mom?" he asked.

"I'm fine. I have some exciting news for you."

Johnnie sat up and grinned. "How ironic, so do we."

"You two go first."

"You want to tell her?" Johnnie asked as he hoisted the covers over his own naked body. "It was your idea you know, Elvis and all."

"Elvis? Are you two in Tennessee? Graceland? That's not far from Atlanta. Are you coming for a visit?"

"No, we're actually in London," Johnnie explained.

Melanie tried to straighten her hair. "We just arrived from Paris."

"Paris?" Mrs. Smith placed a hand on her heart and sighed. "That sounds so romantic."

"Perfect place for a honeymoon." Johnnie grinned.

"You didn't!" His mom clapped her hands, laughing. "You eloped and didn't tell me?"

"That would defeat the purpose of an elopement, Mom."

"Whose idea was this?"

Melanie waved her hand. "Johnnie asked me to marry him. I suggested we not wait."

"That's fantastic! I'm so happy for you two." His mom began to cry.

"Mom, don't cry, please. You're going to make Melanie cry. You know she's a hopeless and emotional romantic."

Melanie wiped away the tears that were sliding down *his* cheeks.

"Yes, I can see Melanie's the big blubbering baby," said a familiar voice. Caesar's dad, who Johnnie called Blue Sr suddenly appeared on screen next to his mom.

"What are you doing in Atlanta?" Johnnie asked.

"That's why I was calling you. Blue has decided to move in with me."

Johnnie's eyes widened, and he turned to Melanie. She was smiling and side hugged him tightly.

"That's great news. We're happy for you, aren't we, Johnnie?"

Johnnie was taken aback. Having watched their sons rise to superstardom together meant his mother and Blue Sr had history. A casual friendship cemented by the fact that their sons were best friends. They'd not seen one another in years until the band's autobiography and the new album was launched. The two of them had hit it off well, with Blue Sr flirting nonstop with his mom. They'd even spent the night together. In the past couple of months, they'd visited one another traveling back and forth between Philly where he and Caesar had first met in high school, to Atlanta where his mom now lived.

"The long-distance thing just wasn't going to work," Blue Sr explained.

"How are Robert and Darren taking it?" Johnnie already knew the answer. His brothers had always hated anything to do with Caesar.

"Who cares?" His mom laughed, then kissed Blue Sr's cheek. "I love this man, and I want to spend as much time with him as possible."

Johnnie smiled. He'd not seen his mom this happy in a long time. His own father, Charles Smith, wasn't exactly the romantic, loving type.

"Do you plan to make an honest woman of her?" He teased the two senior lovebirds.

"Since you asked..." Blue Sr stood, reached into his pants pocket, and pulled out a ring. "I was hoping to get your permission."

Melanie sighed as Blue Sr went to his knee next. "That is so sweet."

His mother squealed in delight. She wrapped her arms tightly around Blue Sr's neck. "You see why I love this man?"

Melanie wiped a few more tears from Johnnie's face. She then handed him a box of tissues.

He wiped his nose with one. "This is sort of sudden, don't you think? You've only been dating a couple of months."

"We're not getting any younger," Mrs. Smith joked.

"I've had my eye on Judy quite a while." Blue Sr hugged her close. "It's no secret I never cared much for your father, Johnnie. Not with the way he treated you. After Caesar died, I didn't see your mom anymore, but she called me every year on his birthday and the anniversary of his death. That meant a lot to me. I knew she cared."

"And he always called me anytime he heard news about you."

"We'd end up talking for hours."

"I'm sure my dad loved that."

Blue Sr winked. "I knew the right times to call. When he wasn't around."

Johnnie was surprised. "So, you've had a crush on my mom all these years?"

"I've always had a little crush on him as well," Mrs. Smith admitted.

"I get it." Melanie sighed. "He and Caesar look so much alike. Beautiful curly hair...mysterious dark eyes..."

"Alright, alright," Johnnie interrupted. "Enough of that."

"He's still so jealous of Caesar," Mrs. Smith whispered.

"Mom, I can hear you loud and clear."

"You two should move to California," Melanie suggested. "You could be closer to us, and I know you'd love being near the beach."

"Now that you mention it," Mrs. Smith said. "We've been talking about that. I want to get back into painting. So does Blue. I remember how you said being at the beach house made you feel more creative."

"We're looking into properties," Blue Sr continued. "But they're pricey. If we sell our two homes, we should have enough to make something happen."

"I'll be happy to help out," Johnnie offered.

"I can't take your money, Johnnie."

"I still receive that allowance from Caesar's estate. I don't need it. With our records selling again, and me doing some studio work, I'm good. Consider it a wedding gift."

"I have your permission then? To make her mine?"

"Yes, Blue Sr. Marry my mom and continue to make her as happy as she is right now."

Blue Sr held up a finger. "On one condition."

"What's that?"

"No more Blue Sr."

Johnnie crinkled his nose. "It would be weird to call you Caesar."

"Well, your mom's been calling me Blue."

Johnnie nodded. "Alright, Blue."

"This is amazing!" Melanie smiled. "I get to plan a wedding. It'll be so much fun."

"I told you we could've waited so you could plan your dream wedding."

"I couldn't wait another minute longer to be Mrs. Johnnie Vega."

"Uh, Mom...Blue." Johnnie grinned, then kissed Melanie. "We're going to need our privacy again."

When Johnnie looked back at the screen, his mom and Blue were kissing. "That's my mom!"

He laughed and switched off the app.

Chapter Four

Past

Johnnie was pushing away tears when Caesar's dad entered the living room.

"What's happened?" the older man asked.

"Johnnie should tell you."

Johnnie sniffled and leaned forward on the sofa. "My dad threw me out."

"What? He can't do that. What did your mother say?"

"She was upset, but he wouldn't listen to her. He never does."

Caesar Blue Sr grimaced. "What caused this?"

"School's kicking my ass. I told him I was dropping out."

Caesar's dad took a seat across from him. "You need your education, Johnnie."

"Music is what Caesar and I want to do. The band is great."

"Caesar's not dropping out." Blue Sr glared at his son. "Are you?"

Caesar shook his head. "Rhett and Kurt aren't either."

"They have decent grades. I don't. I won't graduate. They will."

"Dad, you know the band's good. We're starting to get gigs, and we want to hit the road after graduation."

Blue Sr rubbed his hands together, nodding.

"Can Johnnie stay with us? He has nowhere to go."

"I need to talk to your parents about this."

"My dad won't care." Johnnie scowled. "As long as I'm gone, he'll be happy."

"It's true," Caesar pleaded. "His dad treats him like garbage. He hates that he's friends with me, and that we're musicians."

"I still need to let them know where you are and that you're safe."

Johnnie smiled. "Does that mean yes?"

"With a few conditions."

"Anything."

"You find a job and work part-time. Go to GED classes. And help out around here." Blue Sr held out his hand.

Beaming, Johnnie shook it. "Deal."

Caesar hugged his dad, then Johnnie. "It's like we're real brothers now."

Present

"I now pronounce you husband and wife. You may kiss your lovely bride."

Johnnie smiled, watching his mother get married for the second time. His father had passed away not long after he'd met Melanie. The man had made his childhood a living hell. Which is why once he met Caesar, he spent most of his free time at the Blue household. Blue had allowed Johnnie to bring his drum kit over to the garage, and when the band was formed, Blue allowed them to rehearse there. Blue had encouraged his son's musical aspirations, while Charles Smith had always ignored Johnnie's obvious talent. When his father had finally kicked him out, Blue had been there for him again.

While living with Caesar and his dad, Johnnie had taken a part-time job bussing tables at a local diner. At night he worked on getting his GED. Blue helped him study, and to make sense of things he thought he'd never be able to understand. And when Johnnie passed the test, Blue had helped him celebrate by taking him and Caesar out to dinner. In the two years that he'd lived with him, Blue had been more of a father to Johnnie than his own flesh and blood.

The first Mrs. Blue had passed away from cancer when Caesar was only twelve. Johnnie was happy that both Blue and his mother were able to find love again.

His mother looked simply radiant in the cream-colored dress Melanie had helped her pick out. Her dark brown hair was pulled back into a chignon and her eyes sparkled with a happiness he'd never seen.

Blue, looked great as well. He'd pulled back his shoulder-length silver curls into a ponytail and was wearing an off-white linen suit.

"They're so perfect together." Melanie leaned her head against his shoulder, smiling sweetly.

Tenderly, Johnnie kissed her forehead. "Yes, indeed. I'm glad they moved to California. It's nice having them close by."

The small crowd that was gathered at the beach house cheered as the newlyweds ran into the ocean and began splashing one another. Melanie had helped his mom plan a simple wedding. Even though his mom and Blue lived nearby, the house he'd helped them purchase was about a mile inland and smaller. But Johnnie's private beach had provided the perfect backdrop for a wedding. They'd be having the reception on the deck where a local caterer would feed them a nice dinner topped off by delicious wedding cake.

"This is nice," a familiar voice said. "Thank you for doing this for Mom."

Johnnie eyed his brother Robert suspiciously, then forced a smile. Of the two older brothers he had, Robert was more tolerable. Neither Robert nor his oldest brother Darren had been enthused about their mother marrying Blue, but then again, Robert had always gone along with whatever Darren thought and said. Even though Robert was nearing fifty, he still couldn't think for himself. *Probably why he's still single.* Johnnie had to give him props though. He did show up for the nuptials while Darren had flat out refused to attend.

Smiling sweetly, Melanie grabbed his brother's arm. "Robert, why don't we get some photos of you and Johnnie with your mom and Blue? The photographer won't be here much longer."

Robert grinned. "Sure."

No one can say no to my gorgeous wife. Even a hard-headed brother. Johnnie kissed her.

"Everything is beautiful." Blue glanced over at Melanie, gave her a smile and winked. "Thank you for planning this gorgeous day for us."

Johnnie rolled his eyes. "You're married now. No more flirting."

"I'm married, not dead." Blue laughed and wrapped an arm around Johnnie's mother. She wiped a bit of cake icing from the corner of her new husband's mouth.

Grinning, Johnnie pointed a fork in Blue's direction. "You heard me. No more lady's man."

"Aren't I a lady?" His mother threw her head back and laughed. "Can't he be *my* man?"

"He knows what I mean. He's as bad as Caesar."

Blue held up his glass of sparkling grape juice. "Taught him everything I know."

Johnnie groaned. "That's what I'm afraid of."

"Absolutely nothing for you to worry about, son." Blue's tone turned serious. "I love your mother, and I'll do nothing but make her happy for the rest of our days."

Johnnie was confident he would. Blue might have a way with the ladies, but he was also honest and compassionate. The kind of man who'd nurse an injured bird back to health or open his home to a troubled teenage boy.

"You know, I always thought of you as my second son...and now you truly are."

Johnnie turned away, squeezing his eyes tight. *Not going to cry.*

Blue reached across the table and patted his hand. "Aww. You're not going to cry on us? Not bad boy Johnnie Vega?"

"Bad boy Johnnie Vega has *always* been a big pile of emotions." Rhett smiled. Lush's guitarist sat a few seats down from Johnnie, next to his boyfriend, Jaxson. The two of them had been dating for about eight months.

"Yeah, mostly hostile ones," Kurt added. His wife, Sara, sat next to him.

"Those days are over." Blue squeezed his hand. "How long has it been now?"

"Just celebrated my year and a half mark."

Robert gave him an awkward smile, then cleared his throat. "I'm happy for you. I hope it sticks this time. I know it's hard. Working at the VA, I've seen a lot of PTSD cases. A lot of them are struggling with addiction, as well."

"Thanks, bro." Johnnie gave him a slight nod. Both his older brothers were career military. It seemed like Robert was trying to get along. It was weird but oddly nice.

Melanie stood and pushed in her chair. "If everyone's done eating, we can move inside and let these two lovebirds open their gifts. I know they're anxious to get their honeymoon started."

Blue pulled his hand from Johnnie's, then cupped his wife's cheek with it. He kissed her tenderly. "We sure are."

Johnnie smiled. He'd booked the couple a vacation getaway that included a trip to *Disneyland*. It seemed perfect for a couple that were so young at heart. His mother had never been to a *Disney* park despite being a huge *Disney* movie fan.

"This is the last one," Melanie announced, handing a box to Johnnie's mother. The newlyweds were sitting on the sofa in the living room surrounded by their guests. "It's from me and Johnnie."

"It is?" Johnnie stared at his wife from across the room. Their gift was the honeymoon trip. *What else did Melanie buy them?*

Melanie beamed. "Actually, I'm the one who picked it out. Though I'm hoping Johnnie will approve."

"You've given us so much already." His mom excitedly tore the wrapping paper from the box.

"I promise this one is extra special." Melanie bit her lip. "One of a kind special."

"T-shirts!" Blue declared as his mom pulled out two shirts.

Together, the couple read the shirts' printing. His mom gasped. Blue pumped a fist into the air. Both rose from the couch to kiss and hug Melanie.

"What?" Johnnie asked, perplexed. "Are they vintage Lush shirts or something? Mickey and Minnie Mouse?"

Blue held up his shirt for Johnnie to read. *World's greatest granddad.* His mother came over and hugged him tightly. Hers read, *World greatest grandmother.*

Still confused, he looked at his brother. "Did you knock up some woman?"

Robert chuckled and shook his head.

"Oh God, tell me Darren didn't." Johnnie sneered. "He's the last person who needs to be having more kids."

His oldest brother had three adult children. His wife had left him when they were young, and he'd not remarried. *Because he's a jackass.*

"He hasn't mentioned anything to me," Robert replied, still smiling.

Kurt ruffled Johnnie's hair and laughed. "Man, are you that clueless?"

Johnnie shrugged. "What? I'm lost. Who's having a baby?"

Rhett, Robert, and Blue laughed loudly.

"Looks like *you* did the knocking up." His mom kissed his cheek and patted him on the back. "That's my boy!"

His gaze zipped over to Melanie. *A baby?* They hadn't been trying to have a baby. They'd never even talked about it. Well, once Caesar had mentioned it, but she'd said she was on the pill back then. Caesar had been disappointed to hear that. He'd thought the two of them having a baby was a great idea. *What the fuck?*

Johnnie's head spun, so much so that he thought he might pass out. Slowly, he sank down in the nearest chair. *A baby?* "You're pregnant?"

Melanie came to where he sat, took his hand, and placed it on her lower belly. "Yes."

"But...how?"

Rhett nudged Kurt. "You're right. He *is* clueless."

"I know how it happens." With his free hand, Johnnie rubbed his forehead and groaned. He stared at Melanie and whispered, "I thought you were on the pill."

"You're not happy?" Melanie's lower lip trembled, and her eyes filled with water.

Oh no. She's going to cry.

"He's in shock." Blue ambled over and placed a hand on his shoulder. "Son, it's okay. I felt the same way when Caesar's mother told me she was pregnant. Felt like the wind had been knocked out of me."

A baby? He studied his hand on Melanie's belly. He spread his fingers apart.

"Remember when we went to Sydney and then Tokyo for the book signings? I forgot to bring my pills. I told you."

He remembered. Melanie had even wanted to get her doctor to send her a prescription so she could pick some up from a local pharmacy. But he'd said he didn't care. They'd made love many times on that trip. He'd pulled out. *Most of the time. And now we're having a baby?*

"I'm sorry." A tear slid down her cheek.

"For what?" He stood and pulled her close. "For giving me the greatest gift in the world?"

"You're not upset?"

He looked at her again. "Like Blue said, I'm shocked. I wasn't expecting this."

"I wasn't either." She smiled, still crying. "I found out last week, and I thought this would be a nice time to announce it to everyone. I'm sorry I didn't tell you as soon as I found out."

Her hand went to the necklace she always wore. He'd had it sent to her two Christmases ago while he was in rehab. Three sets of angel wings dangled from it. Caesar's name engraved on one set. The other two had her children's names.

Leila. Lily. Their deaths were the reason why Caesar had entered her life. Because of her grief, she'd stopped living. Nothing mattered to her except work. She'd kept her distance from people, not allowing anyone to get too close. But Caesar had taught her how to live and love again. *He brought her to me. And now here I am...making her feel like shit. For being pregnant with a baby! Our baby!*

Johnnie fell to his knees in front of her. He kissed her belly again and again. He pressed the side of his face against it and was overwhelmed with emotion. Never in a million years had he ever thought he'd be happily married with a baby on the way. It was a dream he'd never had because his life had been nothing but an alcohol and drug-infused fog. *Until Melanie.*

He began sobbing.

Melanie's hands went into his hair, massaging his head. He scrambled to his feet and kissed her repeatedly.

"This is how it happened." Kurt came over and hugged him, then Melanie. "Congratulations you two."

Rhett was next. "Congratulations."
Even Robert came over and hugged him.

"Johnnie?" The ocean water lapped at Melanie's feet as she walked toward his rock. The light of the full moon made her skin look luminous.

He offered a hand to help her up. Then she sat next to him. "It's nearly three in the morning. Are you alright?"

"Couldn't sleep." He kissed her cheek and squeezed her hand. "Too much excitement today."

The truth was he was scared shitless. He'd only been sober eighteen months. *What if I fuck up?* A baby was a lot of pressure. A lot of worries. And stress. He was just getting himself...his life back together. He was being asked to play drums again as a session musician. Life was calm. He and Melanie were in a nice place. A good groove. *What will a baby do to that?*

"You're feeling anxious, aren't you?"

She knew him too well.

"I'd be lying if I said I wasn't worried."

Melanie lowered her gaze. "Remember when we first met? You had trouble sleeping because of your nightmares about Caesar's death. And your cravings for alcohol. Have the cravings come back?"

He stroked her cheek softly. "Baby, they never go away. They're always there. Not as strong as they used to be. I know I can live without it. That I want to live without it. But they're always there."

She nodded, turning from him.

"We've discussed this before. About how I'll always be an addict. That I might have relapses. That I'll have to go to meetings for the rest of my life and stay in touch with my sponsor."

"Are you worried about having a baby and trying to stay sober?"

He pulled her gaze back to his. "Melanie, I never expected to be a father. Caesar, Rhett, Kurt. When we talked about the future, all of them talked about having a wife and kids someday. That was never on my agenda. The only commitment I ever honored was the one to the band. They were the only family I ever wanted or needed."

"And now you're married with a baby on the way."

"It's a tough thing for me to wrap my head around. I never imagined myself in this position. Partly because of my addiction. But, mostly because of my family. I don't want to be like my father. I want to be a good dad."

"You'll be a great dad," she assured him before pressing a soft kiss against his lips.

"I wish I had as much confidence in me as you do." He laughed lightly. "My biggest fan."

"It's like Blue said...the first time is always nerve-wracking." She patted his thigh. "Every new parent goes through it. I did with the twins."

He frowned. *Damn! I'm an idiot!* He was so worried about himself, that he'd not once thought about what she must be feeling. She'd lost two children. Her whole world had been turned upside down, and she'd sunk into depression because of it. She had to be feeling anxious, as well.

He wrapped an arm around her waist. "How are you doing with this?"

"A little scared. Being over forty means I'll have to be monitored. And because I had a c-section last time, I'll most likely have to have one again."

That sounded an alarm. "How risky is this? If anything happened to you or the baby..."

"I found a great doctor. And more women these days are having babies at an older age. We'll both be fine."

"I'll go with you to every appointment from now on."

She smiled and kissed him again. "I'm so happy to be having your baby."

"I bet." He chuckled. "I remember reading in that old journal of yours how you wanted to marry me and have three kids and a dog."

She groaned and hid her face in her hands. "You remember that?"

"I'll never forget reading all those fantasies you had about me as a teenager. Some were quite...stimulating."

She placed her hands in her lap. "How about we stick to one baby and a cat?"

Johnnie rested his hand against her belly. "Do you want a boy or a girl?"

"I'd love a boy who is as gorgeous as his daddy." She smiled and ran her hands through his hair. "Dark, wavy hair...beautiful, greyish blue eyes...beautiful smile."

"A bad boy like me, huh?"

"He won't be bad. Maybe a bit mischievous, and definitely creative like you."

"And his mom." Johnnie closed his eyes and imagined himself playing in the surf with the boy she described. Building sandcastles. Teaching him how to play the drums. Maybe he'd grow up and join a band as he had or become a writer like Melanie. *Like Caesar.*

Opening his eyes, he felt pain in his heart and sighed heavily. "It's been so long since we've seen the dolphins. Not since that night I proposed."

"You said it freaked you out when you heard Caesar's voice in your head."

"It did." Johnnie nodded. "But I'd give anything to hear it again. Or at least see the dolphins. Do you think something happened to them?"

She took his hand again, entwining her fingers with his. "I think Caesar knew we were happy. We got married that night. Perhaps he felt we didn't need him anymore."

"Or maybe he was *very* jealous." He grinned.

She laughed out loud. "Okay, I'll let you think that. He was so jealous that I became your wife, so he took off for good."

"I hope it's not for good. I miss him."

"He's here, Johnnie. I still feel Caesar."

"You do?"

She tilted her head back, closed her eyes, and smiled. "Close your eyes and think of him. You'll feel him, too. His spirit is everywhere."

Johnnie kissed her forehead and closed his eyes. Thoughts of Caesar drifted through his mind. How he'd met Caesar in high school by helping him fight off bullies. The exhilaration they'd felt when they jammed with Rhett and Kurt for the first time. The exhaustion from hauling their equipment from city to city, playing any gig they could get. The excitement when they signed their first record deal. And how that excitement multiplied a million times when they first heard their music on the radio. He thought of the first cars they'd bought. Caesar choosing luxury...while he'd chosen the fast sports car. He remembered Caesar crying over him when he'd overdosed on sleeping pills, begging him to live, and he remembered holding onto Caesar as his friend dangled precariously over the edge of a mountain. Desperately, he'd tried to pull Caesar back to safety, but Caesar had finally told him to let go. Told him he had to live on. *You're needed here.* Caesar had told him. *You'll save someone else someday.*

A strong gust of wind whipped past the two of them. With it came the strong scent of vanilla. Johnnie opened his eyes and stared at Melanie. *Caesar was right!* He *had* saved someone. *Melanie.* Her husband had wrecked their car, killing himself and their two children, leaving Melanie near death. Johnnie's father had suffered a heart attack that exact same day. Because he was living with his parents in Atlanta at the time, he'd been at the hospital with them...the same hospital that Melanie was brought to after the accident. Nurses had come around asking people their blood type, desperate to find someone with O negative. A mother who'd been in a car accident and had lost her family required a blood transfusion. *Melanie.* He'd helped save her life and years later she would arrive at Caesar's Malibu beach house and save his. She loved him, believed in him as no one ever had before. The only other person he'd ever felt that close to was Caesar.

The wind whipped around him again. More vanilla. She was right. Caesar's spirit was here. It was part of Melanie. Melanie had a special bond with Caesar. Something Johnnie knew he could never break. And Johnnie's connection to Melanie...even more special. His blood flowed through her veins. It was that connection that had brought Caesar to her, and then Caesar had pointed her in his direction. The three of them would always share a connection. One that could never be torn apart. Caesar would always be part of them, their relationship. Even if he wasn't here in the flesh as he had been those precious months, his spirit was.

Johnnie leaned over and brushed a soft kiss against her lips. Her eyes opened.

"Do you feel Caesar?" she asked.

He nodded and kissed her again.

"Can we go back to bed now? I'm so tired."

He placed a hand on her belly again. "Is my son tired, too?"

"Your son *or* daughter is exhausted. Grandma and Grandpa's wedding wore us both out."

He helped her down from the rock, and they strolled back to the house. After washing the sand from their feet, they went into the house and upstairs to bed.

"We may have to start sleeping in one of the downstairs rooms in a few months. I don't like the idea of you climbing up and down these stairs."

"It will be good exercise. I'll just take things slower. I want to turn the other upstairs bedroom into a nursery and move my office downstairs."

Johnnie pulled back the covers of their bed. They stripped off their clothes and slipped onto the bed. Caesar's custom-made four-poster bed. After it arrived from London, they'd been able to find someone to sand out his depressing words, replacing them with carved flowers and filigrees that matched the rest of the carvings in the wood.

He turned off the lamp on the nightstand, then scooted himself lower, so he could lie near her belly. He rubbed it. "I still can't believe our baby is in here."

Didn't

"I love your voice, though."

"We have to get him listening to music now."

"Or her?"

Johnnie sighed at the thought of a daughter. A sweet girl like her mother but one who could be feisty and stubborn as well. Long dark curls...with bright blue eyes. A mixture of them both.

Melanie ran her hands through his hair as he began singing again. "Our baby's first words will be, *My daddy is a rock star.*"

"That would be so cool." He kissed her belly. "Every single day, our baby will know how much we love them. And no matter what our baby wants to be when they grow up, I'll tell him or her to go for it."

The tears came, and his body heaved with heavy sobs. Melanie didn't question him. Instead, she welcomed him into her arms and held his head against her heart as his body shook. She, who understood him better than anyone else, knew why he was crying.

He cried for a little boy born Johnathan Smith. The boy whose father hated the fact that he loved music. That father had ridiculed him because he wasn't good at sports like his brothers and punished him because of his inability to do well in school. He cried for the boy who had snuck his first drink at age eleven and who by age fourteen had moved on to smoking weed and taking pills to cope with the fact that his father never showed any affection toward him. He cried for the angry teenager who had finally found refuge with a band of friends that he could call his true brothers. And he cried for the man who couldn't wait to shed the name his father had given him. The man who despite being a worldwide success, still doubted himself and had never thought he deserved the adulation being heaped upon him. The man who had never loved himself until a woman had come into his life and finally made him see just how special and worthy of love he was.

He cried until he had no more tears to shed. Then wrapped in Melanie's arms, he drifted off to sleep nestled close to his unborn child.

Chapter Five

Past

"Where's your little brother?" Mr. Smith asked as he got out of the car. "Didn't I tell you to play ball with him?"

Darren groaned. "He doesn't want to Dad."

"And he sucks anyway," Robert added.

Charles Smith entered his house and roared, "Johnnie, where are you? Get your ass outside and play."

Judy Smith met her husband in the foyer. "Charles, come listen."

She grabbed her husband's arm and pulled him down the hallway to the family room. Their six-year-old son, Johnnie, was playing her piano. No music in front of him. Just creating his own.

"I told you I was not paying for piano lessons. He should be outside throwing a football or hitting a baseball like a normal boy."

"He's not had any lessons," Judy whispered. "He's been teaching himself. Doesn't he sound wonderful?"

Johnnie stopped playing and turned to his parents, looking for approval.

"Get up and get outside!" his dad bellowed.

Present

Johnnie kissed the back of Melanie's hand as the two of them stared in awe at the monitor beside the bed. The 3D ultrasound clearly showed them their baby's facial features.

"This is fucking awesome."

"Johnnie," Melanie complained. "Language."

The ultrasound technician whose name tag read, *Abby,* laughed lightly. "Mrs. Vega, I assure you he's not the first father to say those *exact* same words."

He grinned widely.

"Please, don't encourage him."

"Would you like to know your baby's gender?" the technician asked, smiling.

He glanced down at Melanie. They'd been debating on whether they wanted to know or not. "Guess it's time to make a decision."

"It would help us narrow down names and decorate the nursery."

"Plus, you can have one of those gender reveal things." Johnnie rolled his eyes.

Abby nodded. "They've become quite popular, haven't they?"

"Your *Instagram* followers will love it. They're a sappy, romantic bunch."

"Unlike Dad?" Melanie's eyebrows raised. "Who claims to be unromantic but cries every time he feels the baby move."

Abby smiled. "You two are the cutest."

Johnnie grimaced. "Cute? Ugh! You do realize this baby is rock and roll royalty and will be wearing studded leather diapers."

"Mr. Vega, you are too much." Abby laughed, then looked at Melanie. "Yes or no?"

Melanie squeezed his hand. "What do you say, Dad?"

"I say let's do this, Mom." He squeezed back.

"You heard him."

Abby moved the probe around until the baby's bottom came into view. "Now, if baby will just move a tiny bit for us. Oh! There you are, little man."

Johnnie's eyes grew wide. "Is that what I think it is?"

"Well, if you think it's your son's penis, then you're right. Mr. and Mrs. Vega, you're having a baby boy."

Johnnie felt the tears welling up. *Damn!* He wasn't sure whose hormones were worse. Melanie's or his. *A son!*

"There he goes again." Melanie reached up to wipe a few tears from his cheek.

"Aww. It's sweet." Abby clicked a few photos of the baby for them. "I'll save these to a flash drive for you. Then you can email them or post them to social media."

"Johnnie, where are you? I'm waiting by the cribs?"

Johnnie cradled his phone against his ear as he pulled out his wallet to pay the cashier. "I'm in the electronics department."

"You said you were going to the restroom."

"I did. But I got sidetracked."

"We're here to buy for the baby, not for you."

"I am buying for the baby. I'll be there in a second. I promise."

"You'd better hurry, or I'm picking everything out myself."

Johnnie put the bag with his purchase in the cart with the other item he intended to buy at the front check out. He wheeled the cart as fast as he could to the baby department where Melanie was waiting with her own cart.

"Ta-Da! I'm here, baby."

"What is this?" Melanie asked when she saw the box with the toddler drum set in it. "We're buying for a newborn. This is for ages two to four."

Johnnie shrugged. "He'll be two eventually."

"And what else did you buy?" Melanie examined the contents of the bag. "*Beats?* Johnnie, I said buy for the baby, not you."

"These are for the baby. We're going to put them on your belly so he can listen to music."

She shook her head. "You are too much."

"Isn't that why you love me?"

"*One* of the reasons." She smiled sweetly.

He drew her closer and kissed her neck. "Could another reason be the size of my dick?"

A passing couple gasped, looking mortified.

"Johnnie!" Melanie's cheeks turned pink, but when the couple was out of hearing range, she leaned in and whispered. "Yes, that's another reason, but also because you know how to use it very well."

"Then there's the magic tongue." Johnnie stuck out his tongue and wagged it.

Another couple stared at them with their eyes wide.

"Yes, that, too," she whispered again. "Now, please stop. You're attracting too much attention."

"But I like attention. You should know that," he said loudly. He waved his arm around at the other couples. "It's not like they've never had sex. That's why we're all in this department, isn't it?"

Another father-to-be smiled. "Hell yeah!"

Johnnie gave him a high five. "We're having a boy. Just found out today."

"Same here. Congrats," the man said before moving down the aisle with his clearly embarrassed wife.

"Alright back to shopping, babe." Johnnie walked along the aisle of cribs. He inspected a few before turning to Melanie. "Which one do you like best?"

She ran her hands along the rail of one floor-model. "There's too many to choose from. I can't decide."

"What about this one." He examined the information tag attached to the crib, then looked back to Melanie. "Says it converts to a toddler bed when the baby's big enough."

"That's a great idea." She came to him and read the tag as well. "What color should we get?"

"Personally, I like the natural colored wood."

"But white matches better with blue."

"You're honestly going to decorate his room in blue?" Johnnie huffed and crossed his arms over his chest. "How cliché."

She smiled and yanked his arms down. "Okay, Mr. Vega. What would you suggest?"

"Green." He grabbed the ticket for the crib, then pushed the cart further down the aisle. "Follow me."

He led her to the baby bedding.

"See this." He pointed to a bedding set that had a jungle theme. It was decorated with lions, elephants, giraffes, zebras, and monkeys. "What do you think?"

"How did you know about these?"

"I did my homework." He grabbed the baby comforter. "We could paint the nursery the same green that's in the blanket."

She was staring at him, her mouth open.

"What? You don't like it?"

"I love it." She pressed her lips against his. "And I love you."

He chuckled. "Thick dick. Magic Tongue. Excellent decorating skills. What's not to love?"

She answered him with another kiss. "I'm relieved. I honestly thought you were going to paint the room black and red and decorate it with guitars and posters of bands."

"Wait a minute. That's not such a bad idea." He rubbed his chin. "I could even paint musical notes on the walls."

"No. Let's allow him to be a baby. When he gets older, if he's into music, we can redecorate."

"Whatever you say, boss." Johnnie saluted.

"Now load all this bedding into my cart. Even the little stuffed animals. They can go into the cart with your drum set."

Johnnie placed everything she pointed out into the carts. "What's next?"

"Breast pump."

"We already have two of those." Johnnie held his hands up and went for her breasts.

"Don't you dare." Laughing, she pushed his hands away. "Behave yourself."

"Do you think Johnnie Vega has ever behaved?" Gently, he grabbed her around the waist and pressed kisses against her neck.

"No, but there's a first time for everything." She giggled and snuggled against his chest. "Johnnie let's hurry and finish. I'm getting tired. And hungry."

"Me, too." He continued to kiss her neck. "For you."

"The quicker we shop and get out of here, the quicker we get home, and you can do this and whatever else you want."

He pulled away and raised an eyebrow. "Whatever I want, huh? Promise?"

"Yes. Now come on."

Grabbing the handle of the cart, he pushed it quickly up the aisle. "Breast pumps over here!"

Johnnie drove the car up to the wrought iron gate and pressed the numbers of the security code. He pulled the car close to the front door, so he could unload everything they'd bought. The crib would be delivered in a few days. He hoped to have the baby's room painted by then.

He unlocked and opened the front door of the house, then returned to the car and opened the back door. After they'd left the department store, Melanie had stretched out in the back seat and fallen fast asleep.

"Babe, wake up." He shook her gently.

"We're home already?" she asked groggily, trying to sit up.

"Yeah. If you want, you can lie here while I unload the car."

"I'll help you." With Johnnie's help, she sat up and scooted to the door. "What's that smell?"

"I stopped for food on the way home. You said you were craving Indian, right."

"Yes, thank you. I'm starving."

He helped her out of the car, then handed her the bags of food. "Go in and get started. I'll bring in the baby stuff."

"I want to see if I can get all the parents together for a skyping session," she told him. "I'll be out on the deck."

After he'd brought everything in, he grabbed a special box and went out to the deck where Melanie was sitting at her laptop.

"Here's Johnnie now," she announced. "We can tell you together."

He sat the box on the table and rubbed her shoulders. "Your mom or mine?"

"Both. Dads, too. Three-way call."

He leaned over to see the screen of her laptop. "Hey Mom, Blue...Mr. and Mrs. Davis."

"The sonogram was at noon. We were getting worried."

"Sorry, Mom," Melanie apologized. "We went shopping after the appointment. We bought almost everything we needed for the nursery."

"And a breast pump!" Johnnie grinned and kissed the top of her head.

"Please ignore my crazy husband." Melanie rolled her eyes. "He's been in rare form since we left the doctor's office."

"Can't help it. It's been an exciting day."

"Did you find out if it's a boy or girl?" Melanie's dad asked.

"Yes, sir." Johnnie nodded.

"I told you to call me Carl."

"Yes, Carl. We know. We thought about having a gender reveal event of some kind, but we decided to keep things low key instead."

"Good. Now tell us." Mrs. Davis squealed and clapped with excitement.

"Well, I bought something special to help out." He presented Melanie a white box marked *Suzanne's Bakery*.

Melanie appeared surprised. "What's this?"

"Something else I picked up on the way home," Johnnie explained. "Melanie was passed out in the back seat, so I did a little shopping on my own."

"You left her sleeping alone in the backseat of the car?" His mom narrowed her eyes.

"Mom, the windows are tinted, and the temperature today was cool. It was only two quick stops. I swear."

"I didn't even know." Melanie came to his rescue. "I slept from the time we left the store until we got home."

"She's fine." Blue kissed his wife's cheek, then looked at the screen. "Now let's hear about this baby. Grandson? Or granddaughter?"

Johnnie opened the top of the box and pulled out the cake he'd bought. He held it sideways, so the families could see the decorated top. It was white with blue flowers. In the center was something special he'd asked for.

"It's a boy!" He yelled.

"Johnnie! You did not buy a cake with a penis on it!" Melanie groaned and covered her face.

His mom chuckled. "That's my boy!"

"Sorry, Carl...Mary Jo...hope I didn't offend you." He'd only met her parents once in Jacksonville, Florida where they resided. They seemed to like him, but they weren't used to his crazy ways.

"It's cute." Mary Jo smiled and turned to her husband. "A grandson!"

Carl chuckled. "Johnnie, I don't care what you do, as long as you're taking good care of my daughter and making her happy."

"It's what I live for," Johnnie told Carl.

Mary Jo sighed. "Aww...he's definitely a keeper."

"Melanie's hungry, and we're about to eat dinner. So, we're going to sign off. We'll email you the sonogram photos. There's even one that clearly shows he's a boy if you know what I mean."

Melanie shook her head.

His mom laughed. "Can't wait to see them."

Everyone said goodbye, and then Melanie clicked off the messenger icon.

"I cannot believe you bought a cake with a penis on it."

"Actually, I had them add the penis." Johnnie wrapped his arms around her neck. "It's just some icing. No big deal."

Melanie raked a finger across the penis, gathering icing, then streaked it across his face.

He laughed as he sat in the chair next to her and licked some from his lips. "Mmm...tasty. Does mine taste as good?"

She ran her tongue over some of the icing on his face. "Almost."

"Almost?"

Melanie swiped more icing from the cake and ate it. "This is delicious, actually. Did you bring a knife to cut it?"

"Who needs a knife?" Johnnie took a chunk out of the side of the cake with his hand. He held it up to her mouth, and she took a bite.

She grabbed more with her hand, but when he went to take a bite of it, she smeared it on his face instead.

"You're a very naughty girl."

"Who's in love with a very naughty boy." She licked his face again. "Besides, we never had a wedding cake to do this with."

"You're right. We didn't." He grabbed a bigger chunk and stuffed it down the front of her dress.

"Johnnie!" She jumped up, and the cake slid through her dress and down to the deck.

When she grabbed another chunk, he flew down the stairs and taunted her. "Can't catch me."

She threw the cake hard, smacking him in the chest.

"Okay. Okay. I give up." He climbed back up the stairs, stripping his shirt off. While it was over his head, she smacked him in the bare chest with more cake.

He grabbed her with one hand, cake with the other and stuffed it down the front of her dress and into her bra. He smeared what was left on his hand over her chest and neck.

They laughed and played with the cake until there was nothing more of it.

"Oh shit!" He pointed to the sky. "Seagulls are circling!"

She grabbed the hose and turned on the water, but instead of hosing down the deck, she sprayed him.

Johnnie sprinted over to the table where her laptop and their dinner was. "I dare you."

"That's cheating!" Pouting, she handed him the water hose. "You win."

"Actually, I don't, since I'm the one who has to scrub the deck." He stuck the hose between his legs and made her laugh again.

"You have a penis fixation today." She sat back down at the table, opened the food containers, and made each of them a plate of food.

"It's the whole having a son thing." He continued to clean the deck as she began to eat. "Not going to shower off first?"

"Too hungry." She took a bite of her paneer butter marsala. "This is so delicious. Thank you for getting it for me."

"When you have heartburn and gas later you won't be as thankful." He turned off the hose and sat down with her.

"I know, but I've been craving Indian for days." She broke her naan into smaller pieces. "Besides everything I eat gives me heartburn and gas these days."

"Tell me about it. You fart more than I do."

Her cheeks went pink.

"You know it's true." He took a bite of his chicken biryani. "This is good stuff."

"Alright, Daddy, any ideas of what we should name your son?"

"My son?" Johnnie shook his head as he ran a napkin across his mouth. "Wow...I can't get used to that."

"You'd better. He'll be here in a few months."

"Do you have any suggestions?" When Melanie smiled dreamily, he narrowed his eyes and wagged a finger at her. "Nope. No way. We are definitely not naming our son Caesar."

She shrugged, trying to appear innocent. "I wasn't even thinking about Caesar."

"Yeah, you were. I know that look."

"Two Caesars in our lives is enough."

He was still skeptical. "Uh-huh."

She threw up her hands. "Okay, I concede. Don't you think it would be nice to honor Caesar in some way? Maybe his middle name."

Johnnie sliced a hand across his throat. "I am not naming my son Francisco. He'd have to become a black belt in karate before he ever stepped foot on a playground."

"What about Cisco?"

"Oh, I can hear it now." He groaned and shook his head. "All the kids calling him *Crisco* and asking him what he's frying up today."

Melanie rubbed some icing off his arm with her napkin. "Do you want him to be a junior?"

"Ha! Johnnie Vega, Jr.? Not with my reputation. Don't need any of his school friends googling that name."

"You're not helping here. Surely you don't want him to be Johnathan Smith, Jr."

Johnnie's face twisted in horror at the mention of his birth name. "Fuck no. It must be unique. But sensible."

"Well, we have time. We can look at baby name websites to see what we like."

"You named your daughters Leila and Lily, using the L like their dad's name, Logan. Why don't we find a name with an M to go with your name?"

"Mark? Matthew? Michael? Morgan?" Melanie gasped and smiled. "Or even Michelangelo?"

Johnnie roared with laughed and banged the table with his hand. "You want to name my son after a ninja turtle? You really want him to get into playground tussles, don't you?"

Melanie's bottom lip jutted out. "Michelangelo was a famous artist."

"Kids don't know that."

"Then what about J names? Like Josh, Jared, or Justin?"

"Maybe we should wait until he's born and see what he's like?"

"We could do that. Although we'll need a name for the birth certificate."

"We can go into the delivery room with the top five, then make the final decision when we see him."

She reached her hand out to him. "Sounds like a plan."

He shook her hand. "It does. Now, are you ready to take that shower?"

"Are you trying to get me naked?"

"I'm always trying to get you naked."

"Then you clean up this foodstuff while I shower out here. And take my laptop back inside, please."

He shook her hand again, then covered up the leftovers and gathered all the trash.

"That was quick." She smiled sweetly as he joined her in the outdoor shower.

"But you've already got the icing off you. I was hoping to wash you."

She handed him a bar of lavender soap. "I might still be a bit dirty."

"I bet you are." He rubbed the soap in his hands, creating a rich later. After washing himself, he lovingly ran his soapy hands over her bare chest. Her nipples instantly hardened. "Your breasts are getting huge."

"Just like my belly." She dipped under the water, rinsing the soap away.

"You look beautiful." He ran his hands down the front of her body, gently caressing her growing belly. He flicked his tongue across one rosy nipple. "So different from the putrid green color, you were the first few months."

"I was a mess, wasn't I?" She turned around to face the water.

He moved closer to her, pressing his body against hers. His hands slid back to her belly, then up to her breasts. He squeezed gently, and he pressed kisses against her neck. "My beautiful, wonderful mess."

She turned off the water.

"Are we done here?" he whispered in her ear. He rubbed his hard cock against her ass.

"Can we go upstairs? I want to lie down with you."

"Still tired."

"A little."

"Come on then." He grabbed one of the towels he'd brought outside and patted her down, caressing her skin with the plush terrycloth. When he was done, she did the same to him. When she lingered on his cock, sliding the towel back and forth over him, he let out a moan and grabbed her hand. "Enough of that. Off to bed."

He followed her inside and up the stairs, loving the sway of her hips. With each step upward, he got a small glimpse of her pussy, and it made his dick swell even harder. *God! I love this woman!*

Chapter Six

Past

Judy Smith checked her watch again. "We should've heard something by now."

Johnnie put down the magazine he'd been flipping through. "They'll let us know something soon."

His mother stood and began pacing. He felt terrible. Not because he felt any great love for his father, but because his mother felt so guilty about the man having a heart attack. One minute his father had been chewing him out about pills that were missing from the medicine cabinet, and in the next, he was being wheeled out on a stretcher and put into an ambulance.

"Mom, please, sit and calm down. It's not your fault."

"I should've warned him I was throwing those old medications out."

"He would have found some other reason to yell at me. In case you haven't noticed he seems to enjoy doing that."

Johnnie had been living with his parents for nearly two years. The two longest years of his life. It wasn't the best situation, but he'd finished up a drug rehab program that was in Atlanta. It had been a good program, and he liked his sponsor. His mom loved having him around, and his dad was tolerable, but only because he was clean. Still, he harped on Johnnie about not having a job. Even with the millions he had sitting in the bank. Millions his parents controlled. His dad agreed to sign it back over once he was clean for five years. He often thought about going back to Caesar's beach house, the house he'd come to love, but then he'd have no way to prove to his dad he was sober.

A nurse appeared, and Johnnie thought perhaps they might receive some news about his dad.

"Ladies and gentleman," she addressed everyone in the waiting room. "We have an emergency situation. A woman was just brought in. A survivor *of a terrible car accident. She's lost her husband and two kids. She needs a blood transfusion, but her blood type is rare, and we don't have enough on hand. Is anyone here O negative?"*

"That's your dad's blood type." His mother frowned.

"And mine, too." Johnnie raised his hand. "I'll help."

Present

Johnnie pounded away on his drums, feeling the groove as he jammed to one of Lush's biggest hits playing on the stereo system. Melanie was still upstairs sleeping, but he'd been up for a couple of hours. He'd taken a morning swim before coming out to the rehearsal studio to jam a bit. Recently, he'd been offered a stand-in job with a band whose drummer was having some family problems. As much as he'd wanted to take the job, Johnnie had turned them down. The band was embarking on an extensive American tour, and there was no way he would leave Melanie at this time. His son was due in about five weeks, and he wanted to be by her side.

Besides, they were a young band, probably drinking and carrying on like Lush had done when they were young, single, and touring. That environment wouldn't be conducive to his sobriety. He was nearly two years sober, and he wasn't taking any chances.

When the current song ended, he toweled the sweat from his face. The next song that began playing was one of Melanie's favorites. A song about needing and wanting sex. He smiled, hoping she'd be up soon because he might be needing a little action himself. *Hell, I'll even play the song while we make love.* Hearing Caesar's voice always made her wetter, and instead of being jealous that Caesar's voice turned her on, he preferred to reap the rewards that it brought to their lovemaking.

He tapped the cymbal lightly with his drumstick and prepared for the crescendo of the drums that came after one of Caesar's breathy little teases.

Melanie needs you!

He grabbed the cymbal to quiet it. *Caesar?* It had been nearly a year since he'd last heard Caesar's voice. He listened intently. There was nothing. He shook his head. *I must be hearing things.* Perhaps the music had confused him. He eased into the song, banging out the sexy dance rhythm.

Johnnie, she needs you now!

What the fuck? Immediately, he stopped playing, went to the stereo, and turned it off. Silence.

His jerked his head from one side to the other. "Caesar? Are you talking to me? Are you here?"

Melanie's hurt! Help her!

"Shit!" He threw down his sticks, tore out of the studio, and sprinted to the house, entering through the back door. "Melanie!"

"Johnnie." Her voice was weak and strained.

He rushed to the kitchen, where he found her lying on the floor by the foot of the stairs. He knelt to help her sit up. "What happened?"

"I woke up with intense contractions. They hurt so bad, and they were coming so fast. I got scared and came downstairs to find you. My water broke, and I slipped."

He cupped her face and pressed kisses against it. "I'm so sorry. I should've been with you. Are you hurt?"

"The fall didn't hurt me. I was near the bottom step." Tears began to slide down her face. She pulled her nightgown higher. "I'm not sure about the baby, though."

Nothing he'd ever experienced in his life filled him with the kind of terror he felt seeing the blood that streaked her thighs, and that had leaked onto the floor. "Can you stand?"

With his support, she got to her feet. He helped her over to a chair in the living room.

"I'll call for an ambulance."

She squeezed his hand, then winced in obvious pain. "It will take too long for them to get here. Can you drive me to the hospital?"

"Of course."

"I need my purse and phone. And the bag we packed."

"Let me get you to the car first." He helped her to her feet again and slowly walked her to the car. After helping her into the passenger side, he ran back into the house for her things. He grabbed a shirt for himself, as well. His heart thudded in his chest, and his hands shook uncontrollably as he locked the doors to the house.

"I'm scared, Johnnie," she admitted when he returned to the car and placed everything on the back seat. "It's too soon."

He shut the back door, then leaned over her, giving her a tender kiss. "You and our son will be fine. I promise."

She took his hand, squeezed it, then kissed the back of it. He adjusted the seat into a comfortable position for her, then bolted for the driver's side. He slid in beside her and took a deep breath, trying to hold back tears...trying to calm himself before he attempted to drive anywhere.

He started the car, then turned to her. "I'm sorry I wasn't there. I was practicing in the studio."

"It's okay." She grimaced. "Just get us to the hospital."

And then she gripped her belly and screamed.

"Melanie!" The tears came as he tried to pull her close.

"Please." She pushed him away. "Drive."

"Yes, hang on." He opened the security gate and drove through, not bothering to close it. As he turned onto Pacific Coast Highway, he glanced over at her. "We'll be at the hospital in no time."

She smiled, and a tear fell from the corner of her eye.

He reached over and wiped it from her cheek. Then his hand went to her belly. "You stay put til we get there, little guy."

"I love you, Johnnie," she whispered.

He took her hand and kissed it. "Caesar popped into my head again. He told me you were in trouble."

"Our guardian angel." Her eyes drooped, then shut.

"Melanie?" He stroked her face, but she didn't wake. "Shit!"

Johnnie pulled up to the emergency room's entrance and jumped out of the car. As the doors slid open, he rushed inside, waving his arms in a panic, looking for someone...anyone...to help him. "I need help! Can someone help me, please?"

A security guard approached him. "What is it, sir?"

Frantically looking around, hoping to spot actual medical personnel, he yelled again. "My wife is pregnant, and she's bleeding badly. She's right outside in the car. Please, someone, help us!"

An orderly dressed in hospital scrubs came rushing toward him with a wheelchair.

Johnnie shook his head. "No. She's unconscious. Do you have a stretcher?"

The orderly disappeared, then came back with a stretcher. A nurse was with him. Together, they all raced outside to the car.

"She said she woke up having contractions, and when she came downstairs to tell me, her water broke. She slipped and fell."

"How long has she been unconscious?" the nurse asked.

"Not long after we left home. It was about a fifteen-minute ride."

Another orderly joined them, and he and the two men gently lifted Melanie from the car. Where she had been sitting was stained dark with blood.

"There's so much blood." Johnnie rubbed his face with his two hands, trying to hold it together as the two men moved Melanie to the stretcher.

"Get her into an operating room stat!" The nurse yelled to the orderlies as they reentered the hospital. "The doctor will want to perform an emergency caesarian."

"Is she going to be okay?" Johnnie followed close behind.

"We'll give her and the baby the best care." The nurse took a notepad and pen out of her pocket. "How many weeks along is she Mr..."

His hands trembled, and he stuck them into the pockets of his shorts. "Mr. Vega. Her name's Melanie Vega. We had five more weeks until her due date."

"Anything out of the ordinary happen before this?"

"Nothing. She's forty-two, but her doctor said that wouldn't be a problem. We had the amniocentesis, and things were fine. She's been exercising and eating right. We've been extra careful."

"What's her obstetrician's name?"

"Dr. Velacruz. Maria Velacruz."

When they reached the double doors that led to the operating rooms, the nurse held her hand up. "Mr. Vega, you'll have to stay in the waiting area and fill out the paperwork needed in order to admit her to the hospital."

"Please." Johnnie tried to push past her. "I need to be with her."

The security guard started toward them, but the nurse held out her hand to stop him. "You can see her as soon as it's possible. You have my word."

Johnnie squeezed the bridge of his nose, trying to stop the tears from coming.

She gently patted his arm. "Do you have family you can call? Someone to sit with you while you wait?"

Opening his eyes, Jonnie nodded. His phone. Her phone. *Everything's in the car.* He needed to park the car. *The blood. She's losing too much blood.*

He tried to speak, and his voice cracked. He was losing it. "Nurse. Melanie and me. We share the same blood type. O negative. If she needs a transfusion, I can help. I've done it before. I saved her life before."

The nurse nodded and smiled. "I'll let the doctors know."

Johnnie's lip trembled as the first tears slid from his eyes. He gripped the nurse's arm. "Please don't let her die."

The nurse placed a hand on his back, then motioned to the security guard. "Frank, take this gentleman over to admitting so he can get his wife checked in."

"I...I need to move our car."

"First, I want you to sit down and take a few deep breaths," Frank told him as the nurse slipped through the double doors. "Then we'll get everything taken care of."

Johnnie sat in the emergency waiting room, a nervous wreck. Every few minutes he'd jump up and pace around before returning to the chair he'd claimed earlier. *Why is it taking so long?* Not knowing was driving him crazy. He wanted to see her...to know she'd be alright. *She has to be alright.*

He stared at the ground, his foot incessantly tapping the floor. He closed his eyes and thought of his best friend. *Are you still with me, Caesar? Can you tell me anything? Is she okay?*

But there was nothing. Caesar was no longer in his head. *Was he ever there?* Maybe he'd just imagined it. Maybe it was simply intuition...a feeling that Melanie was in trouble. That something was wrong.

"Johnnie, sorry it took us so long to get here." Blue's voice. "Any word?"

Johnnie looked up to find Blue and his mother rushing toward him. He stood, and his mother wrapped her arms around him. His body began heaving with sobs.

"Nothing," he managed to say. "It's been nearly two hours, and I've not heard anything."

"She'll be alright." Blue patted his back. "Women have been having babies for thousands of years. Much of that time without doctors and hospitals."

Johnnie wiped at his face. "But there was so much blood. I know something's wrong."

"They'll take care of it," Blue assured him.

"They will, honey." Johnnie's mom took his face in her hands and kissed each cheek.

"I'm so scared, Mom. I've never felt this terrified about anything. Not since Caesar. I can't lose her, too."

"Mr. Vega?" A man in scrubs with a stethoscope around his neck approached them.

"Yes." Johnnie started to take the doctor's outstretched hand. "How is she? Is my wife okay?"

"I'm Dr. Stevens. Let's sit for a moment."

No. When you sit, they tell you someone died. His hand dropped back to his side as he started to tear up again. *She can't be dead. I'd know it. I'd feel it. Just like I felt she was in trouble.*

"I'm Mr. Blue, and this is my wife." Blue shook the doctor's hand and then sat. "We're the paternal grandparents. As you can see, my son is very upset."

"I understand." The doctor pulled a chair closer to them and sat down.

Johnnie reluctantly sat as well.

The doctor leaned back in the chair and crossed one leg over the other. "Mr. Vega, we did an emergency caesarian section to deliver your son."

"Is the baby okay?" his mother asked.

"Yes. He's a good weight. A little over six pounds. We'll keep him here a few days to make sure no problems develop and see that he gains more weight, but everything looks good so far."

"Oh, thank goodness." His mother smiled, took Johnnie's hand, and squeezed it. "That's good news."

For some reason, he hadn't even been thinking about his son. Only Melanie. "My wife?"

"She lost a lot of blood, so we gave her a transfusion."

"You should've taken mine. We're the same blood type."

The doctor smiled. "We had enough on hand to help her."

"When can I see her?"

"They're moving her into a room."

"Then I can be with her?"

"Mr. Vega..." The doctor sighed heavily. "I'm afraid she's slipped into a coma."

Blue inhaled sharply. "A coma?"

"We're not sure why. She's stabilized. Vitals all normal. Her brain activity is fine. Because of that, we're hopeful that this is just a temporary condition and she'll wake soon."

A hundred tiny daggers stabbed Johnnie in the heart. His voice rose as he questioned the doctor again. "Can I see her?"

"Yes, I'll have someone escort you to her room. She's in ICU."

"And my grandson?"

"He's in neonatal. You're welcome to see him, Mrs. Blue." The doctor stood again. "Please be assured Mr. Vega that we're doing everything we can for your wife. Dr. Velacruz arrived, and she'll be able to tell you more about Mrs. Vega's condition and what we did for her."

Johnnie stood, politely shook the doctor's hand, and thanked him. Dr. Stevens called over a nurse to take him to Melanie.

"Do you mind if we go see the baby?" his mom asked.

"It's fine," he assured her. "I need to be with Melanie."

Blue wrapped him up in a tight hug. "We understand. Go to her."

Johnnie took Melanie's phone from her purse and handed it to his mom. He punched in her password. "Can you call her parents and let them know what's happening? Maybe take a few photos of the baby to send them?"

"You haven't called them?" his mom asked.

"I couldn't." He rubbed his forehead. "Not until I had something solid to tell them."

Blue patted his arm. "No worries. We'll handle it."

The nurse led him to the intensive care floor and stopped at the information desk. "This is Mr. Vega. He'll be with his wife, Melanie Vega, the patient who was just brought into ICU from emergency."

Another nurse took over, showing him to Melanie's room.

"We'll be right outside if you need anything." She opened the door for him. Another nurse was inside hovering over Melanie.

The room was cold and sterile, nothing like the birthing rooms where they'd planned to be. Melanie was supposed to be in a private room, one with a rocking chair, where she could sit and nurse the baby. Where he could sit and bond with his son. *Everything we planned is fucked up.*

"Are you Mr. Vega?" The nurse asked without even looking at him. She was checking Melanie's pulse and using an iPad to make notes. She was a tiny African-American woman, about five feet tall, with her black hair pulled back into a bun.

Johnnie swallowed hard. Unable to find his voice, he nodded and stood planted at the door. Terrified. He squeezed his eyes shut. *I can't lose her. Not Melanie, too.*

The nurse finally looked at him. "Don't be scared. Her vitals are good. Come over and see her."

His feet refused to cooperate.

"I'm Gailya." The woman smiled warmly. "I promise I don't bite. I want to talk to you about your wife, so come on over. You can put her purse and bag down on the chair."

Finally, his feet moved. He placed Melanie's things on the chair, then slowly approached the bed. When he saw her, tears slipped down his face. Her skin was translucent as if she were already...

No, she cannot die!

"She's so pale."

"She lost a lot of blood. But with the transfusion she's had, the paleness will subside in time."

He reached out and touched her cheek. It was warm.

"You want to know what I think, Mr. Vega?"

Johnnie's gaze returned to Gailya. He nodded.

"Melanie's just tired. She lost all that blood and had to undergo major surgery. Her body needs some rest. She'll wake up when she's good and ready to."

Johnnie wiped the tears from his cheeks. "You've seen other people in comas?"

"Lots of them. I've been working ICU for nearly twenty-five years."

"Can she hear us?"

"Well, the experts argue about that, but it's been my experience that it helps to talk to coma patients. And sometimes when they wake up, they'll say they heard family members speaking to them. So, you should talk away. Tell her all about that sweet baby boy that she's delivered to the world."

Johnnie liked the woman's smile. It seemed genuine. Gailya was friendly and made him feel at ease. And she seemed confident Melanie would recover. He liked that. Melanie thrived on positivity.

"I have more rounds to do, but I'll check-in with you two later."

"Thank you," Johnnie replied.

"When I'm on duty, I'll be your wife's nurse, so we'll get to know one another better. I heard through the nurse's grapevine that you two are famous. You'll have to tell me all about that."

Johnnie forced a smile as Gailya left. Then he turned his attention back to Melanie. She looked small and helpless lying there with an IV in her arm, monitors strapped to her chest. *Famous?* What did that even mean when you were in a situation like this? *Absolutely nothing.* It certainly hadn't prevented Caesar from dying.

He pressed kisses against Melanie's forehead. "I'm here, baby. I came as soon as I could. I had to wait for the doctors to tell me it was okay. I missed you. I love you so much."

He picked up her hand and held it, entwining her lifeless fingers with his. He kissed the back of her hand.

"You did it, babe. We have a son. And we didn't even pick out a name yet. Not even a top-five list like we planned. That means you need to wake up so you can help me decide. If I pick the wrong one, you'll be raising hell with me. Although nothing I choose could be worse than Francisco."

He laughed nervously, and the door opened again.

"Mr. Vega, how are you holding up?" Dr. Velacruz asked as she shook Johnnie's hand. "You don't have to answer that. I know this is nothing like we planned. And seeing her like this must be extremely upsetting."

He choked back tears. "You said everything was fine. That there would be no problems."

"There was nothing in any of her checkups that indicated this would happen." She placed a gentle hand on his shoulder. "An unexpected complication. Her uterus ruptured, Mr. Vega. That's what caused the bleeding."

"Was it because she fell on the stairs?"

The doctor grabbed Melanie's chart and looked it over. "Dr. Steven's noted that she was having contractions before the fall, is that right?"

"Melanie said she woke up with them. Said they were very painful."

"The rupture is what caused the early labor then. It's rare, and most often happens in women with previous caesarian births. The good thing is you got her here quickly. Otherwise, we might have lost her and the baby."

Thank you, Caesar. Or intuition. Whatever it was, it had saved Melanie's life. *And our son's.*

"Speaking of your son. He's doing very well. Has quite a pair of lungs on him. A little rock star, just as Melanie predicted. The pediatrician will be taking over his care from here. And they'll be a specialist taking over Melanie's care."

"We won't see you anymore?"

"If I'm at the hospital, I'll drop by to see how she's doing." Dr. Velacruz returned Melanie's chart to its place on the wall. "But there's nothing I can do for her at this point."

"Doctor?"

"Yes?"

Johnnie couldn't put into words how he was feeling. "Thank you for your help."

"I didn't do much. Dr. Stevens handled most of the work." Dr. Velacruz pulled down the blanket, pulled up Melanie's gown, and touched her belly lightly. The bottom part was covered in a gauze bandage. She lifted the tape and pulled back the bandage.

Johnnie cringed when he saw the staples. The skin around them was already bruising. Dr. Velacruz examined the surgical wound, nodded, then returned the bandage.

"Dr. Stevens did a fine job with the surgery." Dr. Velacruz announced as she covered Melanie once more. Her brow furrowed as she turned her attention back to Johnnie. "There's another thing I need to discuss with you, Mr. Vega."

Johnnie noted the change in the tone of her voice. "What is it? It's bad, isn't it? Just tell me. How much worse can it get?"

The doctor took his hand. "The way we deal with a ruptured uterus that is causing that much bleeding is to remove it."

"How serious is that?"

"Very serious. It solved the problem at hand. And many women have their uterus removed with little physical difficulty. But it can throw off hormone levels and causes some women to have emotional difficulties. Especially because they're unable to have more children. Sometimes they feel like less than a woman."

How will this affect Melanie? They hadn't even planned on this baby. They were both getting older and had no further baby plans. Still.

"I guess we'll cross that bridge later when she wakes up."

Dr. Velacruz smiled. "I have faith that she'll wake soon. She was so excited about this baby. She'll be anxious to see him."

"I hope you're right." Johnnie nodded.

"By the way, Melanie was adamant about breastfeeding. Due to the circumstances, I've taken the liberty of ordering donor breastmilk for your son."

"That's a thing?"

"Believe it or not, yes. Some mothers end up not being able to breastfeed. So, other mothers donate their extra milk to help out."

Johnnie rubbed his forehead. *What would Melanie think of their son drinking another woman's milk?* "She told me breast milk was the best thing to feed babies."

Dr. Velacruz nodded. "She said that to me as well. The nursery will be feeding him the donated milk, and when he goes home, we can put you in touch with the donor bank."

Home? I can't take the baby home. Johnnie shuddered and stared at the floor. *Not without Melanie.*

"Thank you, Doctor," he said without looking up.

She hugged him. "Have faith. Talk to her. Let her listen to her favorite television shows and songs. Perhaps your band's music since she loves it so much."

"I'll do anything it takes. She's my life."

Dr. Velacruz pulled away. She grabbed each of his shoulders, and Johnnie returned his gaze to hers. "And now you've created a life together. Don't forget about your son. He needs you, too."

Johnnie nodded, and the doctor left. He went to Melanie and held her hand again.

"I'm sorry, babe." His bottom lip quivered. "I can't see him yet. You're going to wake up soon, and then we'll see him together. He should see us together. His mother and father. Just like he would've in the delivery room."

"I'll play some music, babe. You'll like that." Johnnie pulled his phone out of Melanie's purse. He scanned through the music and chose her favorite Lush love song.

"I know it's your favorite. One of Caesar's sappy love songs." He laughed lightly and set the phone next to her pillow. "You and Caesar are such hopeless romantics."

Johnnie brushed his fingers lightly through her hair, then kissed her forehead. "I remember the day he wrote it. We were on our first world tour and had a few dates scheduled in Italy. After the shows, we got time off and headed to Venice. Caesar had been looking forward to seeing the city, but I got sick. Had nothing to do with drugs or alcohol. I had a stomach virus. Rhett and Kurt went out site seeing, but Caesar stayed by my side all day long watching over me. There was this large window in the room with a beautiful view of the canals. Caesar watched the people below, riding in the gondolas. He saw a couple he thought might be on their honeymoon. Said they seemed so happy. He began imagining their love story. How they met, their first date, how the guy proposed, what their wedding was like. He wrote the song about them."

Johnnie spent the next half hour playing songs for her and telling her stories of the band. She'd always loved hearing those. When they first met, and he'd been having nightmares about Caesar's death, she would lie in bed with him. He'd tell her band stories until they fell asleep next to one another.

When his mom and Blue entered Melanie's room, he was telling her again how he and Caesar had met in high school.

His mother came to Melanie's bedside and wrapped an arm around his waist. "I'm so sorry this is happening."

"Me, too." Blue ruffled his hair, and the three of them stood staring down at Melanie.

"Were you able to contact her parents?"

"Yes. They're flying out tomorrow morning."

Johnnie nodded. He was grateful they'd made the call. He wasn't sure he could've found the right words. They'd almost lost Melanie once before. *What if they blame me?* Johnnie closed his eyes tight. *It's not my fault...the baby did this. But who put the baby there?*

"Would you like to take a walk and see the baby?" his mom asked and hugged him to her. "He looks just exactly like you."

"That he does." Blue chuckled. "A head full of dark curls. All the nurses are fawning over him."

"I...I need to stay here. In case she wakes up. She needs me. I'm playing her favorite songs and telling her stories, so she'll come back to me. I need her to come back to me."

"Well, let me show you the pictures I took of him." His mom pulled Melanie's phone from her jacket pocket.

Johnnie pushed it away. "Not now, Mom. I have to focus on Melanie and helping her get better."

"Johnnie, I don't understand. This is your son. You should want to see him."

But I don't because I'm a horrible father. How could I let this happen to his mother?

"I can't right now."

Blue rubbed his wife's shoulders. "Hun, it's been a stressful day for Johnnie, and I'm sure he's in a lot of pain right now. Let's allow him to handle things at his own pace."

Tears began to emerge from Johnnie's eyes again. *Blue is such a great father. Unlike mine. Unlike me.*

"Why don't we get some coffee?" Blue kissed his mom's cheek and drew her toward the door. "Or a bite to eat? Then we'll visit the baby again."

She paused, staring at Johnnie, then nodded. "Would you like us to get you something to eat?"

The last thing he'd eaten was an apple before playing drums this morning. But, the thought of eating anything now made his stomach churn. "I'm fine."

His mother hugged him once more and left with Blue.

Johnnie leaned over the bed and sobbed against Melanie's chest. "What's wrong with me?" *What kind of horrible father refuses to look at his new baby?*

"Come back to me, Melanie, please. I told you before I can't live without you. My life meant nothing until I met you. It will mean nothing without you."

His phone began playing the next song on his list. An upbeat number that always got Melanie dancing. Johnnie couldn't control his smile as he remembered her dancing to it with Caesar. He'd watched them dancing naked around the living room before he'd stripped off his own clothes to join in the fun. They'd ended up on the floor, wrapped in one another's arms, each of them taking turns making love to Melanie.

He jerked himself back to standing straight. *Where the fuck is Caesar? He should be here to help her.* If he could come back from the dead and turn into a dolphin, surely, he could help Melanie wake up. *Where are you, Caesar?*

Chapter Seven

Past

Johnnie stood just outside the kitchen, eavesdropping on his parent's conversation. They were talking about him about the fight he'd just gotten into at school. He'd been suspended...again.

"Something's not right with that boy, Judy. Why can't you see that?"

"Nothing's wrong with him. Why do you want him to be like his brothers? Robert follows Darren and does whatever Darren does, but Johnnie's his own person. There's nothing wrong with that."

Johnnie smiled. His mom tried hard to take up for him when his dad was ragging on him, but his dad never listened.

"He's headed for trouble. He barely gets by in school."

"Maybe if you'd try to show him a little kindness, things would change. And take an interest in his music."

"Music is not going to get him anywhere in life."

"He thinks you hate him, Charles. I know you don't. Why don't you show him you don't?"

His dad fell silent and didn't speak. Johnnie knew what his dad was thinking. His mom was wrong. His dad did hate him. He'd tried hard not to hate his dad back, but it was getting harder not to. How could you love anyone who made your life miserable?

He'd show his dad. Music would get him somewhere in life. He was going to be famous. Then maybe his dad would love him.

Present

Mr. Vega, I am about done with you!" Gailya maneuvered around Johnnie as she approached Melanie's bed.

"Why?" Johnnie groggily sat up and blinked his eyes, trying to focus. "What did I do?"

"You slept here again."

"I can't leave her."

Gailya shook a finger at him. "You've been here for three days straight. And quite frankly, you're smelling a bit funky. You need to go home, take a shower, and shave that mess off your face."

Johnnie couldn't help but smile as he stood and stretched out his limbs. Over the last few days, he and Gailya had become fast friends. He rubbed his chin. "It's not that bad."

"Have you looked in a mirror?" She pointed at his face and waved her finger around. "You've covered that gorgeous face of yours with all that scratchy stubble. If Melanie wakes up, she won't even recognize you."

He frowned. "Not if...when."

Immediately, her eyes filled with sympathy. "I'm sorry. You're right. *When* she wakes up."

"Thank you."

"And when she does, she'll get a whiff of you and pass out again." Gailya chuckled as she took Melanie's vitals and checked her over.

Johnnie smiled. "I cleaned up in the bathroom. And my folks brought me deodorant and a change of clothes."

Gailya rolled her eyes. "The bathroom is not a shower. And that deodorant is not working. With all this worrying you've been doing, you know you've been sweating double time."

"What if she wakes up and I'm not here?"

"Your parents or her parents would be. Or one of us nurses. And we'd call you immediately."

Johnnie came to Melanie's bedside and softly stroked his wife's cheek. "I can't leave her like this."

"This is not doing you any good. You need fresh air. You need some decent food. Melanie would want you to take care of yourself."

He'd been eating out of vending machines, and Blue and his mom had brought him a few fast-food meals. That was better than anything he could create on his own at home.

"Didn't you tell me you two had a cat? One that Melanie rescued? Who's taking care of the cat? If something happens to that animal, Melanie's going to be highly upset with you."

Poor CJ. His mom and Blue had been going to the house to feed him and check on things, but CJ was probably missing them, especially Melanie. The cat curled up in her lap every night when they watched television together.

Gailya grabbed his arm gently. Her dark eyes softened. "I heard the baby is being released in two days. Did you go see him yet?"

Johnnie's face flushed hot as his gaze fell to the floor.

"Mr. Vega, I don't understand." She moved back to Melanie and pulled back the covers so she could empty Melanie's catheter bag and check her surgical wound. A feeding tube had been inserted into her stomach. "He's your son."

Johnnie watched the nurse's careful attention to his wife. He felt sick, gutted by guilt. He could not bring himself to face the baby. Not yet. He'd heard about him from everyone. His mom, Blue, and Melanie's parents adored their new grandson.

For months, Johnnie had been so excited to have a baby. *With Melanie.* That was the problem. Melanie wasn't with him. He was alone. And alone, he wasn't ready to be a father. *How can I take care of our son alone? I can barely take care of myself.*

Worst yet, was the nagging feeling that had Melanie not gotten pregnant, she would not be lying here in a coma. She'd be with him. They'd be together at home, him practicing and making music, her writing books. They'd be walking on the beach, relaxing in the jacuzzi, or lying in bed making love. That was gone. He'd have to go home to an empty house and try to live without her. *Because of the baby.*

I'm a monster. How can I blame a baby? Our baby? Yet there was a part of him that did. A part of him that wished she'd never gotten pregnant. *And isn't that my fault? I could have put on a fucking condom. Or let her get her prescription filled.*

"Please don't give me a hard time," he pleaded to Gailya. "I'm working through some stuff."

"I see the trouble written in your face." Gailya jotted some notes down on her iPad, then looked at him. "Just an FYI, they hold AA meetings here in the hospital chapel. On Thursdays, which would be today."

"I'm fine." Johnnie walked to the chair he'd been sleeping in and plopped down. He wiped his face with his hands. "How did you know?"

"Some of the other nurses were talking about who you were, so I got curious. Went home and did a little snooping on the internet."

"Fucking internet." He grumbled.

Gailya came over and laid a hand on his shoulder. "Since you've become a hermit in this room, you should know the story is out there. About Melanie and her condition."

He jumped up. "What? How?"

Gailya sighed heavily. "Hard to keep secrets when you're a celebrity."

"I'm not a celebrity! That was years ago."

"Your band is a pretty big deal from what I could tell. And your wife being an author and director...yes, I'd say the both of you are famous."

"Fuck." He groaned.

"Have you been on *Twitter* lately?"

He shook his head. "I'm not into all the social media stuff. Melanie handles all that for the band and her books. I steer clear of it."

"Get your phone and log on."

Johnnie grabbed his phone off the table next to the bed. He entered his password, then clicked the *Twitter* icon. He'd never had much use for social media, but Melanie had tried to teach him about the different sites. He went to the band's official page.

"Holy shit." There were thousands of notifications with the band, and Melanie tagged in them. He was pleased to see that all of them were positive messages wishing Melanie well.

"You two are well-loved." Gailya smiled sweetly.

"I guess so." It really shouldn't have surprised him as much as it did. The Lush documentary...the autobiography...the new music...were all huge successes. Melanie's romance novels sold well. The fans were out there. Which also meant the press would be as well.

"Have any reporters been hanging around?"

Gailya nodded toward the door. "Ask them."

Blue and Melanie's dad, Carl, entered the room. Carl being over six feet tall, towered over both him and Blue. The man was an intimidating presence. Like Johnnie's brothers, Carl was a military man although he was now retired.

"I'll come back later to check-in," Gailya assured him, then pinched her nose. "Hope you go home and take that shower before then."

Blue hugged him and wrinkled his nose. "She's right. You need a good scrubbing."

"And a shave," Carl added.

"I know. I know. I've heard all about it from Gailya."

"Why don't you go home and get some real rest?" Blue asked, patting his arm. "Some good food and a long shower will do you good."

"Good food?" He shrugged. "Melanie's the cook. Not me."

"I'm sure Judy would come over and cook for you."

"I'm okay, Blue. I am. I need to be here for her."

"If anything changes, we can call you," Blue assured him. "Go home and check on things. Get yourself cleaned up. You'll feel better for it."

"And go see your son," Carl said gruffly, glaring at him.

Johnnie cringed. Melanie's dad was a no-nonsense type of guy, saying whatever was on his mind. Carl wasn't happy that he hadn't gone to see the baby. Or even named the baby. And Carl reminded him of that fact often.

"I will," he mumbled, turning away from Carl's judgmental stare.

"We can go right now." Carl swept his arm toward the door.

"I can't." Johnnie shook his head. "I'm a mess. Dirty...with germs."

"Then do what Blue says. Go home and clean yourself up!"

He quickly changed the subject. "Are there reporters outside?"

Blue nodded. "A few have been hanging around. They've asked questions, but we've ignored them. Kurt said he would handle the band's statements to the press."

"Good." Kurt was great at that sort of thing. He was the most sensible and business-minded of the band. Caesar and Rhett were the romantics...the dreamers. *I'm the hot mess.*

Carl crossed his arms over his chest. "The hospital has been doing a good job keeping them out. But Kurt suggested we get a security guard for Melanie's room."

Johnnie scratched his head. "Security?"

"In case any reporters manage to sneak their way up to this floor," Blue explained.

"If Kurt thinks it's a good idea, I'm okay with it." Johnnie sighed. "Where's Mom and Mary Jo?"

"The nursery." The lines in Carl's forehead gathered together. "Feeding *your* son."

Not again. Maybe he did need to get out, to get away from Carl's wrath. Johnnie went to Melanie's bedside, stroked her cheek, and kissed her lips softly. "I've gotta go for a little while, but I swear I'm coming back. I'm a phone call away. Your dad and Blue are here. Our moms are close by, too. They'll look after you. And if you decide to wake up, they'll let me know."

He grabbed his car keys and phone. "Promise me that if anything changes...anything at all, you'll call me right away."

Blue nodded. "Of course, we will."

He started out the door, but Carl roughly grabbed his arm. "Your son needs you, too."

Johnnie nodded and left. Once on the elevator, he stared at the numbers. He should go see his son. The third floor was where the nursery and all the new moms were. *All of them except Melanie.* He pressed number one.

When he arrived on the first floor, he went to the front desk.

"Johnnie Vega!" the security guard said upon seeing him. He stood and held out his hand. "Can I help you?"

Johnnie had forgotten how it felt to be recognized out in public. After Caesar's death, he'd spent years avoiding the public eye. Now that he was back in it, he had to get used to it all over again.

Johnnie shook the man's hand. His ID read, *Antonio.* "I wanted to say thanks for making sure my wife is safe and that my family has privacy."

Antonio smiled. "I appreciate that. We've had a few reporters try to get in. Luckily not many. But we do have a bunch of flowers and toys that have been received for your wife and son."

"What? No one's told me."

"Well, she can't have them in ICU, and since your son is staying in the nursery, they have no place to put them. They're in a room being held for you. I'll show you."

Together they walked down the corridor.

"When flowers are delivered, they come here," the guard said, opening a door. The room temperature was cool. Inside were pushcarts with flower arrangements on them. A few volunteers were organizing things. They looked up and smiled as he entered. "Your deliveries are in this spare room."

Johnnie gasped when he saw all the flower arrangements, balloons, and stuffed animals. "All this?"

An elderly woman came over holding a basket of colorful flowers. Her badge read, *Tami.* "This one, too."

"Who are they all from?" he asked as he walked inside the room.

"You can read the cards." Antonio plucked a card from one of the larger arrangements and handed it to Johnnie.

Johnnie opened it and read. "It's from the people she used to work with in Atlanta."

He and Antonio began gathering the cards. Some were from fans, others from people in the music business he'd worked with.

Johnnie noticed some of the flowers were wilting. "We can't keep them locked up here. They're meant to be enjoyed. Can you give them to other patients maybe?"

"That would be nice," Tami told him. "Some patients receive no flowers at all. They don't have families. Or their families don't have a lot of money for flowers."

Johnnie bent to pick up a blue teddy bear. "You have a children's ward? Can these toys be used there?"

"You don't want to save any for your baby?" Tami asked.

"He's got plenty waiting for him at home. I'd rather give these to kids who might need them. I'm sure some are a scared by the hospital experience." *Hell, I'm fucking terrified.*

Tami smiled. "That's very generous."

"Save the cards for me, please. You can send them up to Melanie's room."

"I will," Tami said.

He and Antonio walked out of the flower room. He offered Antonio his hand once more. "Thanks again."

Antonio shook it. "Not a problem. You know your parents have been coming through a side entrance. Not a lot of traffic there."

No, I didn't know. He really had been out of touch with the real world the last few days.

"Can you show me?"

Antonio nodded and showed him the way.

Johnnie was opening his car door when he heard a familiar voice.

"Well now, Johnnie Vega finally emerges."

Johnnie scowled at Phil Chase. The reporter had long been a thorn in his side. Chase had covered the band for many years, but instead of focusing on their music, he preferred to write about their private lives. Since Kurt and Rhett were like choir boys compared to him and Caesar, most of Chase's stories involved Caesar's love life and Johnnie's addictions. And after Caesar's death, it was Phil Chase who'd fueled the rumors that Johnnie had been responsible. The man had hassled Melanie a few times while he'd been away at rehab and had even tried to ruin the parties for the release of the band's new material.

Johnnie held up his hand. "Don't fucking start with me, Chase."

"Just wanted to ask how your wife was doing? Any change?"

"None of your damn business," he grouched. Part of him wanted to cry, and the other part wanted to break this idiot's face.

"I guess that's a no," Chase replied. "Have you visited your son yet?"

Shit! How does he know? Maybe he'd figured out a way to get into the hospital. And maybe he'd talked to some of the staff who didn't know what an asshole the guy was. Gailya said the nurses had talked about him and Melanie being celebrities. Perhaps some had talked too much *and* to Phil Chase. *So much for patient confidentiality.* He'd have Kurt talk to a supervisor and remind them to keep quiet.

"Must be a stressful situation. A new baby. His mother in a coma. I hope it doesn't cause you to slide back into any of your old bad habits."

Fuck him! Johnnie slid into the car and slammed the door shut. It was stifling hot from sitting in the lot the last few days, but no way was he going to crack the window. Not even the slightest bit.

Phil Chase grinned and waved to him as Johnnie roared out of the parking lot. Any other time he would have put the reporter in his place, but not now. When it was about him or the band that was one thing, but to talk about Melanie and his son, was a whole other situation. Johnnie was vulnerable, and *yes*, he was stressed. *What if she never wakes up?* He'd tried to be positive at her bedside, tried to think of nothing but her returning to him. But as he drove further from the hospital, he realized that there was a chance she might not ever wake up. That he'd never hear her voice again or feel her touch. He felt the tears well up in his eyes. When they came, he had to pull into a parking lot to get himself together. He rubbed the seat next to him—the place where Melanie had last been conscious. Blue had taken the car in to be cleaned, but in Johnnie's mind, he saw the bloodstain Melanie had left behind. *So much blood!*

"Caesar, what the fuck? She needs you! I need you!" He repeatedly smacked the steering wheel until his hands were red and sore.

Maybe I have to be at the house in order for Caesar to hear me. Was that the connection? The beach house? He wasn't sure, but suddenly he couldn't wait to get home and see if he could conjure up Caesar again.

He started to back out of the parking space and realized the row of stores in front of him included a liquor store. *Damn!* He hadn't even thought about drinking for the last few days. But Chase's words had pushed alcohol back into his brainwaves. A drink or two would certainly relieve some of the pressure he was feeling. He smacked the steering wheel again. *I can't do it! I can't fuck up!* He was so close to his two-year sobriety.

He pulled out of the parking lot and headed home. Sweat beaded on his face, and he cranked the air conditioner up higher. *Whiskey.* That had always been his go-to drink. *No. No. No. I will not fuck up.* Melanie needs me sober.

Your son needs you, too. Her father's stern voice echoed in his mind. What if Melanie didn't wake up? What if he had to raise their son alone? *Will I hate my own son for taking his mother from me? I don't want to be like my father.*

He passed another liquor store and made a quick U-turn.

Chapter Eight

Past

Johnnie stared at the bottle of whiskey in his dad's liquor cabinet and wondered what it tasted like. Seemed like the only time his dad tolerated him was when he'd had a couple of drinks. Imagine that, he thought. Most kids get knocked around or yelled at by parents who have a drinking problem. Yet, Johnnie preferred when his dad drank. It wasn't often enough, though.

He slipped the bottle from the cabinet and opened it. He knew that his older brothers had tasted a few things in here. He'd caught them once, and they'd promised to kill him if he snitched.

He took a sip and nearly spat it out. It was awful and burned the back of his throat. How can anyone drink this shit? He tried one more taste. Still awful. By his fifth sip, it seemed to go down easier, and a warm, fuzzy feeling replaced his normal anxiety. Perhaps that was why his dad seemed mellower when he drank. Perhaps this would help him feel better about having a father who hated him.

Present

Johnnie sat on a stool by the kitchen island, tapping a whiskey bottle with his finger. He'd bought two, but so far, hadn't taken a drink. He'd been desperate to, but after buying the bottles, he'd called his sponsor, Gordon, who'd talked him down. Gordon had suggested coming to the beach house to talk, but Johnnie had declined the offer, assuring his sponsor that he'd be fine. Then he'd called Rhett who was finishing up a tour with a young pop star in Europe. He'd be heading back home soon and was eager to visit Melanie. The two of them had chatted a while about music and traveling.

The next call he'd made was to Kurt who'd been out tending to his horses. Johnnie talked to his young daughter instead...about anything and everything. She'd distracted him with stories of school and Barbies long enough that his craving for the alcohol had subsided.

CJ brushed against his legs and meowed loudly. Johnnie bent over and scratched the cat's head. "I miss her, too, buddy."

The feline stretched his body along the side of Johnnie's leg pleading for more attention.

"Want to go for a walk with me? I feel like a swim." Leaving the unopened bottles on the counter, Johnnie went outside to the deck where he pulled off his dirty clothes. He loved swimming nude in the ocean and luckily with a private beach he could do so as much as he wanted.

CJ stood on the deck as Johnnie sprinted toward the water. "Scared to get wet? Ya big pussy!"

The water was invigorating. He went in about chest deep and rode a few waves in. CJ sat near the water's edge, howling the entire time.

"What is it?" Johnnie sloshed back to shore. CJ curled around his legs, still meowing. "Do you see a big fish you want to catch? If you see that noisy ass dolphin, you gotta tell me immediately. I need a word with him."

Johnnie shielded his eyes and scanned the horizon. Where could the dolphins have gone? Would he see them...see Caesar...ever again?

His fists clenched at his side. *Caesar, where the fuck are you? You must know what's happening with Melanie. Why aren't you coming to help? You helped her before.*

He trudged through the sand, back up to the house, CJ following closely at his feet.

"I'm taking a shower to wash this sand off. Back off or you'll get wet."

CJ sat watching him at the shower stall's entrance as Johnnie lathered up his body and then his hair with soap.

"You're starting to creep me out, dude." Johnnie smiled. CJ usually acted nonchalant about him, preferring the company of Melanie.

"Wait a minute." Johnnie rinsed off quickly, then grabbed a towel to dry himself. After wrapping it around his waist, he bent down to CJ's level. "Caesar, is that you? Are you in there trying to tell me something? Talk to me."

CJ stared blankly at him and then blinked his large gold eyes.

Johnnie straightened and rolled his own eyes. "Talking to a cat. I've lost my damn mind."

The two of them returned to the kitchen. Johnnie's stomach rumbled like a freight train on rickety rails. No more alcohol cravings. Now he was starving for food.

"Let's see," he opened the cupboard. "What can we make since I can't cook worth shit and I doubt you know how to use a frying pan?"

He pulled out a jar of peanut butter. "This should do."

CJ meowed over and over, weaving in and out of Johnnie's legs.

"Is there something up here you want?" Johnnie investigated the cupboards again. "Aha! Tuna!"

Melanie was a vegetarian, and he was not a fan of tuna, so these cans were specifically for CJ.

He showed CJ a can, pointing at the label. "Look! It even says *dolphin-safe.*"

CJ's meowing increased as he snaked around Johnnie's legs again.

He opened the can and put the contents on a small plate, then placed it on the floor for the cat. Grabbing two slices of bread, he toasted them and smeared them with peanut butter. In the fridge, he found apple slices, along with a strawberry banana smoothie drink.

"Damn this is delicious." He licked his fingers and glanced down at CJ. "How's yours?"

CJ ignored him and kept eating.

"That good, huh?" Johnnie checked his phone, but there were no texts or calls from the parents. There were, however, about fifty new posts on *Twitter*. People were sending their love to Melanie.

When he finished his food, he set his plate in the sink. He let out a loud burp that startled CJ.

"Sorry, but after greasy hamburgers and fries, snicker bars and chips for three days, that really hit the spot." Johnnie rubbed his full belly, suddenly exhausted. He hadn't had a good night's sleep in two days, and although it wasn't even noon yet, he wanted to go to bed.

At the bottom of the stairs, he stared at the floor. Three days ago, Melanie had been lying here, in pain. His mother or Blue must have cleaned up the blood, and he was glad. It would have completely freaked him out to see it. *I'd empty those bottles for sure.* Slowly, he moved upstairs to their bedroom but stopped at the nursery door.

Everything he and Melanie had planned was gone to shit. He was supposed to have been in the delivery room, supporting her as their son was born. They were supposed to bond with him together, and then she'd lift him to her breast and feed him for the first time. The next day they'd bring him home and tuck him into bed, beneath a cloudy blue sky, surrounded by jungle animals. They would take turns changing diapers, and Johnnie had promised that when the baby woke in the night, he'd be by her side while she fed him.

He entered the room and looked around. Two years ago, this had been their designated office space where they'd worked on the Lush documentary together. Then the band's autobiography. They'd moved the computer equipment downstairs. The bed where she'd made love to both him and Caesar was in storage.

Hell, we made love to her on all the beds in the house. And a few floors! He smiled thinking back to that carefree time. No worries at all. Just creativity, laughter, and love. Now trouble was all he had.

He left the nursery and entered the bedroom he shared with Melanie. It had been Caesar's old room when he was alive. The bed was made, and he knew his parents had taken care of cleaning up in here as well. He stripped the towel from his waist and slipped on some joggers. Then, he crawled onto the bed and lay back. The mattress felt like heaven after sleeping in a chair for two nights.

Vanilla. Caesar's scent and now Melanie's hit him, and tears slid down his cheek. He sobbed loudly, allowing his sadness to take control. He'd held too much back at the hospital, but now he was free to let his emotions out.

CJ ran into the room and jumped up on the bed. He rubbed against Johnnie, purring loudly.

"Hey, dude." Johnnie sniffed and wiped at his tears with the back of his hand. "Don't worry about me. I'm just a bit down right now. Missing our woman."

CJ licked his face, then settled into the crook of his arm to sit. Johnnie stroked his fur. "I hope she comes home soon, don't you?"

The cat spread his legs and began cleaning himself.

"Yeah, that's attractive." Johnnie chuckled. He patted CJ's head, then lay back and drifted off to sleep.

"Johnnie...son, wake up."

He was being summoned from slumber. Someone was shaking him. Blue's voice. He bolted upright, alarmed. *Why is he here? Did something happen?*

"Melanie?"

Blue patted his arm. "No change. We hadn't heard from you, so your mother sent me to make sure you were okay. Carl's here, too. In the kitchen. The ladies are at the hospital with Melanie."

He yawned and stretched. "What time is it?"

"Morning again. Nearly ten now."

"You're kidding. I slept almost twenty hours?" He shook his head, clearing the cobwebs. "Damn."

Blue sighed then frowned. "Easy to do when you're drunk."

Johnnie slid from the bed and stood. "Drunk? I wasn't drunk."

"We'll discuss it downstairs." Blue left the room.

What the hell? Johnnie went into the bathroom. As he was peeing, it hit him. "Of course, they saw the bottles."

As he walked downstairs, he ran his hands through his hair, attempting to straighten it. He needed another shower and that shave he'd skipped, but first, he had to explain the bottles. Blue would understand. He'd been dealing with Johnnie's problems for a long time. But the last thing he wanted was Carl's disapproval. They needed to unite for Melanie, but so far, he hadn't been able to connect with the man.

As soon as he entered the kitchen, Carl went on the attack. "You want to explain yourself?"

Johnnie couldn't blame him. The man had nearly lost Melanie before. He *had* lost his grandchildren. Then Carl had to watch Melanie suffer from severe depression afterward. And all because of her late husband's drinking.

"Yeah, I can explain. Let me get some water first."

Carl slammed his hand on the island counter. "I won't let another man hurt her the way Logan did. I didn't do enough back then to stop him. I'll be damned if I make that mistake again."

Johnnie's hands shook as he filled a glass with ice water from the fridge. After taking a sip, he stared at the floor, unable to meet Carl's angry gaze. "The last thing I want to do is hurt Melanie. She's hurting now, and I blame myself."

"So, you down two bottles of whiskey?"

"What?" He stared at Carl, confused. "Of course not. I didn't drink anything."

Blue patted his shoulder. "Look, I understand why you did it. What's happening to her is eating you up. But it's not your fault, so don't punish yourself by screwing up your sobriety. I know how hard you've worked at it, and how proud Melanie is of you for getting clean."

Johnnie walked to the counter across from Carl. He took another sip of water. "I know it was wrong to buy the shit. I had cravings, but I beat them. I called my sponsor, then Rhett and Kurt. After that, I was fine. Just hungry and tired, so I ate and went to bed. I didn't touch the whiskey."

Carl marched over to the trash bin, opened the top and pulled out two empty bottles. "Then what the hell is this?"

"I told you I bought them. I didn't drink any of it though. You had to see that they were still unopened when you poured them out."

"I didn't pour them out."

Johnnie's gaze went to Blue. "They were full when I went to bed yesterday."

Blue winced as if pained by his words. "Johnnie, the empty bottles were in the sink when we arrived."

What the fuck? He rubbed his head, racking his brain, trying to remember. *Did I wake up sometime last night and dump them?* He couldn't recall. He'd slept good and hard. He didn't even remember dreaming.

"I swear they were full and unopened when I went to bed. Maybe I got up to take a piss and dumped them. I honestly don't remember."

"Because you were drunk." Carl huffed.

"No, because I've barely slept the past two nights." Johnnie groaned. "I wish I could make you believe me. I know you don't know me that well, but, Blue, you do."

"I do." Blue nodded. "But it looks bad. You're stressed about Melanie, blaming yourself. You bought the whiskey, and we find the bottles empty. If you didn't drink them, or dump them out, then who did?"

A light bulb clicked on in Johnnie's head. *Caesar!* Had he been here? Had CJ sensed his presence? Was that why the cat had been acting so strangely? It made sense. To him at least. He looked from Blue to Carl. He couldn't tell them. They'd never believe Caesar's ghost had dumped the bottles. *They'd think I've lost my mind.* So, he lied.

"Wait!" He tapped the counter with his fingers. "I remember getting up. It was dark. Probably around midnight. I used the bathroom, then checked my phone. Gordon had left a few messages to check-in on me. I dumped the bottles out and let him know I was fine. Texted him."

"Show us," Carl demanded, pointing to Johnnie's phone which was still sitting on the kitchen island where he'd left it yesterday.

Carl's persistence was getting on his nerves. *If I thought anyone was hurting Melanie, wouldn't I be the same way?* Johnnie hesitated. *Shit!*

Blue picked up his phone and handed it to him. "Go ahead."

Damn! I shouldn't have lied. I'm never getting out of this one. Carl's going to hate me forever. Blue will never trust me again.

Johnnie took the phone, put his code in, then handed the phone to Blue. Perhaps Blue could soften the blow. Carl glared at him as Blue scanned through his text messages.

"He's right. There's a few from his sponsor, Gordon. A couple from Rhett and Kurt, too. He only answered the one to Gordon, though. It was at two in the morning though, not midnight."

What the fuck?

Blue handed the phone to Carl, who looked, then grunted.

"We still don't know if he's telling the truth that he didn't take a drink."

"Like Johnnie said, I've known him longer. He realized he was an addict when he was twenty-four. He's never hidden his addiction from anyone since. One thing my son Caesar always said was that

Johnnie Vega always spouts the truth. Even if it's nasty. Even if it hurts. He can be crude and crass, but he's honest."

"You believe him?"

Blue nodded. "But I also think he needs to get himself to a meeting today. Or meet with Gordon."

"I will." Johnnie looked Carl in the eyes. "I promise."

Carl sighed, then nodded. "Sorry I was so hard on you."

"Hard?" Blue laughed. "If Judy had been here, all hell would've broken loose."

Johnnie groaned again. He'd only repaired his relationship with his mother in the last two years. He wanted to keep it happy and strong. He'd disappointed her too many times in the past. "Can we keep this amongst ourselves. Please."

"We can agree to that." Carl held out his hand to Johnnie.

Johnnie shook it. "Thanks. I'm going to shower and shave, then see if Gordon can meet with me. If not, I'll find a meeting."

"We have to discuss something else," Carl announced.

Blue nodded. "The baby's being released tomorrow."

Shit. Here we go again.

"We don't know what's going on in that head of yours, but something is. If you don't want to talk...fine. But we have to make a plan for him to come home."

Johnnie bit his bottom lip. Blue was right, but still, he had no idea how to handle this one. He wasn't ready to be a full-time dad, all alone, with a baby he had yet to see. Plus, he needed to be with Melanie at the hospital.

"Your mom and I talked it over. We know your main concern is Melanie right now, so you won't have much time to spend with the baby. We agreed to take him to our house and watch him until things change with Melanie or at least have calmed down for you."

Relief washed over him. That solved a huge problem. His mom and Melanie had decorated a spare bedroom at his mom's house for when the baby visited. This was the perfect solution.

"We'll cross other bridges when we get there, but for now he can stay with us."

Carl forced a smile. "And if you're so stressed that you're thinking about drinking again, it's probably best he didn't stay with you. Just in case."

Johnnie grimaced. Carl didn't trust him. But the man was right. If he did drink with the baby here, it could be disastrous. Hadn't he been worried about that very thing when Melanie first told him she was pregnant?

"You're right."

"We'll let you get yourself together." Blue hugged him. "See you at the hospital later."

Carl wrapped an arm around his shoulder. "If you need more time away, take it. You know we'll contact you if things change. Sitting and worrying is not helping you or Melanie. Do what you need to do here...get yourself together, then come see her."

Johnnie nodded before seeing the two older men out the door.

First things first, he grabbed his phone and let Gordon know he was okay but asked him if he might like to have lunch and talk. Gordon asked if they could make it an early dinner instead, and Johnnie agreed.

He flipped through his phone messages again, reading the ones Blue had mentioned. The ones Blue had thought Johnnie had read. The one Blue thought he had written.

I'm fine. Poured the whiskey down the drain. Been sleeping mostly. About to head back to bed again. I'll contact you later, and we'll talk.

Johnnie stared at the message. *I didn't write this.* This and the bottles being emptied made him wonder again. *Was Caesar here last night?*

Quickly, he fed CJ, then headed to the beach. He walked along the shore and headed to his rock, where he stood staring at the ocean.

How do I contact him?

"Caesar!" He yelled toward the ocean.

Minutes passed, and Johnnie shook his head. *How did Melanie get him here?* Caesar had been the one to reach out to her in Atlanta, but she'd sent him away when Caesar had learned the truth about her daughters and tried to force her to confront her pain. She and Caesar had already discussed her moving to California and living at his beach house while she pursued her writing dreams. Melanie had decided to pack her things and move, and in doing so had met Johnnie.

They'd had a difficult time getting along at first. The attraction between them was intense. But Johnnie had been too afraid of hurting her and warned her about letting their hearts get involved. Instead, they became friends. That initial lust had turned into love and soon became too overwhelming. Sure enough, once they'd given in to their feelings, he'd screwed it up by cheating on her. She'd been in Atlanta selling the documentary to her former employer, Citizen News Network. And while she was gone, his dad had died. In his grief, he'd turned to alcohol and another woman.

He'd barely been able to get it up, but there was no denying he'd gotten drunk and brought another woman home. Melanie had caught him and told him it was over. It had sent him into a downward spiral that culminated in him holding a gun to his head and threatening to kill himself. For years he'd been slowly killing himself with alcohol and drugs, but that was the first time he'd made a conscious decision to end his life. Melanie begged and screamed for Caesar to intervene. *And Caesar came back again.* Caesar saved the day, knocking the gun from his hand, then knocking Johnnie to the ground.

"Caesar, come on!" he yelled again, throwing up his arms in frustration. "Melanie needs you, man. I need you. I'm lost. Confused. I don't know what to do."

Silence surrounded him.

"What? I have to hold a gun to my head? Seriously, what the fuck?" Johnnie hopped off the rock and stormed back to the house.

He went to the studio and grabbed a pair of drumsticks. He'd last heard Caesar's voice in his head when he'd been drumming, so that was what he decided to do again. He sat down and began playing beats. After a few minutes, he got into a familiar groove. It felt good to be playing. It's what he'd been born to do. Nothing else he'd ever done had ever made him as happy as being a musician. Sober or wasted, there was no greater feeling for him than making music.

Smiling, he twirled his sticks in the air. *Well, except making love to Melanie.*

He crashed his sticks against the cymbals. *I know you helped me, Caesar. You dumped the bottles. You wrote that text. Somehow...with your superpowers.*

Johnnie set into one of his drum solo routines he used to perform near the end of every show. He banged the drums as loud as he could, letting out his frustrations and his stress.

"Damn!" He growled when one of his sticks broke on the side of the snare. He had plenty more, but now his groove had been interrupted.

Back in the kitchen, he got another glass of water and downed it. Then he headed to the office and fired up the desktop. He may as well check emails and pay any bills that needed taking care of. As he sat down, CJ ran in and hopped up on the bed behind him.

Once the computer booted up, his attention was immediately drawn to a file titled *Baby Names*. He hadn't seen it before. Then again, he wasn't someone who could sit in front of a computer for a long time like Melanie. At least not since they'd worked on the documentary together. She could've been working on names for a while and he'd just never noticed.

He doubled clicked. The file was recent. She'd been making a list of her favorites, perhaps to share with him so they could narrow the list down and add his favorites. She'd also included a few notes about why she liked each name.

Duncan Ryan for my uncles. She had written. There were a few more but sitting at number one was a name they'd discussed before, only she'd typed it differently.

Michael Angelo. Johnnie's real middle name and his great grandfather's name. Italian heritage on his mom's side.

Johnnie smiled. His mom's family had come from Italy as immigrants in the late 1800s. Later, his great grandfather had married...much to her family's disliking...a blonde-haired, blue-eyed girl. *Like Melanie.*

Didn't Mom say I looked like her granddad?

Michael Angelo Vega. His son had a name.

He closed the baby name file and saw another labeled. *Caesar and Johnnie.*

"She always puts his name first." He turned to CJ. "In fact, that's how you got your name. I would have called you JC only I didn't have a choice in the matter."

Johnnie turned back to the computer and clicked the file. There were photos of him and Caesar from their days in the band, even a few from high school. Some had been used in the band's autobiography.

There were a few videos here as well, and when he clicked on one, he realized what they were. Before leaving for rehab, he had recorded them for Melanie. He'd figured out how to schedule them to be emailed to her at random times. Then she could remember him while he was away. What made the video even more remarkable was seeing Caesar, his cameraman.

He smiled when Caesar turned the phone's camera toward himself and waved. Caesar had been loved by women around the world. His best friend was extremely good looking. He was the perfect front-man for the band, with a headful of soft curls that reached past his shoulders, deep brown eyes, and a warm smile. He was a master of seduction on stage and off, but he'd never been a player. He just loved women, and women loved Caesar. Caesar was a kindhearted, loving man to everyone. All the fans, young and old, along with everyone he met fell in love with Caesar.

Why won't he come back? Melanie needs him.

Johnnie clicked on another video. *What's this?* Caesar had taken a video of him and Melanie making love? How come Melanie had never shown this to him? He hadn't made it, but perhaps she thought he did. It was hot to watch but made both his heart and his cock ache for her. The camera shifted, and suddenly, Caesar was joining them on the bed. A tear slid down his face, and he wiped it away. Those precious days of having Caesar back in his life and them sharing their love for Melanie would always be special to him, but having Melanie all to himself was even better. *Will I ever make love to her again?*

He missed Melanie and needed to get back to her. He sat on the bed and rubbed CJ. "Let's go for another swim, buddy. Before I have to head back to the hospital."

Chapter Nine

Past

"Where the hell are you taking me?" Johnnie questioned as Caesar pushed him through the doors of a church.

"It's a meeting." Caesar smiled.

"I don't do religion, you know that."

"Me neither. It's not that sort of meeting."

When the two of them entered, Johnnie realized the meeting was already in progress. A middle-aged man stood at a podium talking about heroin.

"Fuck, no!" Johnnie protested. The man at the podium paused, and several people turned in his direction.

Caesar grabbed Johnnie, pulling him into a private corner away from the prying eyes. "Come on, it'll do us both good."

"Are you insane? They'll recognize us, and blab to the press that they saw Caesar Blue and Johnnie Vega at an AA meeting."

"The second A stands for anonymous."

"Money talks. And reporters like Phil Chase will pay for a story that slanders anyone famous."

"I've been here before. There's been no stories."

Johnnie thumped Caesar on the head. "You're an idiot."

Obviously wounded by his words, Caesar frowned. He let go of Johnnie, hung his head, and walked back outside.

Johnnie followed and grabbed his friend's arm. "I'm sorry. But you're the one trying to get sober, not me."

Caesar looked at him, shook his head, and walked down the steps of the church.

Present

"This doesn't feel right to me." Johnnie stood near Melanie's bedside, frowning, shifting from one foot to the other, trying to wrap his head around what the doctor was suggesting.

Melanie's physician, Dr. Chaney, nodded. "I understand your concern. But we've done all we can for her. Most coma patients wake up after a few weeks. She hasn't. I believe moving her to a long-term care facility is in her best interest. It would be a more comfortable situation for both Melanie and your family."

"You've given up on her, haven't you?" Johnnie's hands balled into fists at his sides. His pulse raced. "But I haven't. She's going to wake up."

Blue stood and wrapped an arm around his shoulder. "Stay calm, son."

Gailya cleared her throat. "I know how you feel, Johnnie. But you must think of Melanie. This hospital, with all the noise and chaos, is fine for a while, but these long-term care facilities are very nice, and more like being at home, not a hospital."

"Can she come home then?"

Dr. Chaney and Gailya looked at one another.

"Well? Can it be done?"

"It's not unheard of," the doctor replied. "Especially with the type of coma she's in. Her health is good otherwise. But it would require a lot of work."

Gailya spoke again. "You'd have to hire a full-time nurse. One who'd spend most of the day with you, maybe stay with you. And then there's the equipment and monitors."

Johnnie slipped from Blue's arm and went to his wife's bedside. "I can hire one. And I can help take care of her. Gailya, you've shown me how. I've helped with her physical therapy. I've washed her, changed her catheter bag. You can show me anything else I need to know."

Carl appeared upset. "You haven't even begun taking care of your son, and now you want to bring home Melanie who'll need round the clock care as well?"

He whirled around to face Carl. His brow furrowed. "So, you'd rather have me put her in some home and give up on her?"

"I'd rather you meet your son and take care of him. He needs you. There's nothing you can do for Melanie, but you can do a lot for your son. Like, be a father."

Johnnie knew Carl was right, but that didn't stop him from being upset. How could he make them understand that Melanie was what mattered most to him? The last few weeks he'd been by her side every day, talking to her, playing music for her. He'd even brought her computer and watched movies with her. But there'd been no sign of life. And it broke his heart. It took every ounce of strength he had to stay positive and keep believing in her recovery. And because of his devotion to his wife, he had nothing left to give his son. Besides, Blue and his mother were doing fine with Michael.

"Can we have a few days to decide something?" Blue asked Dr. Chaney.

"Of course. I understand. This isn't easy. Gailya has collected some brochures for you. Look the facilities over and check their websites. Maybe go for a visit. Then you can decide which is the best option for Melanie."

Gailya handed them to Blue.

"If you'll excuse me, I have other patients to see," Dr. Chaney said and patted Johnnie's shoulder. "Let me know when you've made a decision."

"You do what's best for Melanie and yourself." Gailya hugged him. On her way out, she pulled Carl aside and whispered, "Don't be so hard on him. That man is the most devoted husband I've ever seen. You give him time. He'll be a devoted father, too. He's hurting terribly. Let him grieve. He needs time."

Grieve? Even Gailya had given up on Melanie. She'd been his tower of strength these last few weeks. Who would be there for him now? No one seemed to understand how much he needed Melanie back. Every night he sat on the beach, calling for Caesar, only to be ignored. *I have no one helping me fight for her.*

"We can search online and take a look," Blue told him as he flipped through the brochures. "We'll choose a couple to visit."

Carl went to the foot of Melanie's bed. "Only the best for my beautiful girl."

"I'm not giving up on her." Johnnie felt the tears welling up.

Carl glanced at him. "We know that."

"I'm not shoving her in some facility to be forgotten."

Blue grimaced. "The hospital wants her moved, Johnnie. You have to face it."

"She'll come home then. It'll be the best place for her. I'll do whatever it takes to make her comfortable there."

Carl and Blue stared at one another.

"He may be right," Blue finally conceded. "She loves that house. There's good energy there. Even my son felt it."

Carl nodded but didn't say anything.

"Do you mind staying with her while I go to a meeting?"

"Of course." Blue rubbed his shoulder. "You okay?"

"Not really. Lot of heavy shit I need to deal with. I want to check-in."

"You do that." Blue hugged him. "Let me know if you need anything."

"We're going to figure this out, babe. Don't worry." Johnnie pressed his lips against Melanie's. He then put an earbud into each of her ears and put her phone on her chest. He turned on her music. "I'll be back soon, babe. Listen to Caesar and the band while I'm gone."

"Hello, my name is Johnnie, and I'm an addict."

There were murmurings amongst the group as everyone in attendance greeted him.

"I've been coming to these meetings for a while, but I haven't shared anything. Part of it has to do with how many times I've been through this and failed, and part of it is the fact some people consider me a celebrity. I play drums for a band, and I've always been worried that someone would hear me talk and run to the press to give them a story. But that's the least of my worries now. I've been sober for two years. And while I've had cravings during that time, it's been easy to fight them and stay away from the pills and alcohol. Lately though, I've been stressed by the crap happening in my life, and I'm worried that I'm going to screw up and go back to the person I was."

Johnnie glanced around the room. There were a lot of familiar faces, and several he didn't know. Everyone was focused on him. Some nodded. They understood where he was coming from, because they'd been there, too.

"I've been so happy the last two years. I fell in love with a wonderful woman, and that prompted me to get clean. Last year we got married. Something I once swore I'd never do."

Johnnie paused as a few in attendance laughed lightly.

"Then we found out we were having a baby. That scared the shit out of me. My father was an asshole, and I'm worried I'll turn out to be just like him."

He took a deep breath, then exhaled slowly. "My wife had our son, but there were complications, and now she's in a coma. It's been nearly a month, and nothing's changed. And the worst part is, I haven't even met my son. My mom is taking care of him, while I sit by my wife's bedside, hoping she'll come back to me. If she doesn't, I'll have to raise our son by myself and that terrifies me. I want to be a good dad, not like the jerk I had. But already I'm the worst dad. Not even wanting to see him."

Tears began to fall down his face. "I don't know what to do. She's everything to me. And I don't know if I can live without her. Or even if I want to live without her."

He broke down, and several people came to him, circling around, offering their support. He took their hugs and handshakes. These were his people, and he knew they wouldn't judge him.

"You call if you need me. No matter what time of day it is. Okay?"

Johnnie grabbed Gordon's arm, and they pulled one another in for a brief hug.

"You have my word," he assured his sponsor.

Gordon got into his car, gave Johnnie a lazy wave, and drove away. Johnnie swept a hand through his hair. *Now what?* He didn't want to go back to the hospital. Blue and Carl would be harping on moving Melanie, and he wasn't ready to face that decision yet. *I'll go home and sit on the beach awhile. Clear my head.*

"Johnnie Vega, right?"

Rolling his eyes, Johnnie turned to the feminine voice. *Just what I need. A fucking reporter.*

"Thanks for sharing your story today," the woman said. "I hope it helped you."

"The only thing that's going to help is my wife waking up," he snapped.

"I get it. My husband was in a bad motorcycle accident a few years back. He was in a coma for a few months. Traumatic brain injury." She took a cigarette out of her purse, lit it, then took a long drag.

"You're not a reporter?"

She pulled the cigarette out of her mouth. Most of her red lipstick was removed with it. "You really are paranoid, aren't you?"

"Been hounded by too many of them over the years. And for all the wrong reasons."

"Yeah." She flipped back her jet-black hair and took another puff. "I've heard of your band. That's how I knew your name."

"A fan?"

She scrunched up her face. "Nah. Not really. A bit before my time."

Johnnie thought she looked about forty. *How could Lush have been before her time?* Then again, depending on what type of addict you were, your addictions could age you...and not gracefully.

"We have new music out."

"It's not new music." She dropped the cigarette on the ground and smashed it with her boot. "Just unreleased music, right? Now released."

"Yeah, I guess you could call it that." Johnnie was getting annoyed. *What does she want?* "Look, I've got a million things to do."

"Would you like to grab some coffee and talk?"

"I have a sponsor."

She laughed lightly. "That's not what I mean. But I know a bit about what you're going through."

What else do I have to do? It might be good to talk to someone who's gone through a similar experience.

"There's a coffee shop over there." She pointed across the street. "A lot of people hang out there to chat after meetings."

"Do they have food? I skipped breakfast."

She smiled and nodded. "Sandwiches and stuff like that."

"Lead the way."

"So, what happened to your husband?" Johnnie set his tray on the table and took a seat across from the woman.

She reached across the table and offered her hand. "I'm Laurel by the way."

"Oh yeah, sorry." Johnnie shook her hand. "My mind's been a blur for a few weeks now."

"I can imagine." She put cream into her coffee. "My husband, Mario, was hit by a drunk driver coming home from work one night."

"Was he...an addict?"

Laurel shook her head. "No. He drank a few beers if we went out, but nothing like me. I like the hard stuff and pills."

"Same here. I've done everything. Got off the hard drugs about ten years ago, but the pills and alcohol were hard to shake."

"Because they're easy to get." Laurel took a sip of her coffee. "So, two years sober?"

Johnnie nodded.

"A year for me."

"What made you do it?"

"Losing Mario. He left me. Before the accident, he accepted my problems. But afterward, he changed. It made him angry seeing me wasted all the time. Plus, he wanted to start a family but not with an addict."

"Sorry about that." Johnnie took a bite out of his turkey sandwich.

"Everyone has their rock-bottom." She sighed. "That was mine. We were high school sweethearts, and I thought we'd be together forever."

"Has he seen you since you got sober?"

"No. He moved out of state. We're friends through social media, but he has a new life now."

"That's too bad." Johnnie took a sip of his water.

"I get it, though. A drunk driver almost kills him. Then while he's recovering, his wife is stealing his pills. He'd had enough."

"How long was he in a coma?"

"Nearly three months. I'd stay with him all day bawling my eyes out. Then go home at night and get drunk."

"I almost drank a few days after Melanie went to the hospital. I stopped myself, though. I don't know what I'd do if I lost her. She's the reason I got sober...the reason I want to stay sober."

"What about your baby?" Laurel asked as she added more cream to her coffee. "You said your mom's taking care of him?"

"I haven't been able to face him yet."

"Why not?"

"I don't know." Johnnie shrugged.

"You said you were afraid."

"I can't give him what he needs right now. I spend all my time worrying about Melanie, showering her with love, begging her to come back to me."

"Maybe it's you who needs him."

Johnnie bit his lip, trying to hold back tears. "I need Melanie. They want to move her out of the hospital and send her to a facility. Feels like they're giving up on her."

"Mario's family had money. They paid for him to stay at a wonderful place called Malibu Palms."

"I thought about setting up a room for her at our house and hiring a nurse to take care of her there."

"That would be a lot of money."

"Rock star...remember?" Johnnie gave her his trademark grin.

"You didn't squander all your money on drugs and alcohol?"

"Not all of it. I've got enough to take care of her." He chuckled. "What with the previously unreleased music now released."

"You think that's best? I mean if there were an emergency..."

He drifted away for a moment, smiling.

"What?" she asked.

"It's hard to explain...but there's something magical about our house. She loves it there. It would be the best place for her. It's what she would want."

"Guess it's your decision."

"Convincing her dad of that won't be easy." He popped a French fry into his mouth.

"I'm sure you'll find a way." She winked and smiled.

He went back to his food, feeling a bit uneasy. *Is she flirting? Or is it my imagination.* She wasn't bad looking. The single, inebriated Johnnie might have flirted back, but the thought of being with any other woman but Melanie disgusted him. Melanie owned him. Heart, mind, body, and soul.

He quickly changed the subject. "When your husband woke up, was it surprising? Did he just one day wake up?"

"It was a slow process. One day his hands twitched, then his feet. Then he was saying random things, but his eyes stayed closed. Sort of like he was dreaming. One day I walked into his room, and he sat up and asked where I'd been."

"I'm hoping something like that happens with Melanie." Johnnie's phone notified him of a message, and he picked it up. He groaned and put it on silent.

"Everything okay?"

"Melanie's dad was asking where I am." He rolled his eyes. "I swear that man hates me."

Laurel reached over and gently rubbed his hand. "I'm sure he's just worried about his daughter. The same way you are."

Johnnie pulled his hand away, not liking the feel of another woman touching him so intimately. "I better get back to the hospital. Otherwise, they'll come looking for me."

"I'll walk you to your car."

"How often do you make it to meetings?" Laurel asked as they reached Johnnie's BMW.

"I used to come a couple times a month. Lately, it's been more because of the stress I'm going through. When I feel like I'm out of control, I stop by. Or go to one at the hospital."

She placed her palm on his chest. "Maybe I'll catch you again, then."

Laurel's touch made him uncomfortable. Was she trying to be nice...or was it something more?

"Maybe we will." He smiled uneasily.

She hugged him tight, and he felt even more awkward. Reluctantly, he patted her back. When she pulled away and planted a kiss on his cheek, he knew he had to set her straight.

"Look I appreciate you taking the time to talk to me. But you need to understand. I'm dedicated to my wife."

She pouted as she backed away from him. "Don't you get lonely?"

"No. I don't."

"Eventually, you will."

He rubbed his forehead and let out a puff of breath. "Melanie is all I need."

"If she doesn't wake up...what will you do then?"

He narrowed his eyes. "She's going to wake up."

"For your sake, I hope so. But if she doesn't, no one would fault you for moving on."

He couldn't help but laugh. *Moving on?* That was the most ridiculous thing he'd ever heard. Melanie was his reason for living.

He shook his head, unlocked the car's door, and slid in. "Take care of yourself, Laurel."

As he drove away, he knew he'd have to find another meeting place. He couldn't chance running into Laurel again. *What a piece of work!*

Johnnie sat on his rock and inhaled the fresh ocean air. The setting sun warmed his bare shoulders. Tears slid down his face as he remembered how much Melanie loved watching the sunsets with him. They'd spent so many evenings together sitting quietly, watching the sky change colors.

"I'm bringing her home, Caesar. I know that's what she would want. What she needs." He'd already contacted an agency about hiring a nurse for an in-home care job, and they'd emailed a few resumés for him to look over.

"I'll put her in the bedroom that faces the ocean. She'll be able to see the sunsets every day. The stars...the moon." *If she wakes up.* He groaned aloud. *Not if, when.*

"Maybe you'll come to visit her when she's home again. She'd like that Caesar. I'd like it, too. Jealousy or not, there's no denying how much you two love one another."

Johnnie listened carefully for any sign his friend was nearby. But again, there was nothing. Only the sound was of the waves lapping against the shoreline. It was time to face facts. Caesar probably wasn't coming back. *Maybe he can't.* Perhaps he wasn't allowed to return. Caesar hadn't talked about his afterlife. He'd only mentioned having feelings about needing to return to help someone, and he had.

Over the years, Caesar had made several attempts to reach out to him. But Johnnie had always chalked up his Caesar sightings to being under the influence. Rhett, too, had thought he'd seen Caesar from time to time, usually around the anniversary of Caesar's death. But neither he nor Rhett had ever made physical contact or held a conversation with Caesar. *Not until Melanie.* She was the conduit for all things Caesar. The whole band had been reunited because of her.

When she's home, he'll come to her. I know it!

Chapter Ten

Past

Johnnie stepped out into the late afternoon sun and was met by the clicking sounds of cameras. Reporters lined the sidewalk outside of the funeral home where they'd been making plans for Caesar. He turned to Blue Sr who was still at the door and took the older man's shaking hand.

"Are you going to be okay?"

Kurt stepped up behind the two of them. "We don't have to leave right now. We can call and ask the police to clear them out."

Blue Sr seemed haunted. Dark circles had formed under his eyes from lack of sleep the past few days. "Let's just go. They'll always be hanging around somewhere. I want to get back to the house."

Johnnie nodded. Blue Sr had flown to LA to take care of the funeral arrangements. There would be a memorial service before Caesar's remains were cremated and his ashes spread out to sea, off the shore of the beach house.

As they moved toward the sidewalk, reporters rushed in. Phil Chase, a celebrity reporter, approached. "Mr. Blue, do you think Johnnie Vega is responsible for your son's death?"

Before Kurt or Rhett had time to stop him, Johnnie's fist met the side of Phil Chase's face. The reporter fell to the ground in a heap, knocked out cold.

Several reporters gasped audibly.

"I suggest you all back-off," Johnnie growled.

Blue Sr puffed out his chest. "The next one's mine!"

Present

When Johnnie arrived at the hospital the next morning, Antonio met him at the side entrance. Johnnie thought the security guard seemed flustered.

"Good morning. How's it going?" he asked the security guard.

"Did you run into any reporters out there?"

"I didn't see any."

"A few were here earlier bothering Mr. Blue and Mr. Davis. Guess I chased them away."

Just great. Another reason for Carl to dislike me.

"Thanks, man." He shook Antonio's hand. "I appreciate it."

As he walked through the ICU area, everyone's gaze seemed to be glued to him. The nurse at the information desk even shot him a dirty look. *What's going on?*

He entered Melanie's room and went straight to her bedside. Taking her hand in his, he pressed his lips against hers. "Morning, baby. I missed you. I love you so much. I've got so much to tell you. You're going home."

Carl stomped into the room and jabbed a finger in his direction. "You've got a lot of nerve!"

Johnnie turned to Melanie's father. The man seemed ready to punch someone. His chest heaved up and down, and his fists were balled-up tight. Blue entered the room behind Carl, and he didn't appear any happier.

"I'm sorry if the reporters bothered you. My least favorite thing about being a celebrity and another reason Melanie will be better off at home."

"Why haven't you answered your phone? Your mom called you over and over last night." Blue shot a quick glance at Carl. "We tried a few times this morning, too."

Johnnie's eyes widened with alarm. "Is Michael alright?"

"Like you care." Carl scoffed.

"He's my son."

"Really?" Carl closed the distance between them and glared down into his face. "That boy doesn't even know he has a father."

Johnnie's mouth twitched. He was not in the mood to deal with Carl this morning. The man was always on his case, and frankly, he was getting tired of it.

"He's a month old. I doubt he knows much of anything."

Blue came closer and gently tugged him away from Carl. "Where were you when we were calling?"

They don't trust me.

"You know how I am with this thing." Johnnie pulled his phone from his pocket. "I put it on silent yesterday and forgot to change the settings. I didn't check it either. Sorry."

"Guess you were too busy with other things." Carl crossed his arms over his chest and huffed.

"I wasn't drinking, if that's what you're getting at. I went to a meeting, then went home to relax and think. Spent some time on the beach."

"Is that what they call it these days?" Carl grouched.

Perplexed with the animosity he was receiving, Johnnie turned up the volume on his phone. He punched in his security code and immediately saw he had several calls and messages, not just from his family but also from Rhett and Kurt.

"Johnnie, who were you with yesterday?" Blue asked. His dark brown eyes seemed full of sadness.

"What do you mean? I was alone at home. I did some research on hiring a full-time nurse. I even moved some furniture from the bedroom downstairs to get it ready for Melanie."

Carl narrowed his eyes. "Melanie's not going home with you."

"With all due respect, Carl, she's my wife."

"Respect?" Carl closed in on him again, this time poking him in the chest...and not too gently. "You don't know the meaning of the word."

Johnnie took a step back. *What's he so fired up about?* He turned to Blue. "Something's happened. What's going on?"

Blue grabbed his phone and brought up a website specializing in celebrity gossip. He then handed Johnnie the phone. "Kurt called me. Said he'd been trying to get ahold of you. The photos went viral last night."

"I told you we should've gone over to his house and busted up his little party," Carl grumbled.

Johnnie scrolled through the photos. They were of him and Laurel. One of them going into the coffee shop. One of them sitting together, her hand on his. One of them standing by his car. Then one of her touching his chest. Another of her hugging him. And of course, one of her kissing him. The story below was all lies. It was accusing him of seeing another woman while his wife lay in a coma—while his son was in the care of his grandparents.

His stomach churned, and he thought he might be sick. Taking a deep breath, he looked from Blue to Carl. It was written all over Carl's face. "And of course, you automatically believe this bullshit."

"It looks bad, Johnnie," Blue said sadly.

"So now you don't have faith in me either?" Johnnie handed Blue back the phone and went to Melanie's bedside. "Fucking unbelievable."

"Are you going to explain yourself?" Carl asked.

"Why should I? You've obviously already made up your mind about me." He kissed Melanie's forehead. "She's the only one who's ever believed in me. If you think I'd throw that away..."

"You cheated on her before."

He groaned. *Why did Melanie tell her dad about that?*

"I wasn't clean then. I was a mess, in fact. My dad had just died, and Melanie was in Florida with you guys at a party. You know the one. For her birthday."

Johnnie marched back over to Carl. "The one where you invited that asshole claiming to be her ex-boyfriend. The one you thought would be perfect for her."

"You're going to blame me? I'm the reason you cheated?"

"No." Johnnie shook his head, then pointed at his chest. "It was all me. I fucked up, yes. I admit it. Hurting her was the worst feeling in the world. I wanted to kill myself because of it. If it hadn't been for Caesar..."

"Caesar?" Blue interrupted.

Shit! Carl was fucking with his head so much he'd let Caesar's name slip out. Luckily, the two men didn't know about his suicide attempt. He and Melanie had sworn to tell no one other than Rhett and Kurt. Quickly, he thought up a story to cover his slip up. He and Melanie had become good at telling lies where Caesar was concerned.

"I was out on the streets. Completely wasted. But I had a dream about Caesar. He told me to go back to Melanie. That she and I belonged together. When I went back, I swore to her I'd get clean. And I did. Because of her. For her."

"Then who's the woman in those pictures?" Carl barked.

"She was at the meeting I went to yesterday. I spoke about the situation here with Melanie. Afterward, she approached me, saying her husband had been in a coma. I agreed to get coffee with her so we could talk about having spouses in comas."

"So, she's someone you know from your meetings?" Blue asked.

"Actually, I never noticed her before until yesterday."

Carl huffed again. "You two look pretty chummy."

"Why can't you cut me some slack? I have no reason to lie to you."

"You have every reason to lie. Maybe if you hadn't gotten caught."

"Caught doing what? I had a cup of coffee with her. That's it. Right before I took off, she suddenly wants to hug and kiss me."

"Despite having a husband?"

I'm sick of this! Defiantly, Johnnie raised his chin. "It wouldn't be the first time a married woman has thrown themselves at me."

"Oh yes, of course!" Carl threw up his hands. "Because you're the big rock star, Johnnie Vega."

"That definitely has something to do with it."

With a look of disgust, Carl stormed from the room.

"Johnnie, I know you're upset..." Blue took his arm.

Johnnie jerked from his grasp. "I have the right to be upset. Someone wrote a bullshit story about me, suggesting I'm cheating on Melanie, who I love more than anything. And Carl believed every word of it."

Blue sighed heavily. "Unfortunately, he's not the only one who believes it."

Johnnie sank into a chair and logged onto *Twitter*. It was bad. The comments directed at him were ugly. There was even a trending hashtag.

He' a great drummer but a lousy human being.
#johnnievegaisanasshole

He should crawl back under the rock where he lived before his wife made him famous again. #johnnievegaisanasshole

How were he and Caesar Blue ever friends? #johnnievegaisanasshole

He loudly groaned as he sank his head into his hands. "This is some fucked up shit."

"You should call Kurt and figure out a way to handle it."

Johnnie stood again. "I need to go back home. I don't want reporters here at the hospital around Melanie or our families. I'm the story, so maybe they'll go away if I'm not here."

"I don't think it's going to be that easy." Blue put a hand on his shoulder, then pulled him in for a hug. "Are you sure you're not just trying to get away from Carl?"

"It's probably best that we don't cross paths for a while."

"I'll give you one guess as to who's responsible for the story."

"That prick, Phil Chase?" Johnnie fumed as he sat in his car.

"Yeah, I made some calls and found out that it originated with him."

Johnnie thought about the woman...Laurel. How he'd not noticed her at any meetings prior to that one. *Was it all a setup?*

"You willing to do a few interviews and tell your side of the story?" Kurt questioned.

Johnnie switched his phone to his other ear. "I hate the press. You know that. I always fuck up and say the wrong shit. I'd probably make things worse."

"So, you want people to keep believing this bullshit?"

"Of course not."

"Then you've got to tell your truth."

Johnnie leaned back in his seat. "I saw the *Twitter* feed. It's fucking terrible."

"Yeah, it is."

"Will anyone even believe me?"

"You have to try," Kurt told him. "Maybe you can put up a video statement on the *Facebook* page. Something on Instagram, too."

"Can you help me write a statement so that I could practice what to say?"

"Of course. Why don't I come out to your place tomorrow afternoon? We can put something together. I want to visit Melanie, too."

"I can't thank you enough, man."

"Are you really okay, Johnnie?" Kurt asked. "I mean with all your going through with Melanie, and now this mess. It's got to weigh heavy on you. You all right as far as the drinking and stuff?"

"So far, so good."

"Well, hang in there. I'll be out tomorrow afternoon. I'll give you a call before I leave."

"Sounds good. See you then." Johnnie ended the call. He'd lied to Kurt about being okay. The episode with Carl...the shit story...had made his cravings return. With a shaking hand, he wiped the sweat from his brow. In the two years he'd been sober, he'd not felt this sort of need. He was anxious, his heart pounding...and he really needed something to help calm him down.

He scrolled through his phone to call Gordon. *What if he's in on the story with Phil Chase?*

"Damn! I'm fucking paranoid." But he had every right to be. Laurel had popped up out of nowhere and used Melanie's story to get him to talk to her. Something that had seemed so innocent at the time had turned into a fucking fiasco.

Johnnie glanced around the hospital parking lot. *What if Phil Chase is following me? What if he's waiting for me to fuck up so he can tell the world?* He started the car. He needed to get out of here fast.

As he headed home, the argument with Melanie's dad played in his mind. Carl was furious with him. He'd even said Melanie would not be coming home with him. Would Carl fight him on that decision? Johnnie sure as hell didn't want to go to battle in court over it. With his sordid history and this latest disaster, he certainly wouldn't look like a pillar of virtue.

He was so deep in thought that he ran a red light. Several cars screeched to a halt to avoid hitting him. They pressed their horns and Johnnie winced from the blare of the noise. Luckily, no one hit him or any other driver. Even luckier, there were no cops around to pull him over and ticket him. The last thing he needed was to end up in jail or dead. Melanie needed him. *I need a drink!*

Johnnie stared at the new bottle of whiskey he'd bought on the way home. *One drink might take off the edge.* But he was afraid. If he drank one, would he lose control? Or would he be able to stop himself? Having been in show business, he'd met plenty of former drunks who could control themselves around alcohol. They'd have a beer or two, then stop before they got trashed. *Can I do that?*

CJ howled. Happy for a distraction, Johnnie hopped off the barstool. "Hungry, dude? I just fed you a couple of hours ago."

CJ wound himself in and out of Johnnie's legs. Johnnie picked him up, and the cat began to purr.

"I'm glad someone still loves me." He kissed the top of the cat's head. "You're all I've got these days."

Johnnie opened the cupboard where the cans of tuna were. CJ meowed. "Yep. I know what you like."

As he was dumping the tuna into CJ's bowl, his phone began to vibrate on the countertop. It was Carl calling, but he was the last person Johnnie wanted to talk to. A few minutes later, Carl texted him instead.

Meet us at your mother's house. Around six for dinner. It's time we make some decisions about Melanie and Michael.

What decisions? Michael was fine with his mom. Melanie would be fine here at home.

What if she never wakes up? Or worse? What if she...

145

He shut his eyes tight, willing himself not to cry. It would be better here. That was the way Melanie would want it. He was convinced. Even if she died, it would be better if she died in a place she loved. *And she'd be with Caesar.*

"Wait a minute," he said aloud. *What if Caesar hasn't returned because Melanie's already with him?* Was she in whatever world he now occupied? Her body was still here, but her mind? Her spirit? Who knew?

Does he want her all to himself? If she's with Caesar, she's also with her daughters. A family.

In some ways, the thought was comforting. Her being with people she loved and who loved her. But in other ways, it made him pissed as hell.

Johnnie slammed his hand against the kitchen counter. "You can't have her, Caesar. She's mine. You brought her to me. For me. And now you want to take her away? Fuck that! I need her!"

He poured some whiskey into a glass, then walked to the large picture windows that overlooked the beach. "My son needs his mother, Caesar. If she's with you, give her back!"

He drank. The whiskey was like fire in this throat, like it had been the first time he'd tried it at age eleven.

"Fuck!" He threw the glass against the fireplace. It shattered on the stonework. "What is wrong with you? Two fucking years down the shithole!"

Tears fell as he walked back into the kitchen and grabbed the bottle. He slid open the back door and marched down the steps to the beach. "Everyone's right. Melanie's better off without me. So is Michael."

At the water's edge, he opened the bottle again and took a long swig of whiskey. It still burned but it was okay. He needed to feel some physical pain. "She's all yours, Caesar. I don't deserve her. She's too good for me."

He strolled to his rock and lifted himself up onto it. The midday sun was high in the sky. Despite it being October, it was a hot day, and he stripped off his shirt. Then he drank until he passed out.

Chapter Eleven

Past

Johnnie stumbled down a London sidewalk, heading home after a night of partying.

"What's the matter? Can't walk straight?" The woman with him dipped beneath his arm. "Let me help you."

"I'm fine." Johnnie stopped in his tracks. He pointed at the storefront. "I gotta pick up a few things."

The two of them went in. The woman went straight to the candy aisle while he went to the liquor. There was no whiskey at home. He reached for a bottle.

"Haven't you had enough tonight?"

Johnnie looked up, then immediately dropped the bottle. It shattered on the floor at the feet of his dead best friend. "Get the fuck away from me! You're not real!"

"I'm trying to help you, Johnnie."

"You okay, Mister?" the shop clerk asked.

"No, you're not okay." Caesar glared at Johnnie.

Johnnie shut his eyes tight, trying desperately to get rid of this hallucination. He opened them again.

"I'm still here." Caesar flipped back the gold-tinged chocolate curls from his dark eyes and smiled. "Ready to listen to me now?"

Johnnie clumsily ran from the store, leaving a shocked store clerk and his date behind.

Present

Several hours later, Johnnie woke. The sun was setting, and stars were starting to appear in the sky. A strong, cool breeze swept through his hair as he sat up.

"Shit," he muttered, feeling woozy. Immediately, he leaned over the side of the rock and vomited on the sand beside it.

Why did I do this shit again? Easy answer. His wife...the love of his life was in a coma. The idea of raising his son without her terrified him. His father-in-law was disgusted with him. Blue was starting to doubt him. *The entire world hates me.*

"I don't hate you."

Johnnie jerked himself upright. When he saw Caesar sitting on the rock next to him, he scrambled backward, sending himself over the side of the rock and landing on the sand where he'd just puked.

Caesar laughed uncontrollably, his perfectly coifed curls dancing around his face. "You've been hounding me for weeks, and when I finally get here, I still manage to scare the hell out of you."

"Is it really you?" Johnnie blinked his eyes a few times. His vision was a little blurred. "Or am I just drunk?"

"It's really me...and you're *really* drunk." Caesar hopped off the rock and held out his hand to Johnnie. "Get up."

Johnnie took the offered hand, and his friend pulled him to his feet. He stumbled, trying to keep his balance.

"Perhaps you should sit down."

Instead, Johnnie wrapped his arms around Caesar and hugged him tightly. Grief overtook him, and he sobbed.

"I gotcha, man." Caesar rubbed his back, trying to comfort him. "Even if you do reek."

Johnnie drew away. "Where have you been? We've missed you so much."

Caesar rested his forehead against Johnnie's. "You two were so happy together. You didn't need me hanging around."

"But I heard you tell me Melanie needed help."

"Where I was, I felt that she was hurt and needed you. Did you help her?"

Johnnie nodded wiping away fresh tears.

Caesar closed his eyes, took a deep breath, and appeared to be concentrating on something. Then his eyes flew open, and he seemed bewildered. "Johnnie, where's Melanie? I haven't felt her for a while. I can't feel her now."

"You don't know? She's not with you?"

"She's not..." Caesar's eyes went wide. Then he shook his head. "No, she can't be. She *would* be with me."

"When the baby came..."

"A baby?" Caesar gasped and wrapped his arms around him again, lifting him off the ground. "You two had a baby? Let's go see him. Or her."

"A boy." Johnnie pulled away once more and turned his gaze from Caesar's. "I haven't even seen him yet."

Again, Caesar appeared confused. "What? Did she just have him?"

"It's been a month." Johnnie's breath caught in his throat. He coughed to clear it. "There were complications and Melanie slipped into a coma after giving birth."

"And the baby? Is he okay?"

Johnnie nodded. "My mom's been taking care of him."

"He's in Atlanta?"

"What?" Johnnie's brow furrowed. "No. Mom lives in California now. Not far from here. You really don't know what's been going on, do you?"

Caesar plopped a hand down on Johnnie's shoulder and shook him gently. "Let's go back to the house. You can tell me everything. Then we'll go see Melanie and the baby."

"His name's Michael." Johnnie looked around for the bottle of whiskey. He needed to get rid of it.

"Looking for this?" Caesar picked it up and held it out to him. "Why are you drinking again? I thought you got sober."

"I did. Two years. Until last night." There was still whiskey left in the bottle. Johnnie licked his lips, wanting to taste the bronze liquid again.

Caesar opened the bottle. "You want it, don't you?"

"Unfortunately, I do." He wiped the sweat that was beading on his forehead.

Caesar turned the bottle upside down.

"Thanks, a fucking lot."

"You're officially sober again." Caesar replaced the top and handed Johnnie the empty bottle.

"I fucked up, man." Snatching his shirt from the ground, he trudged back to the house. Caesar followed close behind.

"You made one mistake. Fix it. Right now."

"What's the point?"

Caesar shoved him hard, and he fell to the wet sand. "Melanie's in a coma, and you have a son. That's the point."

Caesar didn't help him up this time. Instead, he stormed past him to the house. Johnnie scrambled to his feet and followed. Seeing his friend so angry was rare. Caesar had always been calm and chill, rarely letting anything bother him.

"Take a shower, you smell like puke," Caesar ordered when Johnnie reached the porch.

After cleaning up, Johnnie found Caesar in the nursery sitting in the rocking chair. CJ was on his lap.

Johnnie went to the crib and ran his hand across the top rail. "I found her at the bottom of the stairs, bleeding. She passed out in the car on the way to the hospital."

A tear fell from Caesar's right eye, and he wiped it away.

"Her doctor said it was a ruptured uterus. They removed it and said Melanie should've recovered, but she never woke up."

More tears fell, and Caesar let them.

"I see her every day. I talk to her, sing to her, and I play her favorite songs. But she hasn't come out of it. They want to move her from the hospital...put her in some facility for long-term care. I told them no. She's coming home. She's coming back here. Where we fell in love."

"She'll like that." Caesar's lip trembled, and his voice broke. "I don't feel her, Johnnie. There's nothing. I'm trying so hard to feel her. After you two got married, I still felt her, and she was always so happy with you. Even though I wasn't around, her joy always was there, anytime I wanted to feel it. Now I'm trying, and there's nothing."

Johnnie wiped his own tears away and sniffled. "Everything's falling apart."

"I understand why you got drunk. But promise you won't do it again."

"I can't do that." Johnnie hung his head. "I can only promise to try not to drink."

Caesar stared hard at him. "You *must* do it...for Michael. Where is he? You said your mom has him?"

"He's with her and Blue." Johnnie's head popped back up. "You don't know. My mother...and your father. They got married. They live about a mile inland."

Caesar closed his eyes. At first, he smiled, then he appeared to be in pain.

"Don't worry," Johnnie told him. "It's a good thing. I promise. They're happy."

"It's not that. I can feel them. They're with another couple."

"Melanie's parents, Carl and Mary Jo, are staying with them."

Caesar opened his eyes. "Why isn't Michael here with you?"

Johnnie rose from the chair and went to the window. "You'll think I'm a monster."

"What I think is that you're afraid."

He looked at Caesar and nodded. "I'm afraid I'll hate him."

Caesar gently placed CJ on the floor and walked over to Johnnie. "Why would you hate him? He's a baby. Yours and Melanie's. He was created from the love you two share."

His hands balled into fists. "He took her from me, Caesar. I screwed up, got her pregnant, and then this happened. If he hadn't been born, she'd still be with me."

"You didn't want him?"

"At first, I was scared about being a father. And then as he grew inside her, I fell in love with the idea. I couldn't wait to see him, watch him grow, teach him to play drums. But now I'm afraid I'll see him and blame him. I'm afraid of treating him badly because of it."

Caesar wrapped an arm around his shoulder. "You're afraid of becoming your dad."

Biting his lip, Johnnie nodded.

"You've *never* been like him, and you'll *never* be like him."

Johnnie sat in the rocking chair and sank his head into his hands.

Caesar moved to the crib and picked up a stuffed monkey. "They're angry. Upset. Even my dad is disappointed in you. He believed in you, and you let him down."

Johnnie looked up. "Tell me something I don't know."

"They're making plans, Johnnie. Without you."

"I was supposed to meet with them tonight."

"Melanie's parents." Caesar walked to where he sat. "They want to take Michael back to Florida with them."

"What? No fucking way!" Johnnie jumped to his feet and paced in front of his friend. He knew Caesar could feel things, even see into the near future if he tried.

Caesar pressed two fingers against his temple. "Melanie has a cousin. Maggie. She has a toddler. She's offered to take care of Michael."

"He's my son. They're not taking my son. My mom…"

Caesar snatched his arm roughly. "Think, Johnnie! Our parents are almost seventy. They're too old to be taking care of a baby. Between the four of them, they've been doing okay the last month, but they can't keep it up."

"They're not taking my son anywhere!"

Caesar gripped his other arm and shook him. "Then go get him."

"Where's my son?" Johnnie bolted into his mother's house, looking around frantically. "Where is he?"

His mother held a finger to her lips to shush him. "Mary Jo's trying to get him down."

"He's coming home with me!"

Smiling, Blue rose from a chair. "I'll start packing his things."

"Wait a minute," Carl stood as well. "He'll be down for the night soon."

Johnnie narrowed his eyes. "I don't care. He's coming home, where he belongs."

"Where is this coming from? Suddenly, you want to be a dad?"

"I know you don't think much of me, Carl. But he's my son. And he belongs with me."

Carl lifted his arms out to his sides. "With all the stuff you're dealing with, you think you can take on raising a baby alone?"

Johnnie closed in on Carl and stared hard into the older man's eyes. "I ran from Michael because I was afraid I'd fail him. I'm still scared. But Melanie had faith in me. She said I'd be a great father. So, I've got to have faith in myself and take care of my son. It's what she would want."

His mother wrapped an arm around his waist. "You'll be an excellent father, Johnnie."

"Thanks, Mom."

Mary Jo entered the living room. "What's happening? Blue says you're taking Michael home."

Johnnie stood a bit straighter. "I am."

His mom waved her hand, beckoning Mary Jo to follow her. "Let's get his bottles and milk ready to go."

Mary Jo appeared stunned. She looked at her husband, her eyes full of questions. Carl nodded his head.

Blue soon returned with two baby bags and dropped them in front of Johnnie. "His clothes, towels, and blankets are in this one. Diapers in this one."

Suddenly, Johnnie felt overwhelmed. "We have plenty of this stuff at our house."

"You can always pack him a new bag when he comes to visit." Blue smiled and hugged him. "Why don't you go in and see him? He's quieted down but still awake."

Johnnie felt queasy, his stomach twisting in knots. His heart thudded in his chest. This was the moment he'd once longed for. It was the one he and Melanie had prepared for. Now it terrified him. But it was time. His son needed him. And he needed the strength and love his son would bring to his life.

Slowly, he walked to the bedroom where he'd helped Blue set up a crib just a couple of months ago. The lamp had been dimmed and a night light glowed. A mobile played music above the crib.

With trepidation, Johnnie approached the crib. He couldn't see much, so he reached over to the table and brightened the lamp's light. His son's tiny body was swaddled, but his eyes were wide as he watched the mobile above him move slowly in circles.

He's beautiful. Johnnie felt tears sliding down his face as he gently touched Michael's head.

"Hello," he whispered as he stroked his son's silky, soft dark curls. "Hi, little man. I bet you've been wondering where I've been. I'm here now. Right here with you."

Michael turned to his voice and stared at him. Johnnie thought his heart might burst from the love that was filling it. Gently, he caressed his son's cheek. "Look at you. Aren't you handsome? Your momma's gonna love you."

"Go ahead and pick him up." His mother was at the door.

Johnnie reached in but was unsure of himself. His mother came to the crib and picked up Michael.

"Like this," she instructed, holding a firm hand under Michael's head and another under his midsection. She then passed the baby to him.

"Melanie had me reading the baby books and watching videos, but it's not the same as actually doing it," Johnnie said as he took Michael in his arms for the first time.

"Now pull him closer to your chest and cuddle him."

"Thanks, Mom." Johnnie brought his son to his heart. Michael stared at him, as if in awe.

"Look at him. He's already in love with his daddy." His mother wiped at the tears sliding down her cheeks.

"I love him, too." Johnnie smiled and began rocking his son slowly. "It's like he knows me."

"I'm sure he does. The way you always talked and sang to him before he was born. He recognizes your voice."

"Isn't he beautiful?"

"Yes. He looks just like you when you were a baby."

"I see Melanie." Johnnie looked at his mom. "In his eyes. He has her eyes."

His mother came closer and gazed at Michael. "I believe you're right."

Blue, Carl, and Mary Jo stepped into the room.

"Are you sure you'll be alright with him?" Mary Jo asked. "Making his bottles and changing his diapers?"

"Will you show me before I leave?" He turned his gaze to Carl. "And maybe you can show me how to put him in the car seat properly."

Carl nodded and forced a smile. "Of course."

Caesar was waiting for him at the gate when he returned home.

"Did everything go alright," he asked as Johnnie stepped out of the car.

"Yeah. Can you bring his bags in? And there's a cooler. They're in the trunk." Johnnie clicked the key to open the trunk, then opened the back door and removed a sleeping Michael from his car seat.

Johnnie carried him straight to the nursery. Caesar followed and set everything down on the floor.

"His milk is in that cooler. It needs to go into the freezer. Except for about ten of those bags. I need those in the refrigerator so they can thaw out for him to drink when he wakes up."

Caesar opened the cooler and held up a couple of the bags. "This is how baby formula comes now?"

"It's donated breast milk."

"You're kidding."

"I'm not." Johnnie smiled. "I'll be getting deliveries from the breast milk bank. Since Melanie can't nurse him, it's the next best thing."

Caesar put the milk back and picked up the cooler. "Be back in a few."

Johnnie placed Michael into his crib. The one he and Melanie had picked out together. The baby lay quietly sleeping while Johnnie turned on a lamp nearby, then turned off the room light. He removed all the stuffed animals and put them on top of the chest of drawers.

"Look at him," Caesar whispered. "He's perfection."

Gently, Johnnie stroked the top of Michael's head. "He is."

"How long do you think he'll sleep for?"

"My mom said he usually sleeps in six-hour intervals."

"While you were gone, I set up the monitor. You can watch him while he sleeps."

"I don't think I can leave him alone tonight."

"We could bring in one of the recliners so you can at least be comfortable if you sleep in here."

"That sounds like a good idea."

A few hours later, Johnnie was awakened by the cries of his son. Immediately, he leaped from the recliner and rushed to the crib.

"What's wrong?" Caesar appeared at the door and flipped on the light. "Is he okay?"

Squinting, Johnnie lifted Michael into his arms. "He's fine. Probably just needs to be changed and fed."

"It hasn't been six hours."

"He's in unfamiliar surroundings." Johnnie bounced, trying to comfort Michael. "He'll get on a schedule soon."

Caesar came closer. "You already sound like a pro at this."

"Yeah, well now I have to change him and feed him for the first time by myself. Melanie's mom showed me before I left, but now's the real test."

"Don't worry." Caesar smiled. "I'll help."

"And how much experience do you have with babies?" Johnnie grinned.

"I dated a few single moms."

"Dated or fucked?"

Caesar laughed. "You're right. I have zero experience. But, together, we should be able to handle this."

"We should feed him first."

They made their way downstairs to the kitchen. Before going to bed, Johnnie had filled a couple of bottles with milk so that they would be ready for a feeding. He took one out.

"I need a pan of warm water to put it in."

"On it."

Michael cried louder.

"Guess we're not fast enough." Johnnie gazed down at his son. "Demanding little thing, aren't you?"

Caesar touched Michael's cheek. "Just like his dad."

Michael stopped crying for a moment and looked at Caesar.

"He sees you." Johnnie smiled. "Say hello to Uncle Caesar."

Michael pouted again and began crying.

CJ strolled in and wrapped himself around Caesar's legs. He let out a loud meow. "Is he hungry, too?"

"Always." Johnnie pointed to the cupboard. "He has cans of tuna up there. They're his special treat."

Caesar retrieved one, opened it, and dumped the contents in CJ's bowl.

Johnnie's eyes narrowed. "How come that cat can see you?"

Caesar shrugged. "Wish I had a rule book for the afterlife."

"You'd probably just break them all." Johnnie smiled and then his stomach growled. "Man, I could use some food myself."

"Want to cook something?" Caesar opened the refrigerator. There wasn't a lot there since Johnnie had been fending for himself for weeks.

"Grab that container of stew. My mom sent me home with some homemade cooking."

Caesar grabbed it. "How much do you want?"

"Just heat it all up. Between you and me I think we can finish it off."

While he waited for his food to heat up, Johnnie offered Michael his bottle. The baby instantly latched on and began eating. Caesar grabbed Johnnie's phone and took a photo.

"For Melanie. We have to take lots of videos and photos for her to see when she wakes up."

Johnnie smiled. Caesar had faith that Melanie would recover, and that made him feel at ease. "We will."

"Can we visit her tomorrow?"

Johnnie was about to say yes but then remembered that some people would be able to see Caesar, while others wouldn't be able to. "I'm not sure that's a good idea. It might cause some chaos."

"You're right," Caesar replied, frowning. "I forgot how much trouble it could be."

"You'll see her soon when I bring her home. Besides, there's been reporters up there hounding me and our families. Even Phil Chase."

Caesar groaned. "That idiot's still around?"

"Yep, causing trouble as usual." He filled him in on Chase's latest story. Johnnie hadn't given any thought to his other problems since Caesar had shown up. He'd been too busy getting Michael home and settled in. His stomach churned with worry once again. *Can Kurt and I get control of the situation?*

"That's why you were drinking."

"I can't do that again." He peered down at Michael, and his heart swelled with love. "I have to take care of him."

"You're doing great so far." Caesar touched Michael's tiny hand, and the baby gripped it firmly.

"Definitely a drummer." Caesar smiled.

Johnnie nodded. "I think he's done."

Michael was turning away from the bottle and not eating anymore. Johnnie set the bottle down, then carefully placed Michael over his shoulder to burp him. He gently patted the baby's back.

Caesar raised a fist into the air when they heard a burp. "You did it!"

Johnnie felt something wet sliding down his back. The smell was putrid. He turned his back toward Caesar. "Oh shit, what did he just do?"

Caesar grimaced and held his nose. "That *is* nasty. He threw up or something."

"My mom said he might spit up after he eats. I forgot to put a burping pad over my shoulder."

Johnnie felt Michael's little body tense then relax. Now something wet was running down the front side of his body. "Oh, hell."

Caesar burst into laughter.

"I've got to clean him."

"Just put him in the sink and hose him down." Caesar held up the small sprayer at the sink. "Then go outside and hose yourself down."

"There's a baby tub somewhere upstairs. And some baby wash, washcloths, and towels. We can actually put the tub in the sink."

"What should I do?" Caesar asked.

"I'll go wipe him down with those baby wipe things and get most of the shit off. You prepare his bath stuff here in the sink."

"Be sure to wipe yourself down."

The two men laughed together. Michael began to wail. CJ bolted from the kitchen.

Michael was drifting off to sleep when Johnnie returned him to the crib.

Caesar held up his hand. "We did it."

"Yes, we did." Johnnie smiled and high fived him. "I'm ready for some stew."

"Oh yea, almost forgot about that."

The two of them scurried down the stairs to the kitchen. Johnnie set the baby monitor on the kitchen island before reheating his food. Caesar got a couple of bowls down from the cupboard.

"This is delicious," Caesar marveled between bites. "I remember your mom making this when we were teens."

Johnnie nodded. His mom had always been good to Caesar even though his dad hadn't liked his friend much. The long-standing idea between the elder Smith and his two older sons was that Johnnie was gay. After all, he was into music, not sports or camping—him making a friend like Caesar only deepened their commitment to that theory. The truth was Caesar had always been a favorite of the girls, and he'd helped Johnnie become more comfortable around them. Caesar had even talked a girl into taking Johnnie's virginity.

"How are Kurt and Rhett?" Caesar asked before letting out a loud burp. "Do you see them much?"

"Oh shit! I almost forgot. Kurt's coming tomorrow to help me do damage control."

"That's great." Caesar wiped his face with a napkin. "I can't wait to see him again."

Johnnie smiled. He and Rhett had no problem seeing Caesar, but Kurt hadn't been a believer in ghosts, so it had been harder to convince him that Caesar had returned. *Melanie.* She'd helped Kurt believe, helped him see Caesar. *Melanie is amazing.*

Caesar smiled slyly. "Thinking about Melanie?"

"How did you know?"

"You always get that loopy look on your face when you do. Dazed, confused, and so in love."

"I am."

"She's special."

Johnnie groaned. "Just go ahead and say it. You're in love with her, too."

"No jealousy tonight?"

"Hell no." Johnnie shook his head. "Besides me, you're the next best thing for her."

"I'll let you have that one." Caesar smiled, then frowned. "I'm sorry. I can't help you. That I can't feel her. You know I'd bring her back to you if I could."

Johnnie nodded.

Caesar sighed and pushed his long hair back behind his ears. "I wish I could get on social media with you and tell the world how much you love her."

"That would create a whole new set of problems."

"Can you imagine the four of us performing again for an audience?"

Johnnie chuckled softly. "Caesar...always a dreamer."

"I know it's not practical. Some would see me, others wouldn't. Besides who knows how long I'll be allowed to stay this time."

"You went away before but stuck around...you know...as a dolphin. What's that about?"

"Hard to explain."

"No rule book. I get it."

Caesar stared off into space, obviously thinking, then turned his attention back to Johnnie. "It's like my spirit can go places, but I can't. I can feel things but can't see them unless I'm in a life form of some sort. The dolphins are allowed, being our former selves not so much. Only when we're sent to help someone."

"You came because I drank again." Johnnie sighed. "Was it you who dumped the first two bottles of whiskey and sent those texts to my phone? To help cover for me with Carl and Blue?"

Caesar nodded. "I thought that would've scared you enough to keep you from drinking again."

"It should've."

"You're the gift that keeps on giving." Caesar laughed lightly. "I can't tell you how many times in the past I tried to make contact with you, and it didn't work."

"I always thought I was seeing things because I was drunk or high."

Johnnie put the dirty dishes in the sink. "I'm glad you were given a different mission. To help Melanie."

"It turned out to be another way to reach you."

"Because of our connection," Johnnie replied.

"Because of the blood you shared with her."

Johnnie stared out of the kitchen window and dipped deep into thought.

"What is it?" Caesar asked.

"Leila and Lily? Are they here?"

Smiling, Caesar rose from the barstool. "Come with me."

Johnnie followed Caesar outside. In the moonlight, they stood on the deck together. Caesar closed his eyes and inhaled the ocean air. Two small dolphins leaped into the air and spun in circles.

Caesar opened his eyes and gazed out at the water "I always keep them close."

"Thank you for that. I know it gives Melanie comfort knowing you're watching over them. Although it freaks me out that I've been out there swimming nude around them."

Caesar laughed. "Why do you think I was always harassing you in the water, telling you to put your pants back on."

"Sorry, I don't speak dolphin. I always thought you were trying to get frisky with me."

"Maybe I should have. Maybe then you'd have kept your pants on when you swam."

Johnnie couldn't help laughing now.

"I kept them away if I knew you were swimming naked, or if you were out there making love to Melanie."

"You were there?" Johnnie raised an eyebrow. "I told Melanie you were watching us."

"Let's get back inside." Caesar wrapped an arm around his shoulder. "We can't hear Michael if we're out here."

Johnnie yawned as they went back in. "I need some sleep, too."

"Why don't you take the bed this time. I'll stay in the nursery with Michael."

Johnnie was exhausted. It had been a long day. He picked up the baby monitor from the kitchen. "Alright, I'll keep this nearby though."

"You know, I'm surprised you didn't have a hell of a hangover."

Johnnie scratched his head. "I haven't even thought about it. I was so busy with Michael, I didn't notice."

Caesar patted his shoulder as they climbed the stairs to go to bed. "More important things to worry about."

Johnnie nodded. They parted at the bedroom doors. Johnnie set the monitor on the bedside table before lying down. He smiled, seeing his son sleeping. He touched the screen. *Melanie, you should see him. He's an angel. Sent from heaven.* Johnnie smiled as he heard singing coming from the nursery. *Just like Caesar.*

Chapter Twelve

Past

"Maybe it's time you talked to the press," Rhett said. "Give them your side of the story."

Johnnie rubbed his head and groaned. "Hell no. I have nothing to say to them."

"They're just going to keep speculating and making up stories." Rhett frowned.

Johnnie took a sip of whiskey. "I don't even remember what happened that night."

"If you stopped drinking for more than a minute, maybe you could!" Kurt snapped at him.

Johnnie rolled his eyes. He was tired of Kurt giving him grief about Caesar's death. He didn't want to think about it or talk about it with anyone much less the press.

Kurt jumped up and paced in front of him. "You don't seem to care that people are saying you killed Caesar."

"What is my denying it going to do?" Johnnie demanded. "The police say I didn't, and the reporters are still making up shit about it. If they don't believe the cops, they sure as hell won't believe me. I'm a fucking addict. My word means nothing to those assholes."

"Maybe you should get clean like Caesar did," Rhett suggested. "Like he wanted you to."

"Yeah. Caesar got clean. And look where that got him." Johnnie stood, grabbed his bottle of whiskey, and stalked out of the room.

Present

"Man, it's good to see you," Johnnie greeted Kurt with a hug. "Don't know how I'd handle this mess without you."

"How do you always manage to find trouble?" Kurt ruffled Johnnie's hair. "Guess I should be used to it by now. Although I thought sobriety and marriage would have tamed you."

Johnnie winced at the mention of sobriety. *Should I tell Kurt?* As the two of them entered the house, CJ ran to Kurt and rubbed against his legs. Kurt reached down and scratched the animal's head.

"He's not usually this friendly with me."

"He's lonely. Misses Melanie so much that he's been extra friendly with everyone." Johnnie strolled into the kitchen and to the stairs. He turned, smiled at Kurt, and beckoned him forward. "Come on. I have a few surprises for you."

"Caesar?" Kurt rushed into the room when he saw Caesar in the rocking chair with Michael. He turned back to Johnnie and grinned. "You finally brought Michael home?"

"I had to knock some sense into him first. Literally." Caesar kissed Michael's head. "But it worked."

Kurt bent and gently touched Michael's cheek. "Spittin image of you, Vega."

"Feel his grip," Caesar instructed. "He's already ripped some of my hair out."

"Lucky for you it grows right back," Johnnie said.

Kurt glanced at Caesar.

Caesar smiled and shrugged. "All that ghost, angel stuff."

Kurt stroked Michael's hand with his index finger. Michael grabbed it and held tight.

"He'll be ready for his first sticks soon." Johnnie stroked Michael's other hand.

"It's naptime." Caesar lifted Michael to Johnnie, who took him and placed the baby in the crib.

Johnnie wound up the mobile that was above the bed. "We just fed and changed him. He should pass out soon."

Kurt's gaze zipped from Johnnie to Caesar. "We? Why is Caesar back? To help Melanie? What's going on?"

"Let's go sit on the deck." Johnnie grabbed the baby monitor, and they all walked back downstairs.

"I didn't think I'd ever see you again." Kurt hugged Caesar tight. They held onto one another for a few minutes before parting.

"Some people never stop needing my help." Caesar smirked at Johnnie, then sat down in one of the outdoor chairs.

"So, you *are* here to help Melanie." Kurt sat across from him and crossed one leg over the other.

"I can't even feel her. I'm hoping when Johnnie brings her home in a few days that will change, and maybe somehow I can reach out to her."

"You're bringing Melanie home? How is she?"

"The same," Johnnie replied as he brought out a pitcher of iced tea and some glasses. "But she's coming home. I don't want to send her to some facility to waste away. I'll hire a nurse to come in and help."

"If it were Sara, I'd probably do the same." Kurt looked at Caesar again. "Didn't you say you had to have a purpose for returning?"

Caesar glanced at Johnnie. "Johnnie needed me."

"He's going through a lot of shit that's for sure."

Johnnie plopped down in a chair between the two of them. He knew he had to come clean about what he'd done. Part of recovery was admitting mistakes. "I fucked up bad."

"You didn't punch Phil Chase, did you?"

"Not yet." Johnnie grinned.

"Well don't." Kurt shook a finger at him. "He'll have you arrested, and considering everything that's on your plate right now, that would be the worst thing that could happen."

Johnnie's gaze drifted to the ocean. "After we talked yesterday, I drank nearly a whole bottle of whiskey."

Kurt took off his glasses, closed his eyes, and rubbed the bridge of his nose. Then he slid his glasses back on. He nodded his head slowly. "I was worried that you might drink or take some pills. You've been under a lot of pressure, and I know you miss Melanie."

"No excuse. I shouldn't have done it. I thought I was stronger than that."

Kurt reached over and squeezed his shoulder. "That crap Phil Chase pulled couldn't have helped."

Johnnie shook his head. "Still no excuse."

"Relapses are part of recovery. I'm sure you've heard that."

"You and Rhett were lucky. You two quit all the hard stuff and moved on like it was nothing. Caesar, too."

Caesar squeezed a lemon slice into his tea, then took a sip. "None of us had a shitty father telling us we were nothing and nobody. And your mom even said your grandfather was an alcoholic."

"I know. I know." Johnnie started to tear up. "But I feel like I let Melanie down. I try so hard for her...for us. All this I'm dealing with is nothing. She's the one in the coma. Her life is in limbo, not mine. I'm here. I can still enjoy my friends...my family. I get to see and touch the life we created together. She's missing everything."

Both Kurt and Caesar rubbed one of Johnnie's shoulders.

"He was passed out on the beach when I showed up. I'm helping him get his priorities straight. The first thing was getting Michael here. We'll bring Melanie home. I know you can handle it, Johnnie. You're stronger than you think."

"We've got to handle this ridiculous story Phil Chase got started as well," Kurt added.

"Did you think of any ideas?" Johnnie asked.

"We make a video with you telling me what happened. We'll post it to our social media pages along with some photos of you with Michael. Maybe a few of you by Melanie's bedside."

"Is that necessary? I hate to put the two of them out there like that."

"The world needs to see how devoted you are to her and your son," Kurt explained. "The damage has been done, and we've got to undo as much of it as we can."

"Let's wait until she's here, home with me. No hospital photos."

"I can probably get a news station to come out and do a story of you bringing her home."

Johnnie rolled his eyes, sighed, then shrugged. "Whatever you think is best."

"Well, we need to do things quickly, as soon as possible." Kurt pulled a folded piece of paper from his jacket pocket and handed it to Johnnie. "I wrote something last night. For a video statement. See what you think."

Johnnie unfolded the paper and read. Caesar hovered over his shoulder, reading also.

"It's good."

Caesar shook his head. "It's too rehearsed."

"I need that, so I don't say anything stupid."

"Speak from your heart." Caesar placed a hand on Johnnie's chest. "Say what you feel, and it will all be right."

Johnnie looked at Kurt. "What do you think?"

"Caesar's got a point."

"Let's do it now then while Michael's sleeping. Caesar's taken some photos of me with Michael. We can post those as well."

"Hello, everyone. You all know me, no introductions needed. I felt I needed to respond to a story that's out there. You know the one. That bullshit story about me cheating on my wife."

Johnnie paused a moment. *Maybe I shouldn't curse.* He looked to Kurt and Caesar. They nodded and signaled him to continue. *Hell, it's what I do.*

"Those of you who have followed my band know there's this asshole reporter named Phil Chase who likes to make up lies about me and my musical brothers. Well, he did it again. And unfortunately, too many of you believed it. I understand why. My history isn't the best. I'm not called the *bad boy* of Lush for nothing."

Johnnie stood and went to the crib. Kurt followed with the phone.

"This is my son, Michael Angelo Vega." Johnnie picked up the baby and cradled him close. "When he was born, it was one of the best days of my life and one of the worst. Melanie gave birth and slipped into a coma, and as of now, she hasn't come out of it. For the first three days, I never left her side. I begged her to wake up. I was so focused on trying to reach her and bring her back, that I had my mom and my stepfather taking care of Michael. But it's been a month, and nothing's changed with Melanie. I realized it was time to focus on Michael. So, he's here with me at home, where he belongs and where he will stay."

Gently, Johnnie placed Michael back in the crib. Michael stirred a bit but kept sleeping. Johnnie sat again.

"The stress I've been dealing with is awful. The fight to stay sober while having your world crash down around you is not one many people would win. That's why I was going to meetings more frequently. That's where I met the woman in the photos. She said her name was Laurel. I don't know if that's even true, or something Phil Chase told her to tell me. She said she wanted to talk because her husband had been in a coma. I had coffee with her thinking she could give me some insight on how to deal with my situation. It was only when I started to leave that she came on to me. I told her I was dedicated to my wife. I rejected her advances, then left. I haven't seen her again because I haven't gone to another meeting. I need to go, but this whole thing has left me worried about who's watching me, and what they're willing to do to make me look bad."

Johnnie paused, bit his lip, then stared at the ground for a moment.

"You okay?" Kurt asked.

Johnnie nodded, then lifted his head. The tears had come again.

"Melanie is the best thing that's ever happened to me, and there's no fucking way I'd hurt her or do anything to destroy what we have together. It hurt to have Lush's fans and hers believe I would treat her so badly. But it hurt worse having her family think that of me. I know my past struggles haven't made me the most reliable person in the world. But there's one thing you can be sure of. I love Melanie, and I love our son. They are my life. So, I'm asking our fans to pray to whatever god you believe in. Send your positive energy our way and help us get through this. Because I need her back. And Michael needs his mother."

Johnnie buried his face in his hands and sobbed. Kurt, shedding tears of his own, ended the video.

Caesar wiped back his own tears. He thumped his hand against his chest. The same chest that held no beating heart. "You did it. You spoke your truth."

"Man, this shit moves fast." Johnnie wiped his forehead as he read the responses to his confession. The video had quickly gone viral, and he was trending on *Twitter*, only this time, it was nothing but good comments. People were even apologizing for not believing in him. The photos of him with Michael were getting thousands of likes on Instagram and *Facebook*.

Caesar pointed to a tweet. "That guy says he's a lawyer and you should sue Chase."

Kurt rubbed his chin. "Not a bad idea actually."

"If I wasn't dealing with all this other stuff maybe...I have bigger worries right now."

"Speaking of worries, maybe we should head to the hospital and check-in on Melanie. I want to see her before I head back home."

"You should stay here for the night," Caesar suggested. "We can hang out some more. Maybe jam a bit in the studio."

"I'd love to, but my daughter is performing in a play tomorrow at school. If I don't go, they'll be hell to pay. She's a Daddy's girl and expects Daddy to be there."

Caesar nodded but seemed sad.

Kurt punched his arm playfully. "Rhett's coming home soon. How about if the two of us come back to visit?"

Caesar smiled, then frowned again. "Hopefully I'll still be here."

"I hope so, too." Kurt hugged him.

"Let me get Michael's things ready," Johnnie announced. "They won't allow him up on the ICU floor, so I'll have my mom watch him while we're visiting Melanie."

"I'll be here waiting." Caesar stared at the floor.

"Sorry." Johnnie started for the nursery. He felt bad for Caesar. To be caught in between the land of the living and the dead. *Like Melanie.*

"Hey, Johnnie, do you think we can figure out a way for me to see my dad?"

Johnnie smiled. "Oh wow, Blue would flip. We'll have to figure out a way to get him here alone, though. I don't want to have to explain you to Melanie's parents."

Chapter Thirteen

Past

"What's the verdict?" Caesar asked as Kurt joined them on the beach.

Kurt plopped down on the blanket next to his friends and took the joint that Caesar passed him. He took a hit and passed it to Johnnie. "Dawn's not pregnant."

"Are you glad about that or...not?" Rhett took the joint next.

"Hate to say it, but I'm glad. Even though we've been together for two years, lately things have been going to shit. She's tired of me always being gone. But then we argue all the time when we're together. So, it's probably best."

Caesar nudged his arm. "You seem a bit disappointed, though."

"Might've been nice to become a father."

Johnnie shook his head. "Nah, man, if you two are fighting all the time, that's no place for a baby."

"Johnnie's right." Rhett sighed.

"Do you think you're gonna end things with her?" Caesar asked.

"Looks like it's headed that way. Even she seemed glad she wasn't pregnant."

"Babies and girlfriends," Johnnie huffed. "Who needs them?"

Rhett smiled. "With the way you and Caesar carry on, you're lucky you two don't have hundreds of babies out there."

"Fuck no." Johnnie pointed to his groin. "I wrap this shit up tight."

Caesar fell back on the blanket laughing hysterically.

Johnnie chuckled and took a last puff of the joint. "Are you laughing at me or because this shit is so good."

Caesar wiped the tears from the corners of his eyes. "Can you imagine Johnnie Vega being a father?"

Now Rhett and Kurt laughed and fell back onto the blanket as well. Johnnie shook his head and lit another joint.

Present

"Our flight doesn't leave until seven, but I suppose we should head to the airport."

"Traffic is a nightmare once you get on the freeway," Johnnie told his father-in-law. "Leaving early isn't a bad idea."

"I hate leaving her like this." Mary Jo's eyes filled with tears as she rubbed Melanie's arm. She bent and kissed her daughter's cheek. "I wish you'd wake up for us, honey."

"You're welcome to visit any time you'd like." Johnnie fought his own tears. Melanie had come home earlier that morning. It had taken him nearly two weeks to get everything set up in what was now her room, but he'd done it. And now, Melanie's parents were heading back to Florida. They'd been in California for a month and a half. Things were better between them, but the couple needed to get back home.

"You call us right away if there's any change at all." Carl wiped his own tears away.

"I will." Johnnie nodded as he was pulled into a big bear hug.

"I'm sorry I butted heads with you so much while I was here."

"You love her like I do. I'd be the exact same way if I thought someone wasn't doing right by her."

Carl pulled away and patted Johnnie's back. "I see how much you love her. How you want what's best for her. That's all a father can ask for from a son-in-law. You're doing great with my grandson. I'd say Michael and Melanie are in the best hands."

"Thank you." Johnnie beamed, and he felt tears welling up again. "That means everything to me."

Carl went to Melanie's bedside. "Mom and I are headed home, baby girl. When you wake up, you bring Michael to visit us. We'll take him to *Disney World* and buy him some *Mickey* ears."

Johnnie turned away as Carl broke down. The nurse Johnnie had hired nodded her head and forced a smile. She seemed to be holding back tears of her own.

Blue stuck his head into the doorway. "You folks ready to leave?"

Johnnie's mom came in with Michael. "I know you'll want to hold this little one before you go."

Carl took Michael into his arms and held him close. He cuddled the baby for a bit before handing him over to his wife. Together they all walked out to the driveway.

"Goodbye, little man." Carl kissed Michael's forehead one last time before getting into the back seat of Blue's car.

Mary Jo handed Michael over to Johnnie. "Send us videos and photos. Keep us up to date on everything. He's going to be grown up before you know it."

"Of course." Johnnie smiled. "Thanks for everything. Especially for being there for Michael when I couldn't be."

"That's what family is for." Mary Jo kissed his cheek, then got into the car as well.

"Be careful on the freeway," he told Blue. "And drop by soon. I need to talk to you about some things."

"Will do," Blue answered as he slid into the front seat of his car.

Johnnie laid Michael in the bassinet near Melanie's bed. The baby yawned, and Johnnie gave him his pacifier. Melanie's nurse checked her vitals and then checked the feeding tube in Melanie's stomach.

"How are things going in here?" Johnnie touched Melanie's cheek. "She doesn't seem to be having any adverse reactions to the move home."

"Not at all. Everything looks great, Mr. Vega. I can stay the night if you'd like. I know the first night can be nerve-wracking and with the baby, you've got your hands full."

"I have a friend stopping by later who'll help with the baby." Caesar had been out in the rehearsal studio while the parents were over. He was probably anxious to get out of there. "And call me Johnnie since we'll be spending a lot of time together."

Smiling, the nurse nodded and held out her hand. "And I'm Brenda."

"Your resumé was impressive, so I know my wife is in excellent hands."

"Thank you. You seem to already have a handle on how to care for her."

Johnnie slid his hand down Melanie's arm and took her hand in his. "Her nurse from the hospital, Gailya, was the best. She showed me the ropes. How to feed her, wash her, do her physical therapy. Everything."

"You may not even need me." Brenda pulled Melanie's blanket up to her chest.

"Maybe not. But I hired you full-time and will pay you the full amount, even if you only work a few hours a day."

Brenda nodded. "Being a single mom, I appreciate the flexible schedule."

Johnnie had set up Melanie's laptop on the bedside table. With a few clicks, he started her sleepy time playlist. He kissed her forehead.

"It's Michael's naptime, babe. He's going to sleep here by you."

"Well, if you don't need me, I'll get back home."

Johnnie noted the time on the laptop. "School's out already. Will your kids be alone?"

"They have soccer practice after school. Their dad drops them off. I pick them up."

"I'll see you tomorrow then."

"And if anything changes, let me know. And if there are any problems, call nine-one-one immediately. Don't try to handle it yourself."

"I promise I won't."

Grabbing the baby monitor, Johnnie walked Brenda outside and saw her off. Then he went to the studio.

"I was about to go crazy." Caesar met him at the door. He ran a hand through his long locks. "With my dad here, and your mom. And Melanie. Can I see her now?"

"Yes, come on. Everyone's gone, and I don't like the idea of leaving her alone." They had set up a second camera in her room so that he could watch both her room and the nursery.

At Melanie's door, Johnnie stopped. "I should warn you. She doesn't look like herself."

That gave Caesar pause, and Johnnie thought he might cry. Instead, he bit his lip, then nodded, before following behind Johnnie.

"Melanie?" Caesar went to the head of the bed and rested his palm against her face. Lightly, he slid his hand down to her shoulder, then down her arm. His dark eyes grew full of concern. "She's so thin."

Johnnie nodded, his lip quivering as he stood on the opposite side of the bed. "Wake up, Melanie. Caesar's here, and I know you want to see him."

Caesar brushed a soft kiss across her lips. "I love you, Melanie. I've missed you and have come to visit you again. Can you hear me?"

Michael hiccupped a little and squished up his face. Fidgeting, he whimpered. Immediately, Caesar picked him up.

"Look at this beautiful baby boy of yours, Melanie." Carefully, Caesar unwrapped the blanket the baby was swaddled in and placed Michael face down on top of Melanie's chest. "You and Johnnie did good."

Johnnie sucked in his breath. "I'm not sure if that's a good idea."

"I've got him. He won't roll off." Caesar kept one firm hand on Michael's back.

"I wanted Michael to visit her, but the hospital won't allow babies on the patient floors, especially ICU. Too risky when they're so young."

"Now he can be with his momma all the time." Caesar smiled and kissed Melanie's forehead. "It seems to be calming him down."

Johnnie rubbed Michael's head. His son was falling asleep. "I bet he hears her heartbeat, same as he did when he was still inside her."

Caesar lifted Melanie's arm and placed her hand on Michael's back. Johnnie did likewise with her other hand. Each of them kept their hand on hers to keep Michael steady.

Johnnie leaned in close to her ear. With his free hand, he stroked her hair. "Meet our son, Melanie. Michael Angelo Vega. He's perfect in every way. My mom says he looks like me, but he has your eyes."

"He's got Johnnie's curls." Caesar laughed softly. "But if you let them grow long, maybe they'll look more like mine."

"Caesar's right, babe. You're going to love his hair. He's got so much of it."

"Aww." Caesar cooed. "Your little angel is falling asleep, Melanie."

"Daddy's going to put him back to bed." Johnnie picked up the baby and placed him in the bassinet. He kissed Michael's fisted hand.

"Johnnie," Caesar whispered. "Look."

"What?"

"Is that a smile?"

Johnnie looked down at Melanie. The corners of Melanie's mouth were slightly upturned. "Holy fucking shit! It is!"

Michael began whimpering again. Johnnie patted his back. "Sorry, little man, sorry. Go back to sleep."

Caesar moved closer to her. "Melanie, can you hear us? It's me, Caesar. Johnnie's here, and baby Michael. We're waiting for you to wake up. To come back to us. We love you so much."

There was no response. Michael quieted down and went back to sleep.

Johnnie quieted his voice. "Can you feel her?"

Caesar took her hand in his and closed his eyes. His brow furrowed. Then he opened his eyes again and frowned. "Still nothing."

"But this is a good sign, don't you think? She's never smiled before."

"Take a photo quick before she stops. You can send it to her doctor and see what he thinks."

Johnnie grabbed his phone from the bedside table. "And her parents."

Caesar shook his head. "If you do that, they'll turn right around and come back here."

"And you'll have to go back into hiding." Johnnie took a few photos, then placed the phone back on the table. "I'll send one later."

"Thanks." Caesar caressed Melanie's face again. "I want to spend as much time with her until she wakes up...or..."

"You have to leave."

Caesar winced. "I hope it's not too soon."

"How did it happen before? You know, after I left to go to rehab?"

"We were making love on the beach..."

Johnnie held up his hand and grimaced. "Never mind."

Caesar cracked a wide smile. "Back to being jealous?"

"Always." Johnnie grinned back.

"She's your wife, Johnnie. And you had a baby with her. I'd give anything to be you."

"I'm also way ahead of you in the lovemaking department." Johnnie chuckled. During Caesar's last visit, they'd kept a tally of how many times each of them made love to Melanie.

Instead of showing any jealousy, Caesar smiled and answered, "You're the luckiest man alive."

"I am." Johnnie kissed Melanie's lips, then sat down in the recliner he'd moved to Melanie's room. "She still loves you."

"Does she talk about me?"

"Of course. She even wanted to give the baby your middle name."

"Francisco?" Caesar shook his head. "Thank God you talked her out of that. He would've been bully bait."

Johnnie smiled. "Exactly what I told her which is why he has my middle name instead."

Caesar held her hand up to his mouth and kissed it. He inhaled deeply. "She still smells like me."

"I flew to Thailand and bought her some of that vanilla oil you wore. I'm not sure if she really loves it or wears it because it reminds her of you."

"Maybe both."

Johnnie's mind drifted back to those blissful days the three of them spent together. "I miss making love to her."

"I do, too."

"Go ahead. Tell me how you left her."

Caesar smiled and kissed her hand again. "While we were making love, I got this feeling...like I was being pulled away. I felt sick inside. I knew it was time for me to go. We decided to walk to your rock, but by the time we reached it, she was alone. I could see her from above, but I wasn't with her."

"Then you turned into a dolphin."

Caesar chuckled and placed Melanie's hand on her midsection. "Well, my spirit inhabits the dolphin."

Johnnie breathed deeply. "It's mind-blowing when you think about it. A miracle."

Caesar went to Michael's bassinet, bent, and kissed the baby's head. "He's the miracle."

"I never expected to be a father."

"And I always dreamed of being one." Caesar sat down in the rocking chair. He appeared to be sad. "Funny how things work out."

Johnnie reached over and grabbed his hand. "Michael's as much yours as he is mine. You brought Melanie and me together. Without you, there would be no Michael."

"Thank you." Caesar smiled and squeezed his hand. "And looking after the girls...it's like being their father."

"What do you suppose happened to their real father? Why isn't his spirit with them?"

Caesar sank deep into thought for a few moments. "I don't know. Maybe there is a hell or a purgatory for those that have wronged others."

"Well, I know where I'll end up when I die."

"No Way! You've always been a good person, Johnnie. The alcohol and drugs messed you up because you were hurting inside. But now you're on track. You're making the most of your life."

Johnnie nodded and pushed away thoughts of drinking. *No more of that!* "I'm starving. My mom brought over some lasagna. Think I'll heat that up."

"I'm going to stay here with Melanie if you don't mind."

"Of course not."

CJ suddenly jumped up on the bed.

"Should we allow him up there with her?" Caesar asked.

Johnnie stood and watched CJ sniff Melanie and lick her hand. He then went to the foot of the bed, sat down, and began to clean himself.

"I brought her home so she could be around all the things she loves." Johnnie scratched CJ's head. "Including him."

Caesar patted each of his knees. CJ got the message and left the bed to jump onto Caesar's lap. Caesar stroked the cat, and CJ purred loudly. "We'll both stay with her then."

Chapter Fourteen

Past

Johnnie strolled into the boy's restroom and right into a situation. Four boys surrounding their prey. The kid on the ground already looked pretty roughed up. His abusers simultaneously turned in Johnnie's direction.

"I'm just here to take a piss...carry on."

The four guys nodded and turned their attention back to their hapless victim. Johnnie knew all of them. The four were athletes like his older brothers. Assholes like them, too. The kid they were tormenting was in his English class. What was his name? Caesar Blue. He seemed like a decent guy. Never bothered anyone or caused any drama. He had long curly hair that all the girls loved. Yeah. That Caesar guy got a lot of girls. But for some reason, guys like these four shitheads assumed he was gay. Why? Because he wrote poetry and hung out with girls?

"Fucking faggot," one growled and yanked Caesar by the hair.

"Give me that lipstick, Richard."

Johnnie peeked over his shoulder as they began to smear lipstick on Caesar's face. He zipped up his pants. Enough was enough.

"Is this making you feel more manly?"

One of the brutes turned to Johnnie. "What the fuck did you say?"

"This guy's not even fighting back. Where's the fun in this?"

Another one of the guys stepped up to Johnnie and looked him over, disgust in his eyes. "You like faggots?"

"I like fair fights." Johnnie glanced down at Caesar. "Four against one. Not fair in my book."

The guy in his face poked him in the chest. "This is none of your damn business."

"It is now." Johnnie swung hard, and the guy dropped to the floor, holding his bleeding nose. His friends came for Johnnie, and he managed

to get a few punches in before they overtook him. Caesar jumped on Richard's back and hit the guy upside his head a few times. Good for him, Johnnie thought.

Present

"Michael's just gone down for his nap, so I'm going out to the studio for a while if you don't mind."

"No problem," Brenda assured him. "Everything's under control."

Johnnie knew it was. Brenda was doing a great job. The nurse spent most of her time in Melanie's room, watching over her. When Johnnie spent time with Melanie and Michael in the room, Brenda would take her breaks. Often, she'd sit on the deck reading books enjoying the ocean air.

"I'm taking the monitor with me just in case," Johnnie told her.

Brenda smiled. "Sure thing. Go enjoy making music. I know you need a break from all the caregiving."

Truthfully, he was anxious to get on the piano. Not his drums like he normally did. He'd had an idea for a song floating around in his head all night and all morning long. He needed to get into the studio and work it out.

"Man, I'm so glad you're here. I'm bored to death," Caesar greeted him from where he sat on the floor. Melanie's laptop was in front of him, with a movie playing.

"Can't you go swimming? Do your dolphin thing?"

"I'm afraid if I did, I might not be able to come back. I mean, I helped you, so I don't know how much longer I have."

"Maybe until Melanie wakes up?"

"I hope so. I want to be here for that."

"That song I told you about is swirling around in my brain."

Caesar bounced up and waved an arm toward the piano. "Let's hear it."

"I jotted some lyrics down, too." Johnnie handed Caesar a legal pad he'd written on. Then he sat down at the piano. "I hope I can figure this out."

Caesar read the lyrics, then looked up at him, smiling. "Johnnie this is beautiful. I thought you hated sappy, love songs."

"But Melanie loves them. And this is my love song to her."

Johnnie played a few notes, then stopped. He hadn't played in years. "That's not right."

"Scoot over," Caesar said before plopping down next to him on the bench. "Maybe between the two of us, we can create some Lush magic."

"I want to sing, though."

"Really? After all my failed attempts to get you to take the lead on a song?"

Johnnie chuckled. "Melanie said she loved my voice. I truly want this to be my song to her. Just give me some ideas for the inflections, so it's perfect."

Caesar nodded, and for the next couple of hours, they worked the song. Caesar showed him how to best utilize his voice for the lyrics, and once they had it down on the piano, Johnnie added some percussion to it.

"This could be a new Lush song," Caesar said as they wrapped up another take.

"I should ask Rhett and Kurt to visit, see if they like it. We can add guitar and bass. See how it all sounds. Maybe we could release it as a single."

"You could start singing for the band full-time. Lush could make a comeback."

"We're not a band without you." Johnnie twirled his drumsticks. "And you know I can't give up my drums."

"But I'd love to see you guys keep making music." Caesar held up the pad where they'd written down all their notes. "This song proves you can do it."

"We still make music. In our own way. But we have other things going on, too."

"Yes, you have a son that you'll be teaching how to play drums."

Johnnie pointed a drumstick in Caesar's direction. "You know it. I've already bought him his first set."

"You're kidding!" Caesar laughed. "I can imagine Melanie's face when she saw that."

Johnnie thought back to her reaction that day and grinned. "I'll have to get them out of the box and bring them out here."

The door to the studio suddenly opened, and Blue walked in. "Helloooo, Johnnie! Brenda said you were out here."

Blue stopped in his tracks. He blinked a few times, then rubbed his eyes.

"Blue!" Johnnie bolted from the drum stool and went to him.

Blue's gaze was glued to his son, his brown eyes wide. "Am I seeing things?"

Caesar slid from the piano bench, a wide smile on his face. "Dad. It's me."

Blue put a hand over his chest and began breathing heavily.

Johnnie quickly grabbed his drum stool. "Sit down, Blue. Are you okay?"

Caesar rushed over and wrapped his dad tightly in his arms.

"How can this be?" Blue drew away and stared at Caesar. "Am I dreaming?"

"We didn't expect you," Johnnie told him. "We planned to tell you and prepare you."

"I do need to sit down." Blue took the stool.

"Are you alright, Dad?"

Blue gawked at Caesar with both shock and awe. "We cremated you. Spread your ashes out to sea."

"Do you want to explain, or should I?" Johnnie asked.

"I'll start with meeting Melanie in Atlanta." Caesar pulled one of the large pillows over and sat in front of his dad. "You can take over from when Melanie meets you in California."

Johnnie checked the baby monitor and saw that Michael was sleeping peacefully. "We've got about another hour or two before he wakes up."

"Get your mother," Blue directed Johnnie.

"She's here?"

Blue nodded. "With Melanie."

"I'll get her." Johnnie headed for the door. "May as well tell this story just once."

"I can't get over it." Johnnie's mom hooked her arm through her son's as they walked barefoot along the shoreline. They'd left Caesar and Blue together in the studio.

"It's an amazing thing." Johnnie smiled. "I only wished I'd been sober the other times he reached out to me."

"But then he wouldn't have had a reason to come back to you."

"True but being high or drunk only made his appearances scare the shit out of me, which led to more drinking and pills. I thought it was some sort of punishment for that night on the mountain."

They got to Johnnie's rock, and he turned to steer his mom back toward the house.

"This is a nice spot. Let's stay here awhile." She leaned against one of the bigger rocks and looked out at the ocean.

He smiled. Figures his mom would know which spot was his favorite.

She playfully shoved him. "So, all those stories you and Melanie told me about her dating Caesar long ago were made up?"

"Sorry we lied to you. We didn't think anyone would believe the real story."

"And only certain people can see him?"

"People who believe in spirits can. And those he's come to help."

"What about the nurse...Brenda?"

"We're not even going to try. We can't have her seeing him. It's too risky with him being a celebrity. The fewer people who know about this, the better."

Johnnie's phone vibrated in his pocket. He checked the message. "Michael's awake."

"Oh good, I want to hold him a bit."

"You can feed him and change him if you want." Johnnie grinned and gave his mom a side hug. "I'm a bit tired of seeing baby poop."

"Wait until he's a toddler," his mother laughed as they walked back to the house. "You've got at least two more years of poop to clean."

Johnnie groaned. "Don't remind me."

"What about Melanie? You've done okay cleaning her up?"

"It's different with her."

"Because you love seeing her lady parts?"

"Mom, really?" Johnnie stopped and stared at his mother as if she'd lost her mind. "She's in a coma. I'm not even thinking about that sort of thing."

Now she looked at him as if he were crazy. "Oh, really?"

"Well, I mean I do. But not when I'm cleaning up after her. But you know...when I'm in bed at night...then yeah...I think about her lady parts and how much I miss them."

His mom laughed and lightly punched his arm. "That's my boy!"

Johnnie's cheeks burned hot. "I can't believe we're having this conversation."

"Man, he's wailing tonight. He doesn't seem to want to sleep."

Johnnie paced back and forth in the nursery, trying to soothe Michael. Every time he thought his son might be calming down, the baby would begin crying again. It was nearing eleven, and there didn't seem to be any end in sight. Michael was usually asleep by nine, but not tonight.

His phone buzzed. "Check that for me. I called my mom."

Caesar handed him the phone. "I don't know what this means."

"Video chat." Johnnie pressed the button to accept and then handed Michael over to Caesar.

"Sorry to wake you, Grandma, but someone is not cooperating tonight," Johnnie said when his mom appeared on the screen. "He's usually down by now. But he's been screaming for over an hour. He's not hungry, his diaper's clean. He won't take his pacifier."

"Poor baby, he may be colicky."

"What the hell does that mean?" There was panic in his voice. "Does he need a doctor?"

His mom smiled. "No, he's just got an upset tummy most likely."

"What do I do?"

"Do some research on the internet."

Caesar laughed and walked out of the nursery, bouncing Michael softly in his arms and singing to him.

"Mom, come on."

"Well, there may be some new things to do these days that I don't know about."

"Did any of us have colic?"

"You did. You kept us up quite a few nights with your howling."

"And what did you do?"

"Gave you a warm bath and walked with you until you fell asleep."

"Okay, we'll try the bath."

"Call me again if you need anything."

"Trust me, I will. In fact, maybe he needs to spend a few days with Grandma and Grandpa."

His mother laughed. "Nope, you're stuck with him. Colic, poop, and all."

"Thanks a lot."

"Karma's a bitch."

Johnnie shook his head. "Goodnight, Mom."

"Goodnight."

He found Caesar on the computer in the office, cradling a crying Michael as he searched the internet.

"What did you find?"

"Warm bath. Swaddle tightly. Cuddles and massage. Walk with the baby. Play some music."

"Let's try the bath first."

Once Johnnie set up Michael's tub with lukewarm water, Caesar placed a still screaming Michael inside.

"Wow, he's turning red," Johnnie fretted.

"That's one pissed off kid."

Johnnie took the washcloth and wiped Michael down, trying to soothe him. "Shhh. It's okay, little dude. Daddy's here. And look, Uncle Caesar has your ducky."

Caesar squeezed the duck to make it squeak. Michael stopped for a split second, looked at Caesar, then screamed some more.

"I don't think it's working."

"No, shit." Johnnie picked Michael up and placed him in the towel that Caesar held out. "Let's get him diapered and dressed again."

"Let's try some music," Caesar suggested.

After getting him dressed, Johnnie swaddled him, then placed Michael in his crib. Caesar turned on the mobile, and it began to play a lullaby. Michael's screams stayed steady.

"Maybe he needs different music," Caesar suggested. "Maybe our music."

"It's on Melanie's laptop. Did you bring it back inside?"

"I put it by her bed. Why don't we just put him in the bassinet and let him sleep there again?"

"He's screaming so loud."

"Loud enough to wake the dead...or someone in a coma?"

"Good point." Johnnie picked Michael back up and trudged downstairs to Melanie's room. Caesar changed the music playlist over to Lush.

Johnnie bobbed up and down with Michael. "Listen, can you hear Daddy playing drums? And Uncle Caesar is singing."

Caesar sang along with the recorded music.

Michael quieted down for a few seconds.

"Yes!" Johnnie high fived Caesar. "It's working!"

Michael began crying again.

Johnnie groaned.

"Let's put him with Melanie again."

Johnnie laid his son on top of Melanie as they'd done the previous evening. He held him in place with one hand and caressed him with the other.

"It's working."

"He can't sleep here, though." Johnnie gently picked him up. Almost immediately, Michael's body tensed up, and he began to cry again.

"Maybe in the crook of her arm. He can't roll anywhere from there."

Johnnie placed him on his back nestled between Melanie's arm and her body. Michael hiccupped a few times and then began to quiet down.

"I'm not sure how safe he is lying on the bed with her. Even with the side rail up, what if he falls?"

Caesar rubbed his chin, thinking. "But he doesn't roll over yet."

"I know, but I don't feel comfortable with this."

"He wants to be with her."

Johnnie looked down at his son. His little fist was in his mouth, and he seemed to be falling asleep. Maybe this was the answer, having him with Melanie.

Caesar left the room for a few minutes, then returned with several folded blankets. "We can line the edge of the bed with these. It will be like his crib bumper."

"Okay, but I'm going to stay close by tonight."

"You were planning on that anyway, right? Like last night?"

Johnnie smiled. Caesar knew him well.

Johnnie heard whispers and the shuffling of feet. *What is Caesar up to?* He opened his eyes slightly and tried to focus. The only light in the room was from a nightlight, but it was enough to see the shadows of three figures in the room. Caesar's bouncy curls made his identity obvious, and when he saw the two kids, he knew immediately who they were as well.

"Shh...don't wake up your brother, or your stepdad."

Johnnie opened his eyes wider. When they adjusted to the light, he saw that Melanie's girls had shoulder-length blonde hair and blue eyes just like their mom. They wore sundresses and were barefoot, tracking in sand from the beach. Johnnie wanted to cry. He understood now why Melanie had sunk into depression after losing them. *If anything happened to Michael...*

"What's wrong with Mommy?" one of the twins asked.

Johnnie wondered which was which. They were identical. The other glanced his way, and he snapped his eyes closed, feigning sleep.

She giggled, pointed at him, and whispered. "He's not sleeping."

Caesar glanced at Johnnie. "He's faking, Leila. Let him pretend."

Caesar then pushed the questioner toward the bed. "Lily, your mommy was hurt when she had the baby. She fell asleep and won't wake up."

"Like Sleeping Beauty?" Lily asked.

Leila approached the bed. "Like Snow White?"

"Sort of."

"Kiss her then." Lily tugged Caesar's arm while jumping up and down. "She needs a prince to kiss her."

"I've tried," Caesar replied.

"Do it again!" Leila squealed.

Caesar bent over the bed and kissed Melanie's lips.

"See nothing happens."

With his eyes still half-closed, Johnnie smiled. *Caesar's her angel. I'm her prince.*

Leila shuffled over and poked Johnnie's ribs. "You do it."

Johnnie opened his eyes and set the recliner back into a sitting position. He turned on a lamp nearby. "I've tried, too."

"Please, try again." Leila pulled on his arm. "We've got to wake Mommy up."

Johnnie stood, went to the bed, and kissed Melanie softly. He turned to the girls. "Eww, now I have Caesar's germs."

Caesar smiled at the girls, then kissed Johnnie's cheek. Johnnie stuck out his tongue as he wiped away the kiss.

"Even yuckier."

The two girls giggled.

"This is my best friend, Johnnie. He married your mommy and is your stepdad."

"Why didn't you marry her, Caesar?" Leila asked. "You said you loved her."

"You know why. We've talked about it."

"If Mommy dies, won't she be with us? Then you could marry her."

Caesar inhaled sharply, clearly upset by her words. "Don't say things like that. We want Mommy to stay alive as long as possible. Johnnie loves her and needs her. She's happy with him. Don't you want her to be happy?"

"Yes." Leila bowed her head and stared at the ground. Lily went to her sister and wrapped her arms around her.

Johnnie felt terrible that she'd been scolded. *She just wants her mother.*

"Did you see your baby brother?" Johnnie gently lifted Michael from the bed, trying not to wake him. He sat down on the recliner, cradling Michael close.

"He has a lot of hair!" Lily giggled. "It's dark, like yours. Not like ours and Mommy's."

"Can I touch him?" Leila asked.

"Be very gentle," Johnnie instructed and began to unwrap the swaddling blanket. "We'll try not to wake him."

"He's so cute." Leila touched Michael's hair.

"Because he looks like me." Johnnie grinned. "His name is Michael."

"Hi, Michael. We're your big sisters." Lily shook Michael's hand.

Michael yawned and opened his eyes, but instead of crying, he focused on the two girls staring down at him.

"He sees them." Johnnie looked up at Caesar. "Same as with you."

"Maybe because they're trying to help him and Melanie."

And then Michael smiled at them.

Lily laughed. "He likes us, doesn't he?"

Johnnie nodded and wiped a tear from his cheek. "He must. He never smiles at me or Caesar."

The girls commenced counting their brother's fingers and toes. CJ ran into the room and nudged Leila's leg.

"Look who it is." Caesar pointed at CJ.

Leila sat on the floor and rubbed the cat. "Is this Mommy's cat?"

Caesar smiled. "This is the cat you and Lily found. He was a baby then, remember?"

"He's all grown up." Lily sat down beside her sister and petted CJ as the cat went from one twin to the other.

"Looks like you've been forgotten." Johnnie kissed Michael's forehead. He swaddled the blanket around him once again. "Ready to go back to sleep?"

Johnnie took Michael back to the bed and placed him next to Melanie. The baby put his fist into his mouth again and fell fast asleep.

Lily stood up. "Caesar, I don't feel good."

"I don't either." Leila got up and wrapped her arms around Caesar's leg.

Johnnie's gaze shot to Caesar. "What's happening?"

"They're being pulled back," Caesar explained. He knelt and hugged them both. "It means you have to go soon. Quick, say goodbye to Mommy."

Johnnie lifted Leila, and Caesar lifted Lily so they could both reach Melanie. Each girl gave her a kiss.

"Please wake up, Mommy," Lily whispered. "Michael needs you."

"Johnnie needs you, too," Leila added.

Johnnie couldn't stop the tears that fell. He set Leila down on the ground again, knelt, and hugged her. "I do. I need her so much. I love her so much."

Lily ran over and hugged him. "Take care of Mommy and Michael."

"I will."

Leila wiped at his tears, then patted his head. "Don't cry. Mommy says she'll come back soon. She says she loves you, too."

Johnnie gazed up at Caesar. "What the..."

Caesar bent down. "Did you hear Mommy say that?"

Leila tapped her heart. "In here."

Johnnie hugged both girls tightly. "Thank you."

And then there was nothing in his arms. The girls were gone, the same as Caesar had described to him yesterday. They had just vanished.

The two men stood again and embraced.

"Do you think it's true? What Leila said."

Caesar pulled away and went to Melanie's side. He lifted her hand to his mouth and kissed it. "She must have felt her."

"But you don't?"

"Maybe it's because she's closer to Leila. I don't know."

Johnnie went to Melanie and stroked her face. "Baby, can you hear me? I'm right here. So is Caesar...and Michael. We're waiting for you. Please come back to us."

"Johnnie, look at her hand."

Johnnie glanced down at the hand Caesar was holding. Her fingers were twitching.

"That's it, baby." He snuggled close to her ear. "Come on. You can do this. You can come back to us."

"They stopped."

"Melanie, I love you." Johnnie broke down. "Please, come back to me. I need you."

"She will." Caesar rubbed his back. "Why don't you try and get some more sleep?"

Suddenly he had an idea. "Move Michael to his bassinet for a minute. Then help me move her."

"What are you going to do?"

"Sleep with her and Michael." When Caesar looked at him skeptically, he said, "There's plenty of room."

Once Michael was in his bed, they shifted Melanie closer to one edge of the bed. The railing would keep her safe, and they returned the blankets to make a bumper. Then he crawled into the bed with her.

"Now hand Michael to me."

Johnnie took Michael from Caesar and laid the baby between him and Melanie.

"Be careful. You can't roll over."

"I doubt I'll even sleep. I just want to be with her if she wakes up."

Caesar nodded. "I'll take the recliner."

Chapter Fifteen

Past

"Everyone awake and decent?" Lush's manager, Scott Wilson, walked into their hotel room.

"We're awake." Kurt laughed. "But when have we ever been decent?"

"Especially Johnnie." Rhett nudged Johnnie's shoulder.

Johnnie sat at a small dining table. He rubbed his eyes and sipped coffee, trying to revive himself. The jet lag was kicking his ass. And the valium he'd taken. "Yeah, well at least I don't walk around naked all the time. Like someone we know."

As if on cue, a nude Caesar strolled into the room, stretching and yawning. "What's happening."

Knowing Caesar's habit, the band was prepared. Kurt threw Caesar a robe, and their lead singer wrapped his body up in it.

Scott smiled. "Guys, I've got great news. You're gonna love it!"

"You found me a liquor store?" Johnnie asked. "This hotel charges way too much for whiskey."

"Quiet, Vega!" Scott snapped. "The new single just hit number one in America. After tonight it'll probably be there for England, too."

"What the fuck?" Johnnie's eyes widened. "You're not shitting us, are you?"

"I shit you not."

Kurt, Rhett, and Caesar began jumping around. This was everything he'd ever dreamed of, and now it was happening! He stood, ran over, grabbed Caesar around the legs, and lifted him over his shoulder.

"We did it!" He carried Caesar around the room, his other two friends marching behind him in a line.

When he set Caesar back on the floor, his friend grabbed Johnnie's face in his hands. "This is just the beginning!"

"Fuck yeah!" Johnnie rejoiced. "Now let's find a liquor store so we can celebrate!"

Present

"Any good news to tell us?" Mary Jo asked.

Johnnie frowned, looking at the computer screen where he was facetiming with both sets of parents. Caesar was out in the studio hiding from Brenda.

"Nothing at all. I'm sorry." Johnnie bit his lip, fighting tears.

There had been no sign of life from Melanie in the past five days. She hadn't smiled again. Hadn't moved again. *Nothing.* He felt like ripping his hair out.

"You look worn out, son," Carl told him.

"Is Michael still having problems sleeping at night?"

Johnnie nodded. "Yeah, Mom. I was letting him sleep with Melanie, and that seemed to help, but the past couple of days, he's cried most of the night."

"Maybe Blue and I should come take Michael for the weekend. Give you a chance to rest."

"The guys will be here tonight. They'll want to spend some time with him. We're going to rehearse that song I wrote for her. Maybe sit around and play some live music for her, too."

"She'll like that," Mary Jo told him. "She used to play your records full blast when she lived here."

Carl wiped at his face and forced a smile. "She sure did. I'd go in, and she'd be doing her homework. I have no idea how she could concentrate on her work, but she always made the honor roll."

"Then we'll play extra loud. Maybe I'll even bring my drums in." Johnnie smiled.

"You better not," his mom scolded. "You'll hurt that baby's ears."

"I was kidding, Mom."

"Is that Michael I hear?" Mary Jo asked.

Johnnie glanced at the baby monitor. "Looks like naptime is over. I better go to him."

"I know it's tough, Johnnie." Carl smiled. "But keep doing what you're doing. That photo you sent us of her smile was enough to let me know she's still with us."

"And if she moves again, be sure to get it on video."

"I will Mary Jo. Promise." Michael's cries grew louder. "I have to get going. Talk to you again soon."

Johnnie stopped the app and closed the computer. Feeling defeated, he climbed the stairs to the nursery. When Michael saw him, he immediately stopped crying.

"Look at you." Johnnie's heart swelled with pride as he picked Michael up. If anything could help him to forget his troubles, it was seeing his son. "Did you have a good nap?"

Michael gurgled and babbled.

"Well, now, when did you start talking?"

Michael smiled at him.

"Oh, and now your smiling for Daddy?"

Michael kicked his legs and waved his arms.

"Do you know something I don't know? What are you so excited about? Ready to see all your uncles together?"

He kissed Michael's cheek, and the baby babbled again. "We're gonna make some music for Mommy."

Michael smiled.

"We need to call the grandparents again." Johnnie walked downstairs with Michael and grabbed his phone. "Let's call Papa Carl and Mary Jo first."

"What is it?" Carl asked as he and Mary Jo appeared onscreen. "Did something happen."

Johnnie sat on the sofa in the living room. He cradled Michael comfortably on his lap. "Your grandson has something to say to you."

He held up his phone in front of Michael. When Michael saw his grandparents, he smiled and began babbling again.

"Oh, my goodness!" Mary Jo laughed, which made Michael even more talkative.

"Thanks for calling us back. This is exciting." Carl waved at the camera from his end. Michael waved his limbs again.

"I've never seen him so active." Johnnie kissed the top of his head. "He seems so happy."

"Well, he was a preemie, so he had some catching up to do," Mary Jo explained. "He probably won't stop talking now."

"Oh Lord, now I have a crying, pooping, *and* talking machine on my hands."

They all laughed, and Michael kept smiling. Then he pooped his diaper.

"I appreciate you giving me Saturday off." Brenda grabbed her purse and pulled out her car keys.

"With the guys here, I think we can handle things."

"You'll enjoy having your friends visit. You've been so cooped up here caring for Michael and Melanie."

"Doesn't bother me. They need me more than the rest of the world does."

Brenda smiled and patted his arm. "Yes, but you need to get out more. Michael's growing fast. When I'm here, you're welcome to take him to a park. Or on a shopping trip."

He'd been having groceries delivered, but perhaps it was time to get Michael out more. "Sounds good. He'll be two months old soon. Time to expand his horizons a bit."

"It will be good for him...and you." Johnnie walked her to the front door. She tickled Michael's foot. "See you later, little guy."

Michael kicked his foot and smiled.

"Tell your sons good luck in their soccer game."

"Thanks, I will. They're happy I'm making this one."

"See you Monday morning."

"And don't forget, if you need me for anything...call."

"I will." Johnnie waved.

Brenda waved goodbye and was gone.

A couple of hours later, Rhett and Kurt were pulling into the gate. When Kurt parked the car, Rhett leaped out and ran to Caesar. The two hugged one another tightly.

"When Kurt told me you came back, I couldn't believe it." Rhett sniffed and wiped a few tears away. "I didn't think we'd ever see you again."

"I didn't think I'd be able to come back."

Johnnie walked out of the house, cradling Michael. "Guess you can blame me for that one...and the whiskey."

Rhett drew him close, touching his forehead to Johnnie's. "Tell me it was just that one time."

"Only once. Never again."

Rhett patted his back, then turned his attention to Michael. "Look at him. He's so much bigger than the last time I saw him."

"He's gained a couple of pounds since the hospital." Johnnie laughed. "I think my mom was feeding him spaghetti at her house."

"I believe it." Rhett tweaked Michael's nose, and the baby smiled at him. "Grandma is a great cook."

"Speaking of food." Kurt opened the trunk of his car. "We did a little shopping to make sure you had plenty on hand."

Johnnie walked over and hugged him. "You didn't have to. We could have placed an order, and the grocery store would have delivered it."

"Thought I'd save you some trouble. You have your hands full."

Johnnie gazed down at Michael and smiled. "Literally."

"I'll help bring things in." Caesar grabbed a few bags from the trunk. Rhett did as well.

"This is from Jaxson and me." Rhett pulled out a large gift bag. "You guys weren't able to have a shower, but we got you a few things."

"You didn't have to." Johnnie saw a yellow book that caught his eye. *Curious George.* "I can't believe it. He'll love this."

"I remembered you saying it was one of your favorites when you were a kid." Rhett pulled out a big package of diapers as well.

"We definitely need those." Johnnie laughed.

Caesar nodded to Michael. "That is a shitting machine right there."

"Oh, he's just doing what babies do." Kurt peered down at Michael. "Has he hosed you down with pee yet?"

"All the time. His little wee-wee has a mind of its own."

Kurt bent to put his face next to Michael's. "You're a chip off the old block. Remember all that public peeing you used to do, Johnnie?"

Johnnie groaned. "Hey, it's hard trying to find a bathroom when you're in a foreign country."

Michael waved his arm and touched Kurt's glasses, knocking them askew.

"All of a sudden he's become a wild child today. Talking and waving his arms all around."

Kurt adjusted his glasses. "Then you're going to love what Sara picked out for him. It's in the back seat with the overnight bags."

Caesar opened the back door and retrieved a big box. "Check this out, Johnnie. It's like some sort of entertainment chair for babies."

"A bouncy chair. Deluxe model with lots of different vibration speeds and it even plays music." Kurt took it from Caesar. "And of course, it has a jungle theme to go with his nursery."

"Looks like fun, doesn't it, Michael?" Caesar asked.

"How about we fire up your grill so we can cook a few steaks." Kurt looked at Caesar, who was a vegetarian like Melanie. "And some veggie burgers, too."

Johnnie kissed Michael's cheek. "We'll get right on it, Uncle Kurt."

"He loves that thing," Johnnie marveled watching Michael in the baby bouncer. Once they put it together, they'd set it out on the deck, so he could sit in it while they ate dinner. "This is the greatest invention ever."

"It is. Sara always put the kids in one when she was busy with dinner or cleaning."

"Maybe it will help him get to sleep tonight," Caesar said, then took a bite of roasted carrot."

"Colic is the worst. Janie had it when she was a baby. Thankfully, they grow out of it. Of course, then the teething begins."

"Guess I should prepare for more sleepless nights."

The guys all laughed.

"When are we going to hear this new song?" Rhett asked.

"Let's start fresh in the morning." Johnnie watched Melanie on the baby monitor. "Shouldn't take long to work out the parts and then we can play the song for her."

"It's a beautiful song." Caesar smiled. "Johnnie's going to sing. You guys can release it as a new single."

"Are you sure you don't want to sing?" Kurt asked and stabbed a piece of his steak with a fork. "We could say it's something we dug up."

Caesar put his hand on Johnnie's shoulder. "Johnnie's got this. This is his song to Melanie. It will be great."

Kurt nodded. "I'm sure it will be."

"You know what else I was thinking?" Caesar got up from the table and sat down on the deck next to Michael's chair. "We can do a video. And I could be in it."

"How would we make that happen?" Rhett asked.

"You said only certain people could see you."

"True, Kurt. But maybe I'd show up on video. I have before on those videos we made for Melanie."

Johnnie grinned wickedly, remembering the sex video. "He's right."

"Yeah, but you in a video with us isn't going to fly. People will either think you didn't die, or we found a lookalike."

"No, think about it. I'm still twenty-eight. Same as when I died. Any shots I'm in, I can be alone in them. You guys would be together. I'd be separate."

Kurt pointed his fork in Caesar's direction. "That might work."

"It's genius," Johnnie agreed. "We can say it's old video footage we found of Caesar."

"It will blow everyone's mind." Rhett took a sip of his lemonade.

"Our fans will love it." Caesar stroked Michael's hand until the baby latched on to his finger. He frowned. "And it's a way for me to be part of the band again before I have to leave."

"Any idea when that might happen?" Kurt asked.

Caesar shook his head. "I believe I was sent back to help Johnnie cope with Melanie and the baby. He has it pretty much under control. So, it's only a matter of time."

Johnnie's heart hurt thinking about Caesar's departure. *Do I really have things under control?* Brenda was a huge help. And his parents could always come by and help with Michael if he needed them. So, he didn't really need Caesar, but he sure as hell wanted him here. It made things easier, having his best friend around to talk to. Only Caesar could understand what he was going through because only Caesar loved Melanie with the same intensity he did.

CJ sat at the door and meowed loudly.

"Does he want back in?" Rhett asked.

CJ paced in front of the door and kept meowing.

Kurt threw him a piece of steak. CJ sniffed it but then meowed. He stood on his hind legs and scratched at the door.

"He's been acting weird ever since I took Melanie to the hospital. He misses her. Sleeps at the foot of her bed every night."

Johnnie got up and slid the back door open. CJ darted in and headed straight for the hallway leading to Melanie's room.

What's up with that cat? Does he sense something? "Let me check on Melanie and make sure she's alright."

Johnnie followed the cat into the room. CJ jumped up on the bed.

"What is it, CJ?"

CJ licked her hand, and her arm jerked.

"Oh shit!" He ran over to the camera. "Guys, come in, something's happening. And don't forget Michael."

A few seconds later, Kurt and Caesar were all at the door. Rhett came in right behind them holding Michael.

"She moved again. Her arm this time."

Caesar rushed to the bed, scaring CJ away in the process. He brushed Melanie's hair aside and whispered in her ear. "Can you hear me, babe. Melanie, I'm here. It's Caesar. Johnnie, Kurt, Rhett, baby Michael are all here with you tonight."

"CJ jumped on the bed and licked her hand. She moved her hand away from him."

Rhett patted Michael's back as he bounced him. "This is exciting news. Do you think it means she's coming back?"

"It has to." Caesar took Melanie's hand and kissed the back of it over and over.

Johnnie pulled the rail down and sat beside her. "That woman I was photographed with. Laurel. She told me her husband came out of his coma slowly. Little by little, he began moving until one day he just woke up."

"Do you think she was just bullshitting you?" Kurt asked. "Making up a story? Or was that part of it real?"

"I always wanted to go back to that meeting place and confront her, but I was too worried I'd be photographed with her again. I wish I had now. I could've found out if what she said about her husband was the truth or if it was all just bullshit made up for Chase's story."

"Maybe she wasn't in on it," Rhett offered. "Maybe it was all Chase. He followed you, saw an opportunity to make some shit up, and took it."

"I wonder if Gordon could tell me anything about her?"

Kurt folded his arms in front of him. "You haven't asked him yet?"

"I haven't called him since the story broke about me and Laurel. I had the relapse, then got busy with Melanie and Michael. He's texted and called, but I've ignored it."

Caesar looked at him. "Maybe you should. I'm sure he'll understand. And besides, it was one time."

Johnnie nodded. He should call. The man had been there for him many times. "I should call Melanie's parents, as well. Let them know that she moved again."

Gordon answered on the third ring. "It's about time you called me. Been worried sick about you. Came very close to getting in my car and driving out to your place a few times."

"I'm sorry, things have been crazy busy for me," Johnnie explained.

"Well, I've seen the Instagram posts and tweets about Melanie and Michael. That situation seems to be working out for you."

"Things are good. She hasn't woken up, but she's moved a couple of times."

"Really? That's fantastic."

Johnnie's heart warmed. *It is!* "I'm hoping it means she's coming around."

"Hey, listen, about Laurel and that crazy story that went viral."

"I've been wanting to speak to you about that."

"I questioned her. She said she felt bad about it. Apparently, some guy paid her to talk to you and get chummy."

"I know who it was," Johnnie replied. "Guess the story about her husband being in a coma was all just bullshit."

"I couldn't tell you. She hasn't come around since I asked her about it. But to make up a story like that is crazy."

"I'm sure Phil Chase coached her."

"I'm sorry. She's caused trouble at a few groups from what I hear. She's had a difficult time staying sober."

Johnnie sighed heavily. "Speaking of staying sober. I had a relapse."

"I was worried about that, Johnnie."

"It was one time," Johnnie confessed. "I got drunk, woke up feeling like shit. Went and got my son from my parents and haven't wanted a drink since."

"That's good. I'm proud of you."

Johnnie heard Michael crying. "Hey, I hear Michael. He's been irritable the last few nights. And I've got my band here, so I need to go, but I wanted to call and update you on things."

"Don't wait so long to contact me, Johnnie. Text or call...something. I want to know you're okay."

"Will do."

Johnnie hung up the phone and walked into the nursery. "What's going on in here?"

"He's started again." Caesar handed Michael to Johnnie. "Gave him a bottle, burped him, changed his smelly diaper, and this is the thanks I get."

"Did you try the bouncy seat?"

Kurt nodded. "He wasn't having it."

Johnnie held Michael close to his heart and bounced him. "Poor baby. Let's go see Momma. Maybe that will make you feel better."

"I'll grab my guitar, see if he likes the music."

"Thanks, Rhett." Johnnie kissed Michael's head and strolled down to Melanie's room.

Singing softly, Caesar lightly stroked Michael's back as the baby lay in the bassinet.

"I think it's working," Johnnie whispered as he lifted Melanie's arm, rubbing it up and down to keep the blood flowing and circulating in her limbs.

"Yeah, but what happens when I stop?" Rhett spoke quietly as he strummed his acoustic guitar.

Johnnie shrugged and began massaging Melanie's leg. "We'll see when the song's finished."

Caesar's voice faded away, as did Rhett's guitar. Everyone stayed silent, waiting...hoping. Michael lay quiet.

A loud thud came from outside.

"What was that?" Kurt asked.

"Probably CJ running around, knocking over something."

"He's inside. That came from outside."

Caesar winced as if in pain. He rubbed his forehead. "Someone's here. Someone that's wanting to hurt you, Johnnie."

Johnnie raced to the window that overlooked the beach. It was dark, making it difficult to see anything. Then he saw a shadowy figure dash away from beneath the window, scrambling back up the beach—leaving the scene.

"He was right at the window watching us." Johnnie motioned for Caesar and Rhett. "Come with me. Kurt, call the cops and keep watch over Michael and Melanie."

Kurt nodded and took his phone from his pocket. "Be careful."

Johnnie grabbed his own phone, then he, Caesar, and Rhett sprinted down the hallway and out the backdoor.

"He headed that way." Johnnie pointed to the right of the deck. He turned on the flashlight function of his phone.

"I can catch him," Caesar said before disappearing in a blur.

Wide-eyed, Rhett turned to Johnnie. "Did you know he could do that?"

Johnnie shook his head and picked up speed.

The found Phil Chase lying on the sand just past Johnnie's rock. He was curled in a fetal position, holding his ankle, and muttering curse words. Caesar stood nearby. He smiled at Johnnie, then held a finger up to his lips.

Chase can't see Caesar.

"What the fuck are you doing here on my property?"

"I think my ankle's broke. I need to get to a hospital."

Johnnie pointed the light in Chase's face. "And you think I care?"

Chase shielded his eyes and moaned, clearly in agony. "Please, help me. I tripped over a rock or something."

Johnnie and Rhett looked over at Caesar who nodded, then laughed.

"Apparently your own damn feet." Johnnie chuckled.

"It's not funny. I'm in pain, damn it!"

"Pain?" Rhett questioned and tapped Chase's non-injured foot with the toe of his sneakers. "Like the pain you've inflicted on my friends with your harassment and fake stories?"

Chase grimaced. "Look, I'm sorry. Please help me get to a doctor."

Johnnie narrowed his eyes. "The police can get you to a doctor."

"You called the police?"

"What the hell did you think would happen if you got caught snooping around my house?"

"I was only trying to get an update on the band...and Melanie."

"Fuck you." Johnnie spat on the ground next to Phil. "You've been a pain in my ass for too long. Now you'll pay."

Caesar was holding his head again. "He has photos."

"Where's your cell phone?"

Chase's eyes grew wide. "I left it in my car. I swear."

Caesar pointed at Chase. "Check his jacket pocket."

Johnnie kneeled next to Chase. The reporter was wearing a bomber jacket, and Johnnie checked the front pockets first. But then he felt a bulge in the jacket, so he opened it and checked the inside pocket. There, he found a small camera. He stood and handed it to Rhett.

Rhett turned on the camera and began checking the photos that had been taken on it. He showed Johnnie a close-up taken of Melanie lying on the bed. And another of Michael's face as Johnnie held him.

"I ought to break your other ankle," Johnnie snarled at Chase.

Rhett then pointed out a photo to him that showed the band singing to Melanie and Michael.

"You've got a lot of fucking nerve, Chase." Johnnie swore when he saw Caesar on camera. "Can you delete them?"

Rhett nodded and hit the buttons until he found the delete all function. "I'll take out the memory card, too."

"Fuck that." In a flash, Caesar grabbed the camera and hurled it into the ocean where it made a small splash.

"You owe me a camera, Starr!" Chase growled. "I can't believe you did that!"

Rhett put his hands on his hips and smirked.

Johnnie shook a fist at Chase. "How dare you sneak onto my property and take photos of my wife. She's in a coma for God's sake. And our son, too? You have no shame, do you?"

Phil was panting, sweat running down his face. "She's a story...you're a story."

"No...we're not!" Johnnie's face burned hot. "We're two people going through the most difficult time of our lives, and you think you have a right to somehow be part of that?"

"It's my job to inform people of celebrity news."

"You mean celebrity gossip." Johnnie huffed.

"Kurt keeps our fans updated on what's happening," Rhett added. "The people that need to know, do know."

In the distance, a siren could be heard.

"The police will be here soon," Rhett said.

Phil Chase groaned.

Johnnie glared at Chase. "That woman you paid to have coffee with me..."

"I don't know what you're talking about."

"Don't lie. She told my sponsor some guy paid her. I'm betting it's you since you wrote that shit story about me dating her."

Chase smiled through gritted teeth. "She's an addict, like you. Think anything she says is true? I doubt a court of law would."

Johnnie went to kick Chase's wounded ankle, but Rhett grabbed him and pulled him away.

"Don't," Rhett spoke low. "You know this asshole would press charges. Then you'll be the one in court."

"Listen to your friend. He's always had more sense than you. Except for that whole gay thing."

Caesar kicked Chase's ankle instead. Not hard, but enough to make some new pain shoot up the man's leg. Chase howled and held onto his ankle.

"Fuck me!" he yelled as tears mingled with the sweat.

"I'll be in the studio until the police leave," Caesar announced.

Johnnie and Rhett nodded.

Chapter Sixteen

Past

Johnnie scanned through the notebook Caesar handed him. "You wrote all these poems?"

"Yeah." Caesar nodded, then took a sip of his soda. "It probably sounds stupid, but I love words. I love playing with them, creating with them, fitting them together in unique ways."

Johnnie turned a page and read one of Caesar's poems. Some sappy love bullshit. But hey, it got his new friend a lot of girls, something he sure as hell wasn't any good at doing.

"You know some of these would make great song lyrics." Johnnie flipped through the pages again. So many potential songs just waiting to be created.

"Really? You think so? I love music. I play piano and a little guitar. My dad taught me. He and I have been singing songs together since I was a baby."

A great dad? Gets girls? Caesar was everything Johnnie wished he could be. "I play piano, too. Taught myself. But drums are my thing. I love playing them. I want to start a band someday."

"Someday?" Caesar smiled broadly. "Why not today?"

"Yeah." Johnnie grinned and nodded. "Why not?"

Present

"Sounds like you guys had an exciting night," Blue said as he hauled a large duffel bag into the kitchen.

"Excitement I could've done without." Johnnie smiled, taking the bag from him.

"The good news is Phil Chase won't be bothering us for a while." Kurt came into the kitchen carrying Michael. "Johnnie's called an attorney to have a restraining order put on him."

"There's my grandson." Judy squealed and immediately went for the baby. Kurt handed him over. She kissed each cheek, and Michael smiled. "Oh, isn't he just Mr. Personality!"

"Until tonight, when the screaming starts again." Johnnie went into the living room and placed the bag next to the coffee table.

Caesar came in with a video camera. He showed it to his father. "This is my old one. Not sure if we need it, but we did charge it last night. And I found some blank tapes we could shoot on."

Blue examined the camera. "This one will be best for the shots of you. They'll have an older feel to them."

"We rehearsed the song all morning," Johnnie informed Blue. "It was great. Everything clicked. So, we can start recording whenever you get things set up."

"I'm ready to go when you guys are." Blue pulled out his newer video camera as well as a digital camera. "Thought I'd take a few photos as well while we're all together."

"Can I be in those, too?" Caesar asked.

"I don't see why not. We can tell anyone who sees them we photoshopped you in from old photos."

Rhett came in carrying some papers. He laid them out on the coffee table. "This is a storyboard of sorts that we created last night. What do you think?"

Blue looked it over. It combined shots of the band in the rehearsal studio with shots of Caesar walking along the beach and playing in the water.

"What about Melanie?" Blue asked. "The song is about her, right?"

Johnnie shook his head. "I don't want video of her lying in a coma."

"Can we incorporate her another way. Old video footage...photos?"

Caesar looked at Johnnie. "Instead of making it just about Melanie...why not include all the guys? Kurt with his family. Rhett with Jaxson. You with Michael."

Blue smiled. "I like that idea."

"You'll have extra work, going out to Kurt's house and Rhett's apartment."

"I'm retired. I think I can handle it." Blue winked. "In the meantime, you better brush up on your editing skills."

"It's been a while." Johnnie smiled, remembering how he self-taught himself to edit video, during the time he and Melanie put together the band's documentary. "We'll also have to find someone to get Caesar's film into data files for the computer."

"It will all work out, Johnnie," Caesar assured him. "We better get started, though."

Judy entered the living room, holding a nearly sleeping Michael. "Yes, you boys get to work. I've got the baby and Melanie taken care of."

"And the food, too, right?" Caesar wrapped an arm around Judy. "I can't wait to have more of your home cooking."

Rhett smiled. "Same here."

"It's unanimous," Kurt added, then motioned for everyone to follow him. "Caesar, we can film some of your scenes first."

Caesar nodded. "I'm going to put on that old swimsuit of mine I found. That way, even what I'm wearing is from the past."

"This footage is great so far." Johnnie was huddled up with his friends going through Blue's video from the day.

Kurt burped. "Excuse me. But that food was fantastic."

Judy was sitting on the loveseat with Blue as she fed Michael his last bottle for the night. "Thank you. It was fun feeding you boys again."

"A lot easier than when my jackass father was around."

"Johnnie," Blue admonished. "Let's not speak ill of the dead. What's done is done. We've all moved on."

Johnnie nodded, then nudged Rhett. "Let's clean the kitchen."

Blue took Michael over his shoulder to burp him. "He seems so calm tonight. Maybe he'll sleep for you."

Johnnie sighed. "Last night he did okay once the police were gone and things calmed down again."

"And we sang for him," Caesar added. "We plan to do that again tonight. Sing Melanie her song."

"Make sure to record it." Blue smiled. "Then you can keep playing it for her every day until she wakes up."

Judy stood. "I'm going to go say goodbye to her. Be right back."

"I'll go with you, Mom."

"Sure...leave me stuck with clean up."

"I'll help you out," Kurt told Rhett, and the two of them went into the kitchen.

"How are things *really* going, Johnnie? Are you doing alright?"

Johnnie hugged his mom. "Aside from the colic and sleepless nights, I'm okay."

"I don't mean with Michael. I knew you'd do great with him, but with Melanie. Are you sure you can handle this by yourself? It's so much work."

"Caesar's been a big help."

"What if he doesn't stay around?"

"I'll figure it out and get it done."

"You can call us if you need to. Don't feel bad if you have to reach out for help. It's a lot for anyone to take on by themselves. Don't let it overwhelm you."

Johnnie laughed lightly. "You mean, don't get drunk again."

His mom wagged a finger at him. "That, too."

"Since I brought Michael home, the thought hasn't even crossed my mind."

"But it might."

He nodded. "I know. And I'm positive I can handle it."

Judy ran her hands through his hair, and sadness filled her eyes. "Honey, what if she doesn't wake up?"

"She will, Mom."

She frowned. "There's always a possibility."

"She smiled. She moved her finger, then her arm. I know she's fighting to come back to me."

"I hope you're right." Judy picked up Melanie's left hand and held it. "Where's her wedding band?"

"The hospital took it off."

"And you haven't put it back on her?"

"I haven't thought about it. And she's lost so much weight, it probably won't fit."

"She should have it on."

Johnnie kissed his mom's forehead. "You're right."

Blue stopped at the door, holding Michael out in front of him. "Someone needs a bath."

"He shit all over himself again?"

Judy laughed. "Karma. Let's get him cleaned up...again. Then Blue and I have to get home to take our own showers and get to bed."

"I like the sound of that." Blue winked at Judy.

Johnnie covered his ears. "Too much information!"

"Well, he's not crying tonight." Kurt placed Michael in the bouncy chair and turned it on to a nice low vibration setting.

"No, but he's wide awake." Johnnie handed Kurt his acoustic base. "Let's hope the music puts him to sleep again."

"Look what I found." Caesar entered the room with some bongos. "Maybe you can play on these."

Johnnie took them. "Where did you find them?"

"In the closet of the spare bedroom. Bought them years ago. Try them and see what sort of sound they have."

Johnnie took a seat near Michael and tapped on the drums. Michael waved his arms and legs around. "This will work. Although we'll still only be able to do the softer songs."

"Aren't the love songs Melanie's favorites?" Rhett asked.

"True."

After nearly an hour of playing and singing, Michael was slumped over in his chair.

"Let me get him into bed." Johnnie unbuckled him, then lifted him out. He walked him over the bassinet and placed him in bed. "That was almost too easy."

"Maybe he's done with his bout of the colic," Kurt offered.

"Let's hope so." Johnnie pressed a kiss onto Michael's forehead, then went to Melanie's bedside and did the same to her. "Love you, baby. This next song is very special. It's brand-new, and I wrote it just for you. I'm going to sing it to you."

Caesar sat down on the other side of the bed and took her hand. He held Johnnie's cell phone up in the other, waiting to record. "You're going to love it. It's brilliant."

Johnnie sat back down in the chair and took up the bongos again. He worked on the beat a bit, then called out, "One...two...three."

"Wasn't that beautiful, Melanie?" Caesar stroked her cheek. Then he looked at Johnnie, his eyes wide. "Johnnie."

"What?"

Caesar held Melanie's hand up. Instead of her fingers lying limp, they were wrapped around Caesar's. "It's not tight, but still, she's holding on."

Johnnie rushed to her side. "Melanie?"

Caesar stroked her cheek, then pressed his lips against hers. "That's it, Melanie, come back to us."

Rhett and Kurt joined them.

"I love you, Melanie." Caesar kissed her over and over. Melanie's hand went slack again. Caesar choked back tears. "No, baby. Come back to us, please."

"Damn it!" Johnnie yelled. Michael fidgeted in his bassinet and whimpered.

"Johnnie, calm down," Rhett told him.

Johnnie tore out of the room, rushed down the hall, and stormed out the back door. On the beach, he raised his fists skyward. He wanted to tear the world apart. Instead, he screamed, shouting into the black sky over the seemingly endless ocean.

Caesar came and stood beside him. "Let it out."

He screamed again and threw punches in the air before turning back to Caesar. His chest pumped up and down.

"This is fucking bullshit, Caesar! She doesn't deserve this. She's the sweetest, kindest person I've ever met. Why is this happening to her?"

"I wish I knew. I wish I could feel her the way Leila did. Maybe I could give you some answers."

"I lost the two people I love the most. First, you...and now her."

"She's still here, Johnnie."

Johnnie paced, then stopped and kicked at the sand. "Yeah, you're dead, and I can talk to you. She's not, and she can't communicate. None of this makes any fucking sense."

"I'm sorry you have to go through this. But you have to be strong...for Michael."

Johnnie jerked Caesar by the arms. "It's like I said on that damn mountain. It should've been me. I've done nothing but fuck up my life for so long. I've slowly poisoned myself, and yet here I am. Still alive and miserable."

"And that night on the mountain I told you that you had more left to do. I told you that you'd save someone, and you did. Melanie lived because you were there for her all those years ago. Giving her your blood. There's still more for you to do. You must raise your son. You must be the father you never had. No matter what happens to Mclanic, you will always have a piece of her. You created Michael with her. Your love is so powerful it created a life, Johnnie. That's something. That's the most amazing thing you've ever done in your life."

Johnnie fell into his friend's arms and sobbed.

Johnnie entered the kitchen and found Rhett and Kurt having some juice. "Sorry about that, guys."

Kurt came over and hugged him. "It's okay, man. You're allowed to be upset. Angry even. I can't imagine what you're going through."

Rhett patted his back. "We're always here for you. Anything you need."

"My brothers." Johnnie pulled Rhett into the hug, and then Caesar joined in as well.

Suddenly Caesar pulled away. "Oh, no."

"What is it?"

"I have to see Melanie."

"Caesar, what's happening?"

Caesar turned back to Johnnie as he walked down the hallway. His face was panic-stricken. "I have to go."

"Shit. No. You can't." Gutted, Johnnie followed him down the hallway. Rhett and Kurt did as well.

Something made Johnnie stop at the door. *Give him privacy.* He watched as Caesar kissed Michael's head.

"I love you, little man. Take good care of your daddy. He needs you."

The knot in Johnnie's gut tightened. "I need you, too, Caesar."

"You've got this." Caesar smiled at him. He then put Melanie's bed railing down and climbed on with her. Pressing his body close to hers, he lifted hers just enough to put an arm behind her and cradle her. "Believe in yourself, the way Melanie believes in you. She sees what I've always seen. A great man who's funny, creative, loyal, and honest. The best friend anyone could ever have. One who can do anything he sets his mind to."

"Thank you." It was true. No one had ever believed in him the way Melanie and Caesar had. It was time to stop giving into doubt and insecurity. *Time to be the man I was always meant to be. The man Melanie expects me to be. The man Michael needs me to be.*

Johnnie came to the bed and grabbed Caesar's hand. "I'll miss you."

Caesar nodded. The moonlight spilling into the room, made his tears glisten against his cheeks. "I'll miss all of you."

Rhett and Kurt came to the bedside. Their eyes were misty.

"It hurts having to say goodbye again," Rhett said.

"It does." Caesar's bottom lip trembled as he pulled Melanie closer. "I want to lie here and hold her until I'm gone."

"We'll leave you alone with her." Johnnie let his friend's hand go...let Caesar go...knowing he no longer needed his best friend. *I've got this!*

As he, Rhett, and Kurt left, Caesar began singing Melanie's favorite love song.

Johnnie bounded upstairs to his room. He opened the jewelry box that he'd put Melanie's wedding band in. *She should be wearing this. She's my wife.* He scurried back downstairs and into Melanie's room. She was alone in bed. It was quiet, except for the steady breathing from her...and Michael. Their child created from their love. Caesar was right. She wasn't gone. And no matter what happened, a part of her would live on in Michael. And even if it hurt like hell…he would go on. *For my son.*

"You're missing something, baby." Johnnie held up her hand and slid the band of gold onto her ring finger. It was loose, but he left it there, and laid her hand back down on the bed beside her. He kissed her softly and stroked her face. "I love you, Mrs. Vega."

Melanie's smile returned.

"You sure you don't want to take some of these leftovers with you?" Johnnie asked Rhett. "You know you love Mom's cooking."

"I'm good," Rhett said and sipped some coffee. "You keep it for yourself. You're not going to have a lot of spare time for cooking."

"Even when I have spare time, I don't do much cooking." Johnnie smiled and turned to Kurt. "When do you think we can get into a studio to record the new song?"

"I have a friend who's a producer. He'll get us some time, and I'll let you know. We should do it as soon as possible, though. Keep this positive vibe going."

"As soon as you give me a head's up, I can arrange for Mom and Blue to come take care of Melanie and Michael."

Rhett set his coffee cup down. "We should start some teasers on social media."

Kurt nodded. "Hopefully Blue got some great photos of the band. We'll use some of those."

"We'd better get going soon. I've got to get some rest and pack for my next gig." Rhett was about to start another tour with Sam Dean, a popular pop star. Tonight, he'd be leaving for New York City. "You sure you'll be alright all alone with Melanie and Michael?"

"Brenda will be back to work in the morning. I'll be fine."

Kurt slapped him lightly on the back. "Yes, I believe you will be."

Rhett hugged Johnnie, then bent to Michael's level. "Keep us posted. Send photos of Michael. He's going to grow so fast. I don't want to miss it."

"Been taking lots of photos. For Melanie." Johnnie bent and lifted Michael from his bouncy seat. "We'll walk you out to the car."

Kurt and Rhett collected their overnight bags, and the trio walked out to Kurt's car.

"Maybe Jaxson and I will adopt a little girl. Then you'll have a ready-made girlfriend." Rhett stroked Michael's cheek, and the baby smiled.

"When he starts playing drums, he'll have plenty of girls to choose from."

Kurt kissed Michael's forehead. "If you'd rather play bass, buddy, your Uncle Kurt has you covered."

"Bass? Pffft! Not a chance," Johnnie scoffed.

Chapter Seventeen

Past

Carrying his favorite book, four-year-old Johnnie crawled onto his father's lap.

"Shouldn't you be in bed?"

Johnnie patted his book. "Read my book."

His dad took the book, opened it to the title page, and frowned.

"Please, Daddy."

His dad put a finger on the first word of the title, then tried to say the word. But he was wrong.

"Cu-ri-ous George." Johnnie smiled as he tapped his small finger against the page. "He's a monkey. He's funny."

His dad flipped to the first page and began reading. At first, Johnnie was confused, but then he listened intently.

"You didn't say the words right," Johnnie said when his dad closed the book. "Momma tells it different."

His dad shrugged.

"I like your story better." Johnnie hugged his father, then crawled off his lap, took his book, and went to bed.

Present

"See the ocean, Michael?" Johnnie pointed toward the crashing waves. The air was chilly, but Michael was wearing his footed pajamas and a little knit cap with a skull on it. *A gift from Rhett.* Johnnie had the baby carrier strapped to his chest as he walked barefoot through the sand along the water's edge.

"It's beautiful, isn't it? Your mommy loves it here. She came to live here a couple of years ago, and that's how we met. We fell in love right here."   .

Michael's eyes were wide open, as he took in the new surroundings. Johnnie had taken Brenda's advice about getting Michael out of the house. So far, Johnnie had stayed near home. In the garden, they watched birds and butterflies together with CJ. In the studio, he'd played the piano for Michael who listened intently, cooing with the music. He'd taken Michael to his mother's house for a brief visit, and they'd stopped at the food market on the way back.

He's also taken him in for a doctor's appointment—a checkup which also included Michael's vaccinations. As for the colic, just as his mom and Kurt had told him, the doctor said it had to run its course.

It had been a week since Caesar left...since Rhett and Kurt had returned to their homes. Kurt had booked them studio time for the following week. Rhett would have a two-day break from the tour and would fly in to record Melanie's song. *Heaven Sent.*

"Because an angel brought her to me." He kissed Michael's head. "And because we created our own heaven right here...together."

Johnnie continued strolling down the beach, pointing out seagulls and pelicans to Michael, picking up shells and rocks for the baby to see. Michael took it all in with wide eyes and smiles that warmed Johnnie's heart.

Although he hadn't been a great student, Melanie had, and he knew that she would want their son to start learning about the world. *I'll teach him everything I know, and we'll learn the rest together.*

Carefully, Johnnie crawled up on his rock with Michael.

"This is my favorite place in the world, Michael. It's so peaceful here. I can think and dream."

Johnnie sighed heavily. *What are my dreams?* After Caesar and the guys left, he'd stayed close to Melanie, hoping for another sign she'd wake up. He kissed her, cuddled her, sang to her. He held long conversations with her and played the new song over and over. Melanie smiled, but there was no other movement, no other sign of life from her. *Maybe there never will be.*

As much as he wanted and needed her, he knew he had to accept that she might always be like this. Like their parents had told him, his main focus *had* to be Michael.

"I will give you the best of everything." He touched Michael's hand, and the baby gripped his finger. "I will be the best father any kid has ever had."

In the distance, flashes of grey moved through the ocean at lightning speed. Johnnie shielded his eyes so he could see.

"Look who's come to entertain us." Johnnie unhooked the baby carrier and took Michael from it. He positioned the baby so that he was facing the ocean.

"Hmm. Maybe that's not who I thought it was." Johnnie noted there were more than three dolphins. It was, in fact, a true pod with closer to twenty animals in it. "Look at them go, Michael."

Several members of the group lined up and rode a huge wave in. Before coming too close to the shore, they dove back under and swam back out.

Michael waved his arms and legs. His mouth opened wide as he watched the dolphins play. When one leaped into the air and splashed down hard, the baby laughed.

"Did you just laugh, little man?" Johnnie turned the baby to him. Michael smiled. "You did, didn't you?"

Michael laughed again.

The dolphins swam away—all but three of them. Johnnie turned Michael back around to see them.

"I think we might personally know these three."

Johnnie watched along with Michael as the three sped through the water and made a succession of jumps. The large one vocalized loudly.

"Say hi, to Uncle Caesar." Johnnie waved Michael's hand. "Tell him thank you for the show."

Michael smiled, gurgled, then tensed up and let out a little grunt. The dolphin vocalized again, bobbing it's head up and down.

"Not funny!" Johnnie shouted. He strapped Michael back into the carrier. "Man, you stink. Let's get you back home for a cleanup. Then Daddy will read you a book so you can take a nap."

As he entered the back door with Michael, Brenda appeared, smiling. "Did he enjoy the beach?"

"We had a great walk," Johnnie answered. "Until he pooped all over the place."

"I just folded a bunch of his clothes and put them in the nursery."

"You didn't have to do that."

"Well, Melanie's such a quiet patient to work with, sometimes I get a little bored. I don't mind doing a little housework."

"I appreciate it. I'm going to clean him up. Then it's lunch and naptime for this little guy."

"Are you going to do some drumming today?"

"I'm going to try and take a nap myself. I'm beat."

"Is he still having trouble going down at night?"

"Yeah. I'll be glad when this colic shit is done."

"I can always stay here a few nights a week when my kids are at their dad's house. We can sleep in shifts."

An attractive, single nurse who stays at my house overnight? *No way!* That was drama he didn't need to create. He'd not give anyone a chance to question his motives again.

He shook his head. "Thanks for the offer, but my parents can always take him or help out if I need it."

Johnnie trotted upstairs to the nursery with Michael.

"You're lucky this carrier is machine wash safe." Johnnie screwed up his face looking at the mess Michael had made in his diaper, on his clothes, and on the carrier. "How can you sit in shit looking all cute?"

Michael laughed as Johnnie laid him on the changing table.

"I've got to start watching my mouth around you. Your mom will kill me if your first words are *fuck* or *shit*."

Michael gurgled, creating spit bubbles.

Johnnie glanced down at his own shirt. "Just great, you got me, too."

He undressed Michael and cleaned him up with baby wipes. He gave his son a big smile. "Don't you pee on me, little man."

Michael flailed his legs and arms, smiling back. Johnnie pulled his own shirt over his head, then dropped his pants and boxer briefs to the floor.

"You're gonna take your first big boy shower with Daddy because we both reek."

Johnnie picked Michael up and grabbed one of the baby's hooded towels. He stood at the nursery door, listening for Brenda. When he heard her running water in the kitchen sink, he knew he could safely scoot naked across the upstairs hallway and into his and Melanie's bathroom. Then, he turned on the water so it could warm up a bit.

"I'm getting good at doing this one-handed thing." Johnnie tested the water in the shower. "Feels just right, little man."

He stepped in, keeping Michael turned away from the showerhead, letting only a little water trickle onto his son.

"What do you think?" Johnnie smiled.

Michael pouted. His bottom lip began to quiver.

"Aw, you're not going to scream, are you? You hate your little tub. I thought you might like the big boy shower. Watch, Daddy loves getting his hair wet."

Johnnie tilted his head back and wet his hair. "See, it's fun. It makes your hair curl up like Uncle Caesar, and all the women love his hair, even your momma. When he was around, she didn't even notice that my hair curls, too."

Johnnie put a little water in his hand and trickled it over Michael's hair. "See that's not so bad, is it?"

Michael turned red, opened his mouth, and let out a horrifying scream.

"Okay, maybe it is bad." Johnnie looked around for soap. "Damn, I forgot to bring the baby wash. We'll use Mommy's soap. It smells good. Lavender, just like your baby soap."

Quickly he cleaned a screaming Michael with the soap. Then he washed his own chest and belly.

"Okay. Enough of that, we're done." Johnnie turned off the water. He cradled Michael close to his chest, trying to comfort him. "It's okay, baby. Daddy's got you."

Michael cries began to quiet down. Then Johnnie felt something wet and warm sliding down his chest. "Dude, I said not to do that. I guess we're not done."

Johnnie turned the water back on. "Go ahead and scream."

Michael did.

"Okay, no more peeing," Johnnie said when he turned the water off again. He opened the shower door and grabbed Michael's towel. "Let's get you dry."

He wrapped the baby snuggly in the towel. Then realized he had no towel to dry himself with. Brenda had probably put them in the wash. *How am I supposed to dry off?*

"Be careful, Daddy," Johnnie said aloud as he stood on the plush bathroom rug trying to air dry. Michael was still crying. "We can't slip and fall."

Suddenly, Brenda appeared at the door. Her gaze raked over his body before she moved backward down the hallway. "Oh, I'm sorry. I thought you were just washing him."

Damn! "I thought I could shower with him. He hated it worse than his own tub."

"Do you need any help?"

"He's fine, just angry. But I forgot to bring in a towel for myself. I don't want to walk on the floor and slip while I'm holding him."

"I'm throwing one in, get ready to catch it."

The towel came in, and he caught it. He dried off the best he could with one hand. "Are you still there?"

"Yeah, need something else?"

"I really didn't think this whole thing through. Can I hand him to you?"

"Sure."

"Let me close the door a little. Then I'll pass him to you." Johnnie shut the door a bit, hid himself behind it, then handed Michael off to her.

"I'll get him diapered and dressed for you."

"Thanks."

"The best thing is George didn't stay at the zoo. George and the man with the yellow hat had more adventures together. How about tomorrow we go to the bookstore and buy all the books?"

Johnnie sat in the rocking chair with Michael. The baby had been fed and changed again, and now his eyes were droopy. He was ready for his nap.

Brenda stood at the doorway of the nursery smiling, her arms crossed in front of her, watching him with Michael. For the first time, he felt uneasy in her presence. She'd seen him naked. And instead of being flustered or upset about it, she'd taken a few seconds to check him out.

"That was quick."

"The walk on the beach and the shower seem to have tired him out."

"Probably overstimulated by all the new experiences."

Johnnie nodded, silently wishing she'd go away. "Did Melanie have her physical therapy yet?"

"I was about to get started. Did you want to help?"

Michael yawned. Johnnie stood and placed him in the crib. He turned on the mobile, then put Michael's pacifier in his mouth.

Johnnie looked at Brenda, then quickly averted his eyes. "I'm going to have that nap."

Brenda laughed lightly. "You don't have to be embarrassed, Johnnie. I'm a nurse. I've seen many naked bodies over the years."

Johnnie felt his face warm as he walked to the door. "Well, I was a rock star who showed his naked body to a lot of different women over the years. But things are different now."

Brenda moved so that he could pass. He went downstairs and poured himself a glass of juice. Brenda came in and stood at the kitchen island.

"You really love her a lot."

"More than anything."

"Don't you get lonely?"

What the fuck? Hadn't Laurel asked him the same thing?

"I get lonely for her. I miss her smile, her laugh, her hugs, her kisses. I miss her stubborn streak. How feisty she is. How romantic she is."

Brenda sat on a stool and placed her elbows on the table. "What will you do if she doesn't wake up?"

"I'll focus on my son. Raising him the way Melanie would want."

"I've worked with a lot of people in your situation. Most promise to stay faithful. Few have."

He grew agitated. She'd been a stellar nurse. *Why is she starting this shit now?* "Did you sleep with them?"

Brenda appeared shocked by his question. "What? Of course not. They were my employers."

Johnnie nodded.

"Wait? Did you think because I saw you naked, that I was coming on to you?"

He shrugged.

Brenda shook her head. "Guess those things I've read about your enormous ego are true."

"It's hard not to have an ego when you're in the business I'm in."

"Yeah, I suppose you're used to women coming at you from all sides."

"One of the job's perks. Even the ugliest rock stars can get gorgeous women to sleep with them." He took a long drink.

"Well, you're not one of the ugly ones."

"I guess not." He wasn't sure if he should feel flattered or worried. "I was just one of the wasted ones."

"Is that why it took you so long to settle down?"

"Never met a woman I loved more than pills or alcohol. Until Melanie."

"She must be very special." Brenda slid a hand through her auburn hair, pushing it back from her face.

"She is."

"I used to take care of an Alzheimer's patient whose husband divorced her so he could marry again. He still took care of his first wife, but he knew there was nothing that could be done for her. She didn't even know him. Her family wasn't upset with him. Even they understood."

What is she getting at? "Is this story supposed to mean something to me?"

"I don't think people would fault you for moving on."

"Apparently, you didn't see social media's take-down of me when they thought I had stepped out on Melanie while she was in the hospital."

"I didn't mean now, but perhaps in the future."

Johnnie shook his head. "Never going to happen. She's the only one for me."

"Even if she died?"

Frustrated, Johnnie threw his empty glass down in the sink. Luckily, it was plastic. "Why are you talking to me like this? I pay you to take care of Melanie...not ask me about my sex life. You should be in there helping her, not out here trying to pull some psychological bullshit on me."

"I'm trying to help you. You've got a tough road ahead of you. Sometimes it helps to let off some steam and sex is a great way..."

Johnnie walked to the opposite side of the island from Brenda. He glared at her. "I thought you weren't coming on to me."

"I'm not. I mean, not really," Brenda stammered, and appeared uncomfortable. "I don't mean you should move on now. But later..."

A sudden, loud crash came from Melanie's room. Johnnie dashed to the room. Her laptop was on the floor.

"Shit!" He picked it up. Luckily, all her writing was on the desktop in the spare bedroom. She mainly used this one for music and surfing the net. *How did this happen?* It had been sitting on the end table for days playing music for Melanie. Which it wasn't now.

"What was it?" Brenda asked as she followed him into the room.

"Did you move her laptop?"

"No, it's been right where you put it, on the nightstand."

"You're absolutely sure you didn't touch it? Didn't move it an inch?"

"I had no reason to move it. I don't touch it. Ever."

Did Caesar do this? To draw me away from Brenda and her stupid questions? There were no coincidences in this house. He looked at

Brenda. Was she hoping to worm her way into his life? Why? She has a family. *But she is divorced.*

"Why are you thinking that you and I would ever be a thing?" He set the laptop back onto the nightstand. "Have I given you that impression?"

"No, you're always nice and respectful."

"Have I ever acted out of line with you?"

"Never."

Johnnie lifted his arms out to his sides. "Then, why me?"

"Maybe because you are so nice. And of course, attractive, too."

"You barely know me. And what you do know is that I'm devoted to Melanie. She's my wife, and nothing and no one will ever change the fact that I love her, and I only want her."

"I understand." Brenda's gaze dropped to the floor.

"I don't think you do. You've compromised this working relationship by questioning my feelings and offering yourself as some sort of surrogate. I can't have you here anymore. I'll be happy to give you recommendations since you've been a great nurse up until today."

"Johnnie, I'm sorry." She looked up again. "Forget I said all that. I enjoy working here. And you've allowed me to spend more time with my kids."

Kids. Johnnie's face twitched as he felt a touch of sympathy. He looked down at Melanie again, then to the laptop. *Is it a sign?* "I can't trust you with her."

"What?"

"If you hurt her in some way."

Brenda's mouth dropped open. "I'd never do that."

"Honestly, I don't know what you're capable of. But I do know what the media is capable of, and how false stories can get out there and ruin lives. And I have to protect Melanie."

"I would never lie about a client I worked for. Not even a celebrity one."

Johnnie decided he couldn't take any chances. Not after last time. He swung his arm toward the door. "I need you to leave. I'll give you two weeks' pay to help get you through to your next placement."

"Do you need us to come over?" Johnnie's mom asked.

"I think I'll be okay for the rest of the day."

"You think?" Johnnie heard Blue ask. His mom must have clicked on the speakerphone.

"The nursing center will send a replacement tomorrow. They'll be here until I hire someone new."

"It's a shame Brenda didn't work out," Blue said. "She seemed to be doing fine."

"I couldn't risk it, Blue."

"I understand. She crossed a line."

"I couldn't trust her around Melanie. Especially after she mentioned Melanie dying."

"What a horrible thing to even bring up with someone's family."

"It's done and over with, Mom. I appreciate you guys taking Michael for the weekend. I need to catch up on sleep. We'll be recording next week, and I want to be fresh and ready to go."

"What time should we pick him up?" Blue asked.

"Tomorrow around dinner time, maybe?"

His mom laughed. "How about we bring you some dinner?"

"I was hoping you'd say that."

"How about we bring take out?" Blue asked. "Perhaps some barbeque? We'll eat together and then take him on home with us."

"Just be prepared to be up most of the night."

"Between the two of us we can handle it," Blue assured him. "Just make sure you have that shaking chair ready to go."

"Of course." He laughed. "I better check on Melanie and Michael. He'll be waking soon, and I have to do her physical therapy."

"See you tomorrow."

"Thanks again." Johnnie hung up as he walked to Melanie's room. CJ was sleeping at the foot of the bed. He pulled back her blankets and moved his eyes over her from head to toe.

He sighed, pushing back negative thoughts, and trying to find a way to stay positive.

"Hi, babe. Ready to exercise." He put down the bed railings, then tried again to turn on her laptop. It wouldn't work.

"Damn!" He hoped it could be repaired. Again, he wondered how it ended up on the floor.

"I'm sorry. Your computer is toast. Should I get your phone? Or maybe I'll just sing for you."

For the next hour, he sang to her as he worked the muscles in her legs and arms. Gently, he rolled her onto her side, mindful of her feeding tube. He rubbed her back. The idea was to keep her circulation in good health. Even if she did wake, it would take a while for her to have strength enough to sit up or walk, let alone make love to him.

He kissed each of her fingers as he massaged her hands. "One day we'll get there, babe. I know it."

"Remember our first time together? I do. Like it was yesterday. You'd fallen and hit your head. Scared the shit out of me. I called an ambulance to take you to the hospital. You got seven stitches. When I brought you home, I put you to bed and then crawled in with you. We both took a nap, and when we woke up, I couldn't hold my feelings back any longer. I had to have you, had to be inside you, and most importantly, I had to tell you I was in love with you."

He placed her hand on his heart. "I get excited thinking about that day. I was so scared, Melanie. Scared to open my heart to anyone.

Scared I'd hurt you. But being inside you was the most wonderful feeling. Better than any drug I'd ever taken."

He chuckled. "And as you know, I've tried everything."

Johnnie sat on the bed. He kissed Melanie tenderly, then lay down beside her. He stroked her face lightly.

"We're recording your song next week. I know it will be a hit. Caesar, Rhett, and Kurt believe it, too. Blue took a lot of video of the band. He even took some of Caesar alone. Blue will download it all into the computer, and then we'll create a new music video for the band. Caesar will be in it. Can you believe that?"

Johnnie felt himself losing it as he caressed her face. Tears slipped from his eyes and fell onto Melanie. "I hate seeing you like this. You hate it, too, don't you? Being caught between two worlds."

"I know you're fighting hard to come back to us." Johnnie took her hand in his and kissed her forehead. "Baby, if you're tired of fighting and need to go, I'll understand. If you want to be with Caesar, that's fine by me. He loves you, and he'll take good care of you, the same way he's doing with Leila and Lily. I'll always be here, taking care of our son. You won't ever have to worry about him. He'll be loved. By me, your parents, my mom, Blue, Rhett, and Kurt."

He kissed her lips again. "I'll be alright, Melanie. I love you so much. But I know I can make it on my own and take care of myself. I've been keeping the house clean...the clothes washed. CJ has gained so much weight from all the food I've been feeding him. I even learned how to make scrambled eggs without burning the house down. And...no more cravings. There's just no time for them."

"I don't want you to go, Melanie." He snuggled closer. He placed his palm over her heart, feeling it beat. "But I also don't want you to have to live like this. You deserve so much more. You were so full of life and seeing you like this...it's just not fair, babe. So, you make the decision. Either come back to me or let yourself go. Be with Caesar and the girls. As long as I know you're happy and loved. That will be enough for me. Michael and me...we'll be fine. I promise."

Melanie's chest rose as if she were taking a deep breath.

Sssssss, was the noise she made as she exhaled.

Johnnie's desperate despair suddenly flipped to exhilaration and hope.

"Melanie? Baby? Are you trying to say something? Caesar? Is that what you're trying to say? Caesar's close, babe. Lily and Leila, too. The dolphins are here. When you wake up, we'll go see them. I took Michael out to see them earlier. He loved them. They made him laugh for the first time."

He kissed her again. She uttered no more sounds, though.

Michael however, did. Cries came from the nursery as he began to wake from his nap.

"Someone's up from their nap. I'll get him and bring him to you."

After changing Michael, Johnnie grabbed Melanie's cell phone and earphones, then returned to her room.

"Momma's been trying to talk. Can you say hello to her?"

He placed Michael near Melanie. The baby kicked his legs and flung his arms around, gurgling and smiling.

"Hi, Mommy. We came to say hello and bring your music to you. But it's lunchtime so we're going to eat, then we'll be back to talk to you some more."

Johnnie turned on her phone and brought up the Lush playlist for Melanie. He covered her ears with the earphones.

He waved Michael's hand. "See you later, Mommy. Enjoy Daddy's music for a while."

Johnnie needed to tell Melanie's parents the latest developments. *Lunch first.* While he fixed himself a sandwich, Michael sat in his bouncy chair. The baby stared at the toys attached to it and even reached his hand out to touch one. Johnnie smiled.

"You're getting so big. Soon you'll be eating peanut butter and jelly with Dad."

CJ came in and circled the baby's chair. He sat down next to Michael and stared at him. Then he licked his face.

"CJ, don't do that. He doesn't need cat germs."

Michael laughed and kicked his legs.

CJ meowed, and Michael laughed some more. Johnnie grabbed his phone and took a video of their exchange. Michael began babbling, CJ responded with meows.

"You two apparently speak the same language." Johnnie laughed. He quickly sent the video to all the grandparents, along with Kurt and Rhett. Then he posted it to Lush's *Twitter* and *Facebook* pages. *Perhaps the fans will get a kick out of this.*

After making Michael's bottle, he grabbed his plate and drink and took them to the spare bedroom. Then he gathered Michael and brought him into the room. Time to *FaceTime* Melanie's parents.

"Did you see the video I just sent?" Johnnie asked Carl and Mary Jo. Michael sat on his lap, having his bottle.

"It was adorable," Mary Jo gushed. "Those two were really talking to one another."

"How are you doing, Johnnie?" Carl asked. "You look exhausted."

"I am. I got a couple hours sleep last night. I'd planned to take a nap when Michael went down for his, but something came up with Brenda."

Johnnie explained what happened with the nurse.

Carl's brow furrowed. "Are you going to be alright all alone with Melanie today?"

"I can handle it. The interim nurse will be here tomorrow, and Michael's going to spend the weekend with my parents, so I'll be fine."

"You be sure to take care of yourself, son," Carl told him. "You won't be of any use to either of them if you get sick."

Johnnie nodded, then grinned.

"What is it?" Mary Jo smiled back. "Some good news to tell us?"

"She was trying to talk earlier."

Mary Jo gasped.

"Are you sure?" Carl asked.

"She only said one sound, though. An S sound."

Carl appeared confused. "Like she was hissing?"

"I honestly think she was trying to say Caesar. I was talking about him right before she did it."

Mary Jo and Carl looked at one another.

"I know what you're thinking. Maybe I'm overreaching. Maybe it was nothing. But just maybe...it was everything."

"I hope you're right, Johnnie." Carl started to tear up.

Johnnie saw that Michael was finished with his bottle. He put the baby over his shoulder to burp him.

"He's getting so big." Mary Jo brushed back tears as well. "Please promise us you'll bring him to visit even if..."

"Even if it means leaving Melanie." Johnnie turned his gaze from the computer.

"That's a tough request, I know," Carl told him.

"Maybe Blue and my mom could bring him. Perhaps for his first birthday."

"That would be wonderful."

"I'm going to finish my lunch and then let Michael spend some time with Melanie. I'll call you if anything else happens."

"Thank you, Johnnie. And make sure you get some rest this weekend."

Johnnie saluted. "Will do."

He turned off the camera and held Michael up. "Time to see Mommy again."

By eleven that night, Johnnie was ready to have himself committed. Michael had been having crying bouts for hours. He'd tried everything—placing Michael in his bouncy chair, walking him around the house and out on the deck, playing music for him, putting on an animated kid's movie, lying him next to Melanie. He thought about taking him for a car ride which always seemed to knock him out, but he couldn't leave Melanie alone.

Sometimes you have to let them cry it out. His mom had told him that when he'd called her again, but he hated seeing his son so frustrated...so red and angry. Maybe it was time to make another appointment with his pediatrician. *Maybe it's more than just colic.*

He paced the floor of Melanie's room, singing to Michael, trying to get him to calm down. He thought his legs might give out. He was drained.

"I wish your Uncle Caesar was here." *I'd sleep then.*

Although Caesar slept, he really didn't need to. Caesar had spent a few nights comforting Michael when he was like this. Johnnie would pass out in the upstairs bedroom while Caesar kept the screaming baby downstairs. Listening to Michael now, he wondered how he'd ever slept through all the crying.

"Alright, Grandma, we'll try your idea." He swaddled Michael up tight, then placed him on his back in the bassinet. He tried to give the baby his pacifier, but he refused it. "Sorry, dude, but maybe Grandma's right. Maybe it's time for you to learn to calm yourself down."

Johnnie scooted the bassinet over to the reclining chair. He could gently rock Michael and get some rest at the same time. Michael kept screaming, but the rhythmic motion of rocking the bassinet, soon lulled Johnnie into a stupor. Despite Michael's continued cries, Johnnie drifted off to sleep.

Chapter Eighteen

Past

"*I wonder if that woman from the accident yesterday survived.*"

Johnnie wondered, too. As he walked with his mom to his dad's room in ICU, he took note of everything going on. She had to be here somewhere. If she was alive.

A few rooms down from his dad's he saw a chaplain with a man and woman. The woman sobbed uncontrollably, as the man tried to console her. They were wrapped so tight in one another's arms that Johnnie couldn't see their faces.

"That poor family," his mother said as they approached the scene. Johnnie held back, letting his mother go ahead of him. He wasn't anxious to see his dad anyway.

"Take strength in the fact that your daughter survived," Johnnie heard the chaplain say. "And an angel sent from heaven saved the day, donating his blood so that she could live."

Johnnie couldn't suppress a smile as he walked past. An angel from heaven? Ha! The man had no idea, and he wasn't about to inform him. He was curious about the woman, but the last thing he needed was for the press to know what he'd done. He was tired of being a story.

Still, it felt good to know he'd saved her life. Other than music, his life hadn't afforded him many opportunities to feel good about himself. So, he'd allow himself to bask in this good feeling for a little while.

Present

"Johnnie."

Johnnie stirred in his sleep. He smiled, dreaming of Melanie. Of her calling him to bed. She wanted him. And he wanted her. He approached the bed, and she pulled back the covers, revealing her long, tan legs, her luscious curves. His cock ached to be inside her. *It's been too long.*

"Johnnie."

But Michael was screaming, calling for him in a very different way. Johnnie forced his exhausted eyes open. *Shit! When did I fall asleep?* Had Michael been screaming this entire time. *How could I sleep through this noise?*

"Johnnie."

He blinked, adjusting his eyes to the light. "Sorry, Melanie. I gotta get up. No sex dreams tonight."

"Johnnie...please."

He bolted upright and flew from the chair to Melanie's side. She was staring up at the ceiling, her blue eyes wide open.

"Melanie?"

"The...baby. He's crying."

Johnnie grinned so widely it hurt. He cupped her face as tears threatened to erupt. "No, that's what we call screaming bloody murder around here."

"He's probably hungry. Give him to me."

Oh shit! She's confused.

"Johnnie, hurry. I can't stand hearing him cry. He's been crying for so long. Where were you?"

Johnnie lifted Michael out of the bassinet, then held him over his shoulder. He rocked him, and Michael quieted down to a few hiccups and some soft whining. "I fell asleep, babe. He's been having trouble sleeping which keeps me awake half the night."

Melanie lifted an arm toward him.

"Do you remember what happened, Melanie?"

She looked at him strangely. "Of course, I remember. We had a baby."

"Melanie, you fell, and I took you to the hospital."

"And then we had a baby. Let me see him, please." Melanie raised her other arm.

"Melanie, be careful. We need to talk first."

She persisted. "Help me raise the bed so I can hold him. Where's the button."

"You shouldn't be sitting just yet." *Can she even sit up?*

In his arms, Michael squirmed and whimpered.

"Johnnie, please, I need to hold him. He needs me."

Johnnie found the remote on the bed. He'd never even used it before. He pressed the up button slowly. Melanie's upper torso started to rise with the bed. When it got too high, she started to slide sideways slowly. She struggled to balance herself.

"That's what I was afraid of," he told her.

She grimaced. "I feel so weak. What's wrong with me?"

"Hold on, babe." Johnnie immediately put the bed back down.

He strapped Michael into his bouncy chair. "I'm going to need you to be a very good boy. Sit here quietly while I talk to Mommy. I'm begging you, kid. Do right by me this one time, okay."

CJ ran into the room and immediately approached Michael. The baby's eyes grew large, and after a few more hiccups, he got quiet.

"Thanks, CJ, you're a lifesaver. Please entertain him for a few minutes."

CJ immediately rubbed against the chair. Michael sat entranced, sucking on his tiny hand.

"Try this instead." Johnnie put the pacifier to his mouth, and this time Michael took it.

"Johnnie, talk to me. What are you doing?"

Johnnie sat on the bed beside her and took her hand. "I'm here, Melanie."

"Where's my baby?"

"In his bouncy chair watching CJ."

"We're home?"

Johnnie raised the bed again. This time he kept his body close to Melanie, holding her against him. "Look around. It's the downstairs bedroom. I put you in front of the window so you could see the ocean."

Melanie pushed her blanket away from her. "Why am I in a hospital gown?"

"First things first." He held her hand to his mouth and kissed it over and over. "I love you so much, and I've missed you."

"I didn't go anywhere, Johnnie." She started to cry softly. "Please tell me what's happening."

Johnnie grabbed his phone from the nightstand and dialed 911 for an ambulance.

Melanie's eyes widened. "Johnnie?"

When Johnnie hung up, his own tears fell. Overcome with emotion, he took a deep breath, trying to get the words out. "I almost lost you. There was so much blood. The doctor said you had a ruptured uterus. You had an emergency c-section. During the operation, you went into a coma."

"A coma?" She sniffed. Her bottom lip quivered. "For how long?"

"Almost three months."

She buried her head against his body and cried. Johnnie looked over at Michael. The baby had fallen asleep. CJ was napping on the floor next to him.

"It's okay. You're back now. That's all that matters." He kissed the top of Melanie's head. "But you're weak, so we have to take things slow."

"Who's been taking care of the baby?"

Johnnie chuckled. "What do you mean? I have, of course."

"By yourself?"

"Is that so hard to believe?"

She looked up at him, and her lips curled upward into a smile. "Yes."

She's beautiful. He pressed a kiss against her lips. "Well, believe it or not, I've fed him, burped him, taken him on walks, sang him to sleep, taken him to the pediatrician, changed all his shitty diapers...come to think of it, I've changed a few of your shitty diapers as well."

Melanie looked under the covers again. "Oh, no. How embarrassing."

"You owe me. I'm not changing another diaper for at least three months."

"So, you've been taking care of me *and* the baby?"

"You already know how incredible I am."

"Apparently, even more so than I ever thought."

"Do you think you can sit up by yourself?"

Melanie adjusted herself. "Maybe."

"If you start to fall over, yell."

"Where are you going?"

He eased away from her. "To get Michael for you."

"Michael?"

"Yes." He slid from the bed and removed Michael from the chair. Then, he brought the baby to Melanie. "Michael Angelo Vega."

Johnnie sat back on the bed and held Michael close to Melanie. "I hope that name's okay with you."

"It's perfect, Johnnie." Melanie wrapped her arms around their baby and pulled him close to her. She checked each of his fingers, then pulled his socks off to see his toes.

"They're all there, I promise. No one's lost any limbs under my care."

"He's beautiful, Johnnie."

"Of course." Johnnie rolled his eyes and grinned. "He looks like me."

Melanie lightly touched Michael's dark curls. "He does, doesn't he?"

"He's had no health problems. Except for colic. But he eats well and has been gaining weight steadily."

Melanie frowned. "I didn't get to breastfeed him."

"I did the next best thing. He's been drinking donor breastmilk."

"A bouncy chair? Donor breast milk? You *have* been taking good care of him."

"The chair was a gift from Kurt. Can't take credit for that one."

"Kurt's been here? What about Rhett?"

Johnnie nodded. "There's so much to tell you, Melanie. But let's just enjoy this moment, right here, right now with Michael."

CJ jumped on the bed and walked to Melanie.

"And this knucklehead of course."

Melanie laughed as CJ butted her head and rubbed himself all over her.

"He's been a big help as well. Michael loves him."

Melanie kissed CJ's head. "Thank you."

"No kiss for me, yet?"

Melanie gazed up at him and smiled. "You said I had to take things slow."

"Slow kisses are phenomenal."

"I know what will happen if I kiss you, slow or fast."

"True. But I also know you have to fully recover before I jump your bones again."

Melanie held up an arm. "I am all bones, aren't I?"

"Don't worry. The weight will come back."

"Tell me everything I've missed."

Johnnie heard sirens in the distance. "We've got plenty of time. In fact, we have the rest of our lives."

Melanie's lips met his, and they kissed over and over until Johnnie left the bed to let the paramedics into the gate.

Chapter Nineteen

Past

"When was your first time? What was it like?"

Johnnie squeezed the excess water out of the sponge. He was helping Caesar wash his dad's car. "My mom let me drive her to the grocery store. Wasn't a big deal since it's only a few blocks from our house."

Caesar squirted Johnnie with the hose. "I'm talking about fucking, not driving."

"Oh." Johnnie went back to scrubbing.

"Well?"

Johnnie ignored Caesar.

"You're still a virgin?"

"Don't remind me."

"What's the problem?" Caesar rinsed the soap from the side Johnnie had just washed. "You like girls, right?"

Johnnie nodded, then frowned. "I'm no good at talking to them."

"I'll help you. That is...if you want to get laid."

"Are you kidding me? Damn straight I want to get laid."

Caesar pushed his curls back from his forehead. "Some of my female friends have been asking about you."

Johnnie's eyes widened. "No, shit?"

"You seem surprised."

"No one's ever been interested in me."

"They say you always seem angry," Caesar told him. "But they also say you're good looking. And then there's the drumming thing which they find sexy."

Johnnie felt his face warm. He'd never thought of himself as handsome or sexy.

"What's your type? I'll pick one out for you."

"Type? Female and breathing."

Caesar burst into laughter. "Well, that's easy."

"Curves. I like girls with curves."

"I can accommodate that. Maybe my friend Cara."

Johnnie knew who exactly who Cara was. She was hot. "You think she'd have sex with me?"

Caesar shrugged. "She had it with me...so why not?"

"I'll be a nervous wreck."

"Have a glass of wine. It will relax you."

"I might need five or six." Johnnie's brow furrowed, but then a slow smile crept across his face. "Shit! I'm getting laid!"

Caesar tossed back his head and laughed. "Yes, you are!"

Present

"All cleaned up, Mommy," Johnnie announced as he walked into Melanie's hospital room carrying Michael.

Melanie had been admitted to the hospital so that her feeding tube could be removed through surgery. Other than that, she'd been given a clean bill of health from her doctor and would be going home tomorrow.

"And then I told him he better get his butt home and clean up. He was smelling up the whole ICU ward."

Gailya and Melanie laughed together.

"Gailya! It's so good to see you." Johnnie handed Michael over to Melanie and then hugged her former nurse tight. When he pulled away, he smiled and said, "Are you telling her all my secrets?"

Gailya poked him in the chest with a finger. "Every...last...one."

Johnnie chuckled and squeezed her even tighter.

When they parted, Gailya sat back down on the edge of Melanie's bed. "And look at this handsome little man. He's grown so much. And that hair!"

"Just like his daddy's." Melanie beamed.

Gailya looked up at Johnnie. "Yes, I believe he's going to look just like his daddy."

"Well, then he will be very handsome." Melanie tickled Michael's chin, and the baby smiled at her.

"Handsome and a great man as well," Gailya added. She placed her hand on Melanie's shoulder. "In all my years of being a nurse, I've never seen a husband more devoted or more in love with his wife."

Johnnie's face warmed. "Aw shucks."

Gailya eased off the bed again and went to Johnnie. Then she turned back to Melanie. "Don't let this one get away."

"Never," Melanie promised.

"My break is over, so I better get back upstairs. I'll come say goodbye when I get a chance."

Johnnie hugged her once more. He couldn't help himself as tears began to fall. "Thank you for everything you did for her."

Gailya pulled away and held his hands. "You did it. Your love...your dedication brought her back."

Johnnie nodded and hugged her again.

"You take care of yourself, okay? You have two people who need you."

"And a cat."

Gailya laughed, kissed his cheek, and then disappeared out the door.

"Wake up, babe." Johnnie sat on the bed and tickled Melanie's foot. "I have a surprise for you."

Melanie opened her eyes and tried to sit up. "Is Michael okay?"

"He's fine." Johnnie placed a pillow behind her, propping her up. "Mom and Blue picked him up about ten minutes ago."

"Did you pack everything he needed?"

"There you go again forgetting who took care of him for the last few months."

"Sorry. I worry so much about him."

Johnnie nodded, knowing it was due in part to her losing Leila and Lily, but also knowing it was a normal part of being a parent.

Melanie had been home nearly three weeks with no complications. She was eating well, gaining weight, and her new nurse had been coming during the week to help with her physical therapy. His parents had spent a lot of time with Melanie the past week, helping take care of her and Michael while he'd been away recording with Rhett and Kurt. Although their recording plans had been delayed by Melanie's recovery, the single was now done. And he'd completed the editing of the video here at home when Melanie was asleep or playing with Michael.

She started to move, and he helped her slide to the edge of the bed.

"I can do it." She slowly slipped from the bed and then placed her weight on her feet. When she teetered, he put his arm around her waist. She pushed his arm away. "I've got this. Watch me"

Johnnie smiled. *Feisty as always.* She was fighting to get back to normal. He watched with admiration as she slipped a dress over her head, and then shuffle over to the door of their bedroom. When she got to the top of the stairs, she turned back to him.

"Are you going to help me get downstairs?"

He grinned. "I thought you had this."

"I haven't done the stairs by myself. You'd know that if you'd been here with me, instead of going off to do some secret project with Rhett and Kurt."

"You knew I was a rock star when you fell in love with me." He laughed and put his arms around her. "Sometimes, I'll be doing projects that involve music."

"Your new project is helping me get down these stairs."

He started to lift her, then stopped. "Perhaps you should go to the bathroom first. I don't need you peeing on me when I pick you up. I get enough of that from Michael."

She laughed. "Perhaps I should."

Once she was finished in the bathroom, he swept her up in his arms, carried her downstairs and out the backdoor.

"Where are you taking me?"

"I thought you might like some ocean air." He took her to a blanket that he'd spread out under a large umbrella.

"You bought an umbrella?"

"Yes, I knew we'd need it to keep the sun off Michael." He set her on her feet, and she sat down.

"It's a little chilly out here."

"Already thought of that. I'll be right back." He ran to the deck and then back to her. After handing her a sweater, he set down a big basket filled with food and bottles of juice. There was also a new laptop with a bow around it.

"What's all this?"

"I thought we'd have a picnic." He took out all the food. There was a variety of cheese, crackers, and fruit.

"Yummy." She grabbed a slice of cheese, put it on a cracker, and stuffed it in her mouth. "I'm starving. It's like I haven't eaten in years."

He leaned in close to her and cupped a breast. "Keep filling out these curves. I don't want you to get hurt when I finally fuck you again."

She took a sip of orange juice. "Mmm...sex. Something else it feels like I haven't done in years."

"It'll take me years to make up for all the sex we've been missing."

"Promise?" she asked coyly.

He kissed her tenderly and then handed her the laptop.

"I took your old laptop in to be repaired. The guy told me it could be fixed, but it was a dinosaur and that I should buy you a newer model. He was able to extract all your files, and they're inside the house on a flash drive."

She took the bow off and opened the new computer. "This is nice. Thank you."

"Turn it on. There's a file I've uploaded that I think you might enjoy."

"Are you dancing naked for me?"

He smacked his forehead. "Damn! I knew there was something I forgot to do."

Melanie laughed, then turned on the computer, and immediately saw the file marked *Heaven Sent*. She clicked on it.

"Listen to the song first."

"I love this song," she said as the music began. "It's one of my favorites."

Johnnie's eyes narrowed. "There's no way you know this song."

She tilted her chin up. "Superfan, remember?"

"Melanie, this is a brand-new song. It's what I've been working on with Rhett and Kurt."

"But I know it." She hummed the melody and then sang the chorus.

"I wrote this song for you about a month ago. That's me singing. Not Caesar."

"How would I know it then?"

"We played it for you live when you were in a coma. Then I played it for you all the time after that. It was a rough cut but not much different than this. You must remember it from that time."

"Is that possible?"

"Gailya told me it was. She's the one who told me to talk and sing to you every day and so I did."

Melanie closed her eyes, smiling blissfully as she continued to listen to the song.

When the song ended, he stroked her cheek, and she opened her blue eyes. "I love you, Melanie. You are truly my gift from the heavens."

"From our angel, Caesar." She took his hand and kissed it.

"Speaking of Caesar. Click on the other file. It's the music video."

Melanie watched intently, appearing thoroughly entranced by the video, especially Caesar. She touched the screen when a close-up of his face was shown. "He's so beautiful."

Johnnie smiled. Apparently, Melanie was thinking they'd done some clever editing to put old clips of Caesar in. He was glad she was fooled. It meant their fans would be as well.

Suddenly, she gasped. "He came back?"

"What?" Johnnie feigned surprise. "How did you know?"

Johnnie hadn't yet told her about Caesar's return or about his getting drunk again. He'd been searching for the right way, the right moment to tell her. *If there is one.* He thought the song and video might be a good segue way to news that she might react badly to.

Melanie went back in the video and paused it. It was a scene of Caesar sitting on the beach. Behind him was the deck. And on the deck...sat CJ.

"That little devil." Johnnie laughed. "I'm glad you caught that. We're going to have to edit him out. It's supposed to look like old video footage to the fans."

"Caesar was here, then? When I was in a coma? Did he come back to help me?"

Frowning, Johnnie shook his head. "I haven't told you everything that happened, Melanie. He actually came back to help me."

"With Michael?"

"He did help with Michael, but that's not the reason he came back. You see, things were worse than I told you. Seeing you in that coma every day, and not being able to reach you. And I was terrified of being a father alone without you. My parents were taking care of him because I couldn't. Then the crap with Phil Chase making up stories about me dating someone else."

She sighed heavily as she hung her head. "Was it pills or alcohol?"

"Whiskey. Just once. I drank until I passed out, and Caesar came back to help. He insisted I get Michael from my parent's house and get myself together for you and our son."

Her hands began to tremble. "I see."

He took them in his. "Since bringing Michael home, I haven't wanted another drink. Then you came back. All I care about is you and him."

She fell quiet.

Johnnie's pulse raced. "I understand if you're angry with me or if you want to banish me to the rehearsal studio."

Melanie laughed. "Why would I do that?"

"I let you down. You have a right to be upset."

"I'm upset with myself." A tear slid from her right eye. "I put all that stress on you."

He wiped it away. "It's not your fault. I let things get to me when I should have been stronger."

"It was a lot to deal with."

"Still no excuse. I'm just glad Caesar came when he did and that I was able to get myself together."

"How was he?"

"Truly heaven sent. He helped me so much with Michael."

"So, it wasn't just *you* taking care of Michael."

"I guess I did fudge a bit on that detail." Leaning back, Johnnie took a bite of a strawberry. He scanned the horizon and grinned.

"Then it wasn't only dreams I was having about Caesar."

Johnnie rolled his eyes and groaned. "You dreamed about him?"

"Still jealous." She laughed.

"Always."

"I dreamed of you, too. And my parents. Judy and Blue. Rhett and Kurt. Only I guess none of it was really a dream. I felt you all with me."

He looked at Melanie. "Did you dream of Leila and Lily, too?"

"What?"

"Caesar brought them one night to see you. I spoke with them. They could see me and Michael...even CJ."

"How is that possible? They weren't able to see me or hear me when Caesar brought them before."

"I'm not sure." Johnnie sighed. "Maybe because they were trying to help you. In fact, it was Leila who told me that you were coming back to me. She felt you, even when Caesar couldn't."

"What do you mean?"

"After Caesar warned me you were hurt, he said he couldn't feel you any longer. But Leila did."

Melanie shook her head. "I'll never understand this spirit thing."

"Me neither." Johnnie shrugged, then pointed over Melanie's shoulder. "Like now. Caesar's standing right behind you and you haven't seen him yet."

Melanie twisted her body and let out a scream of excitement.

Johnnie laughed. "Oh, so you *can* see him."

Melanie tried to scramble to her feet but was too weak and stumbled.

"Hold on there." Caesar laughed lightly. "Be careful. Let me come to you."

Caesar bent to Melanie and hoisted her to her feet. He hugged her for a long time. Then the two of them gazed into one another's eyes.

"What are you doing here?" Melanie caressed Caesar's face.

Caesar cupped her chin. "I cheated and came to see you."

"Are the girls here?"

Caesar pointed to the ocean where two dolphins were zooming through the water. "I can't stay long, but I had to see you. I'm so glad you're alright. Johnnie and I were so worried about you."

"I've missed you." Melanie pressed her lips against Caesar's. As she kissed him again and again, he softly caressed her back. His hands drifted down to her butt, and he pulled her close.

Johnnie felt a pang of jealousy and fought it off. This was a magical thing, and he'd enjoy it—even if he did have to interrupt them.

He stood up. "We were just watching the video."

"Is it fantastic?"

"It is." Johnnie nodded, grabbed the laptop, and pressed play.

"How do you like Johnnie's song?" Caesar asked Melanie, his arms still wrapped possessively around her waist.

"It's beautiful. And the video is so sweet with everyone and their families."

"He wrote it for you and insisted on singing it."

"Because I love his voice." Melanie looked at Johnnie. "And him."

She left Caesar's arms and wrapped her arms around Johnnie's waist. She held up her ring finger to Caesar. "I guess you know we got married and had a baby."

Caesar nodded. "I'm happy for you. Michael's beautiful. I'm glad I got to spend time with him. Hopefully, I can check-in from time to time."

"We'd like that," Johnnie said and set the computer back onto the blanket.

"Are you sure? Because you were turning green with envy a few minutes ago."

"We're you?" Melanie pulled his gaze to hers. "There's no need to be jealous. I belong to you, Johnnie."

"Then you don't want to run your hands through that mess of curls on his head while you're making love to him all day and night?"

"I didn't say that." Melanie smiled. "But I can take all those feelings for him and make love to you instead."

Caesar grinned. "Hmmm, perhaps it's time I leave the two of you alone."

"No," Johnnie said. "Stay as long as you can. Melanie's still recovering so we have to refrain from making love for a little while longer."

"Really? Because my doctor said whenever I'm ready, I can get back to it. And since Michael's not here to interrupt, perhaps we should take advantage of the situation."

Johnnie looked from Melanie to Caesar. "She's kidding, right?"

"I don't think she is." Caesar caressed Melanie's face. "And if you don't take her up on the offer, I will."

"Not a chance." Johnnie pushed Caesar gently. "She's my wife remember."

Caesar playfully pushed him back. "I do remember...that you're the luckiest man in the world."

Johnnie hugged his friend tight. "That I am...that I am."

"Now go make love to her before she changes her mind," Caesar whispered in his ear.

Johnnie swept Melanie up in his arms. As he carried her back to the house, she waved goodbye to Caesar and blew him a kiss. When Johnnie turned to say goodbye, Caesar was gone.

"Baby, are you sure about this? As much as I love you and want you, I can wait."

Melanie slipped her dress over her head and stood naked before him. "I don't want to wait."

"You can barely walk."

She crawled onto the bed and lay back against the pillows. "Who's walking?" He started to get onto the bed with her, but she held up a hand.

"What?"

"Take your clothes off...slowly. I want to watch."

He grinned. "I'm a drummer, not a stripper."

"I've seen concert footage of you, stripping off your sweaty t-shirts and throwing them into the crowd."

"Only when I borrowed one of Caesar's shirts."

"Do it."

"Okay, boss lady." He slipped his shirt over his head, swung it around, then tossed it to her.

"Nice chest." She smiled.

"Am I making you wet?"

His dick hardened as she moved her hand between her legs and touched herself.

"Yes, I'm wet. But then again, it could be because I saw Caesar."

He shook a finger at her. "You're going to pay for that one."

"Pants. Now."

"And if I say no?" He turned away from her but could still see her in the mirror over the chest of drawers.

She spread her legs further apart. "Then you don't get any of this."

Down went his joggers.

She sighed. "Amazing ass, Johnnie Vega."

"Should I dance around? Do you want to see the magic tongue?" Johnnie shook his butt and wagged his tongue while moving in a slow circle.

"Definitely a drummer." Melanie covered her mouth and laughed. "Not a stripper."

He turned back to her and grabbed his hard cock. "Maybe it's this you want to see?"

"Yes, a close-up view please."

He crawled onto the bed and in between her legs. "Still my number one fan?"

"Always." She put a hand on each side of his face and brought her lips to his.

"I don't want to hurt you." He stared down at the two scars on her abdomen, then traced his finger along the long one from her cesarean. "Are you sure you're okay?"

"I'm fine." She pulled his gaze back to her own and kissed him. Her mouth opened, welcoming his tongue. He placed his cock at her wet entrance and slowly pushed himself in. Without warning, she gasped, and her pussy tightened around him.

"Already?" He smiled as he continued moving inside of her.

"Couldn't help it. It's been so long."

He stroked her face. "Too long."

"You are a bit heavy."

"Why didn't you say something?" He quickly moved away.

"Let's change positions." She turned to her side. "How about like this?"

He cuddled up behind her, lifted her leg, and slipped inside her.

"That feels wonderful, Johnnie."

"Does it?" He swept her hair to one side and kissed her neck. His hand wrapped around her waist and moved to her nipples. He rubbed one between his fingers. "You like it even more now, don't you?"

"You're going to make me cum."

"That's the plan." He chuckled. "Should I move a little faster? Are you good?"

"Better than good. But I can't see you. I can't kiss you."

"What should we do about that?"

"Let me ride you."

He lay back on the bed and then helped her straddle him. "Let me know if it's too much."

"Your cock feels so amazing." She ground her hips into his slowly.

"Fuck, you're so wet." He reached for her nipples once again.

"You know what I want."

He sat up and took a nipple into his mouth, sucking and licking it before moving to the other.

"I'm going to cum again."

"Should I cum with you?"

Instead of answering, she grunted and ground into him even harder. He left her breasts and kissed her lips instead. He felt her pussy tighten on him and held her body against his as he moved his cock inside her.

"I love you so much," she whispered, her body trembling in his arms.

Her words were all he needed for his release. He held her for a while, then eased her down beside him.

"Guess Caesar really did get you revved up for me."

"Stop being jealous."

Johnnie sat up. His gaze whizzed around the room. "You know he's out there, somewhere, watching us, wishing he were me."

Damn straight!

"Oh shit, he's in my head again." Johnnie rubbed his forehead, then laughed. He stared up at the ceiling. "Can we please be alone? This is our first time in months. It should be special. Between the *two* of us."

Tell Melanie I love her.

"No. You should've told her on the beach."

"What's he saying?"

"Nothing."

Remember who saved your ass when her dad thought you'd gotten drunk.

"Damn it!" Johnnie fell back onto the pillow. "You win. Caesar says he loves you, Melanie."

"I love Caesar, too." Melanie smiled and cuddled closer. She pressed her lips against his. "And I love you even more."

"You hear that?" Johnnie shouted.

Caesar's laughter filled his mind. *I love you, too, Johnnie. Be happy, man. You deserve it.*

Johnnie's eyes filled with tears.

"What is it? What did he say? Are you alright?"

Johnnie wiped his tears, then grinned slyly. "He said you love me more because my dick is thicker."

"Johnnie Vega stop lying!"

"He said to fuck you a few times for him."

She rolled her eyes and groaned.

"He said he loved both of us and wants us to be happy."

"We will be once you make love to me a few more times."

His hand traveled to the juncture between her thighs. She moaned when he slipped two fingers inside her. "Let's make some magic then."

Chapter Twenty

Past

Johnnie stared at the folded letter from his father. Caesar had looked into his future and told him it was coming. Along with the money that his parents had controlled for nearly sixteen years. He and Melanie had flown to Atlanta so his mother could sign over the money to him. When his mom gave him the letter, he'd put it aside, saying he'd read it later. At the time he had no intention of ever reading it.

He'd gotten up early this morning, before Melanie. He couldn't bear to say goodbye to her face to face. Instead, he'd written her a letter and left it with Caesar to give to her. Then Rhett had driven him to the rehabilitation center in Arizona. It was a beautiful facility, and the staff had been welcoming, but he missed Melanie. He kept reminding himself that in order to have a future with her he needed to be here. And this time he needed to succeed.

Johnnie was no stranger to rehab, so it wasn't a surprise when his counselor said that they would get to the root of his problem. Johnnie already knew what that was. His father. It's why he had brought the letter with him. An apology letter is what Caesar had told him.

Johnnie unfolded the paper. He had thought that his mom might have written it for his dad, but this was definitely the untrained scrawl of his father. He'd written it on his death bed.

Johnnie,

Im a man of few words. And truth is, I dont right good. I wasnt good in skool ether. Win you were in 2ⁿᵈ grade, yor teachr told us you needed to be in a spechal class. I said no. I didnt wont peeple sayin my sun was stoopid. But then I called you stoopid. A long wit othr bad names. Im sorry. I was wrong to treet you bad. I no it hurt you. Made you hate me and hate yurself. I prey you stop drugs and drinking so much. You hav talint and hav dun grate things despit having a dad who is bad to you. It made me prod win I herd peeple talk abot yur band. I liked the musik you made.

I cant xplan why I treeted you bad. It was how my dad treeted me. To make me tuff, a man. It was wrong and agin Im sorry.

I love you,

Dad

Present

"Just arrived home. Thanks for talking to me while I drove."

Rhett chuckled. "Are you kidding. If something happened to you, I'd have to face the wrath of Melanie for letting you drive home this late at night as exhausted as you were."

"We'll talk again soon." Johnnie hung up, punched in the security code on the gate, and drove through. Once the gate closed again, he parked near the front door.

He'd been exhausted but had made the drive from LA anyway. Rhett had helped him acquire a gig as a session drummer for an up and coming rhythm and blues singer. For the past week, they'd been recording, but once they'd finished, Johnnie wanted nothing more than to be back home. *Back with my family.*

Feeling revived, he grabbed his suitcase from the back of the car and dragged it behind him to the front door.

He smiled when he heard the television on. *Melanie's still up.* He couldn't wait to see her and hold her in his arms. And Michael, too. A week was too long to be away from them. Especially with Michael's first birthday right around the corner. Melanie's parents would be flying out and together with his parents, they'd all be going to *Disneyland* to celebrate.

"Honey, I'm home!" he yelled as he came through the door.

"We're in here," Melanie yelled back.

Leaving his suitcase by the door, he went into the living room. Michael was sitting on a blanket on the floor, surrounded by toys. He looked up when Johnnie entered and smiled.

"Daddy's home!" Johnnie held his arms out to his side.

Michael laughed and squirmed around on his butt.

"We were watching cartoons, Daddy." Melanie rose from the couch and came to him.

"I've missed you." He wrapped her in his arms, holding her close, pressing his body against hers. His cock immediately came to life.

"So, I see," Melanie purred in his ear.

They kissed over and over.

"He's ready for bed, right?" Johnnie whispered in her ear.

"I think he sensed you were coming home. He didn't want to sleep. Maybe now I can get him down."

"I hope so." Johnnie's hands traveled down her back, then squeezed her butt.

"Guess, Daddy's ready for bed, too."

"No, Johnnie Vega is ready for bed. He's had a hard week beating on drums for hours a day, and he needs a little appreciation from his number one fan."

Melanie laughed lightly. "Let's get Michael to bed then."

When they looked down, Michael was pulling himself up using the coffee table for balance.

Johnnie knelt. "Look at my little man. Almost ready to walk."

"Da da da da," Michael babbled. His blue eyes lit up with excitement as he bounced.

"Oh shit!" Johnnie's heart fluttered. "Is he saying Daddy?"

"We've been working on it all week."

And then Michael let go of the table, held out his arms, and took his first steps toward his daddy. When he started to teeter, Johnnie swooped in and scooped him up in his arms. Michael squealed with laughter.

"I can't believe it. He walked. Is that the first time?"

Melanie nodded and started to tear up. "I guess he's been waiting for you to get home so he could show off."

"A showoff?" He tweaked Michael's nose. "That's Johnnie Vega's son alright."

Michael put a chubby hand on the side of Johnnie's face. "Da da da da."

"Da da loves you so much." Johnnie brushed his son's thick dark hair away from his forehead. The baby's curls nearly touched his shoulder now, and he wondered if he'd ever be able to convince Melanie to cut them. *Probably not.*

"Let's get you on the floor for more practice." Johnnie placed Michael near the table, and the baby grabbed onto the sides again.

"I thought we were getting ready for bed."

"He's probably too excited now."

CJ ran over to Michael and rubbed against him.

Johnnie wagged a finger at the cat. "Be careful, don't knock him over, you crazy cat."

Michael laughed and reached for the cat. "Sss...sss."

Johnnie looked at Melanie. "Be honest, was his first word Da, or has he been trying to say CJ as well."

"Ma, ma, ma, ma." Michael stammered out, looking up at Melanie and waving his arm at her.

"Apparently, he's been learning lots of words while I was gone. You know what this means?"

"What?"

"He'll be singing soon."

"Hold that thought." Melanie grabbed the remote and quickly switched the TV over to *Spotify* where she pulled up her list of Lush songs. She selected a danceable number.

Michael immediately began bouncing and rocking to the song. When Caesar's vocals began, Michael created his own sounds to go along with the song.

"Well, I'll be damned." Johnnie rushed to his suitcase. He returned with a pair of drumsticks.

"Really, Johnnie? Don't you think it's too soon?"

"Never!" Johnnie handed one to Michael. His son's bright blue eyes widened as the baby reached out and took it in his hand.

"Watch this, Michael." Johnnie tapped the other stick softly against the coffee table so as not to scare his son.

Michael squealed and began banging the table with all his might, making lots of noise.

"Yes! You got it!" Johnnie held his arms up in victory. Michael did the same and promptly fell on his butt, narrowly missing the edge of the coffee table.

Melanie walked over, picked Michael up, and took the stick away from him. She handed it back to Johnnie, and Michael immediately screeched with anger.

"Mommy, you're ruining our groove."

"Tomorrow the groove can continue. Out in the studio."

Johnnie laid the sticks on the table. Michael continued to scream. Melanie handed Michael to him. The baby kicked his legs and squirmed in his arms.

"I'm going to take a shower. You get him down since you got him all riled up."

"Me? You're the one who took the stick away."

Melanie whispered in his ear. "Because I want my big, thick stick."

"Alright, Michael, it's time for bed." Johnnie tickled his son's belly as they walked upstairs to the nursery. "Let's read *Curious George*."

Michael's cries of protest turned to giggles. He clapped, then stared at his hands, in awe of the noise he'd made. His head wobbled forward and back in a nod. "Ja Ja Ja."

Heaven Sent

Lyrics by Johnnie Vega

No need to see a halo
No need to see any wings
No need to read the scriptures
No need to hear angels sing
To know you're a precious gift
Sent from heaven above
To heal my wounded heart
And fill it with your love
You took away my sadness
Replaced all of my pain
With you there's only joy and laughter
Our love
It has been ordained
The stars kissed you with their beauty
The moon hugged you with its light
The sun touched your soul with kindness
The winds caressed you with delight
There's no need for a halo
or any feathered wings
No need for a book of devotion
No use in divine harp strings
I know you were sent from Heaven
An angel's gift to me
And when I feel your touch
Honey, I'm in extasy
You are heaven sent
Sent from those skies of blue
You are heaven sent
And my heart
It belongs to you

About the Author

A Florida native and graduate of the University of North Florida, Cherié Summers has spent the last two decades teaching reading and writing. Her previous publications include a short story in *Children's Digest* and newsletters for nonprofit organizations. *Heaven Sent* is Ms. Summers sixth book. All have been inspired by her favorite musical icons.

She wrote the first draft of her first book when she was eighteen, but it wasn't until she turned fifty that she began getting serious about pursuing a career in writing.

Writing is only one of Ms. Summers' creative passions. She is also an avid photographer, specializing in portrait photography of animals, nature, and people. Another creative outlet she revels in is belly dancing. She teaches the art of Middle Eastern dance through her local community education program. She also enjoys traveling to music concerts and pop culture conventions with her daughter, Kayla. Atlanta is a favorite destination, and Ms. Summers' dream is to move there when she retires from her day job.

Made in the USA
Columbia, SC
03 March 2021

33487074R00167